THEY ALMOST ALWAYS COME HOME

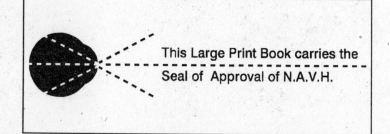

THEY ALMOST ALWAYS COME HOME

CYNTHIA RUCHTI

THORNDIKE PRESS

A part of Gale, Cengage Learning

Detroit • New York • San Francisco • New Haven, Conn • Waterville, Maine • London

GALE
CENGAGE Learning™

Thorndike Press, a part of Gale, Cengage Learning.

Thorndike Press® Large Print Christian Romance.
The text of this Large Print edition is unabridged.
Other aspects of the book may vary from the original edition.
Set in 16 pt. Plantin.

LIBRARY OF CONGRESS CATALOGING-IN-PUBLICATION DATA

Ruchti, Cynthia.
   They almost always come home / by Cynthia Ruchti.
     p. cm. — (Thorndike Press large print christian romance)
   ISBN-13: 978-1-4104-2893-6
   ISBN-10: 1-4104-2893-1
   1. Married people—Fiction. 2. Missing persons—Investigation—Fiction.
3. Wilderness areas—Fiction. 4. Canada—Fiction. 5. Large type books.
   I. Title.
   PS3618.U3255T48 2010b
   813'.6—dc22   2010016018

Published in 2010 by arrangement with Abingdon Press.

Printed in the United States of America
1 2 3 4 5 6 7 14 13 12 11 10

*This book and my life are dedicated to
the Rescuer,
who risked everything to lead me
out of the wilderness. I am His forever.*

*My life and this story also belong
to my husband, Bill,
whose Quetico wilderness trips
sparked the idea. Bill blessed me
with key plot points and then complained
that his name isn't on the cover.
I told him his last name would be on the
cover of every book I write.*

ACKNOWLEDGMENTS

If my mother holds this book in her hands, it will be because she prayed it into existence and because the Lord stayed *His* hand from calling her home, though she's tiptoed on the edge of eternity far too long in her estimation. In many ways, she served as my novel-birthing coach, cheering me on and reminding me how to breathe. Thank you, Mom. *(Author's note: That's how this paragraph was written during the novel's creation. The day came when, with inexpressible gratitude, I laid an advanced copy in Mom's hands. Two weeks later, she took her final breath.)*

I choose to believe it was not merely the air conditioning in the room that made my editor, Barbara Scott, rub her arms and say, "Ooh! I have goosebumps!" while listening to the pitch for this story. The moment is a sweet, sustaining memory. I didn't know at the time that I was gaining not only an editor but also a sister and friend. What a grace-gift!

Abingdon Press — its authors and publishing team — have made this experience a journey of unending joy.

Thank you, Wendy Lawton and the Books & Such Literary Agency family, for embracing me, nudging me, and feeding my hope. I'm honored to know you and be counted among you.

The role American Christian Fiction Writers (ACFW) has played in my writing life and my faith is immeasurable. Amazing friends and mentors, storytellers and publishing colleagues, fellow board members — thank you for your impact. This story — and I — grew in your light.

My critique partners — Julie, Terri, Rachel, Melody, Laura, Margaret, Sally, and newcomer Karin — deserve recognition for their patience with me, their insights, and their "the sting won't last long" critiques.

Becky, the Lord knew exactly what I needed when He sent you.

This book was nurtured by the faithfulness of Fiction Friends, my writing prayer partners — Michelle, Dorothy, Diane, Shannon, Robin, and Jackie. Thank you for waiting with me.

Adventurer Mike Knuth offered his valuable *voyageur* perspective on the wilderness details, for which I am grateful. His experience added to the story. His enthusiasm for the story created a smile that has yet to fade.

In their individual ways and corporately, Kathy Carlton Willis, Twila Belk, and Cec Murphey blessed me and this book with a depth of encouragement every novelist craves.

Thank you, Western Wisconsin Christian Writers Guild, for teaching, inspiring, and holding writers accountable to write.

Bless you, Yay Rah Rah writers, for yay rah rah-ing.

Thank you, Jackie, for wearing out your knees for me and for cheering loudly no matter what the project, as long as it brings the Lord glory.

Amy, I wept for Libby in this story because she didn't have a daughter like you.

Matt, you taught me that "middle" child means "middle of my heart." (I might have read that somewhere, but it fits you.)

Luke, a third child with a creative mind! How was I so blessed? May the lyrics of your life be a praise song.

Grace, Ben, Hannah, Andy, and Josh, the art of telling stories took on new meaning with you on Grammie's lap.

Special thanks to Kelly and Mark at the Second Wind Country Inn in Ashland,

Wisconsin, for creating a scene and a place in which to write it.

Bill, with whom I have shared many moons in the same canoe, thank you for signing up for the journey of loving me for life.

1

From the window [she] looked out.
Through the window she watched for his
    return, saying,
"Why is his chariot so long in coming?
Why don't we hear the sound of chariot
    wheels?"
— Judges 5:28 NLT

Do dead people wear shoes? In the casket, I mean. Seems a waste. Then again, no outfit is complete without the shoes.

My thoughts pound up the stairs, down the hall, and into the master bedroom closet. Greg's gray suit is clean, I think. White shirt, although that won't allow much color contrast and won't do a thing for Greg's skin tones. His red tie with the silver threads? Good choice.

Shoes or no shoes? I should know this. I've stroked the porcelain-cold cheeks of several embalmed loved ones. My father and grandfather. Two grandmothers — one too young to die. One too old not to.

And Lacey.

The Baxter Street Mortuary will not touch my husband's body should the need arise. They got Lacey's hair and facial expression all wrong.

I rise from the couch and part the sheers on the front window one more time. Still quiet. No lights on the street. No Jeep pulling into our driveway. I'll give him one more hour, then I'm heading for bed. With or without him.

Shoes? Yes or no? I'm familiar with the casket protocol for children. But for adults?

Grandma Clarendon hadn't worn shoes for twelve years or more when she died. She preferred open-toed terrycloth slippers. Day and night. Home. Uptown. Church. Seems to me she took comfort to the extreme. Or maybe she figured God ought to be grateful she showed up in His house at all, given her distaste for His indiscriminate dispersal of the Death Angel among her friends and siblings.

"Ain't a lick of pride in outliving your brothers and sisters, Libby." She said it often enough that I can pull off a believable impression. Nobody at the local comedy club need fear me as competition, but the cousins get a kick out of it at family reunions.

Leaning on the tile and cast-iron coffee table, I crane everything in me to look at the wall clock in the entry. Almost four in the morning? I haven't even decided who will sing special music at Greg's memorial service. Don't most women plan their husband's funeral if he's more than a few minutes late?

In the past, before this hour, I'm mentally two weeks beyond the service, trying to decide whether to keep the house or move to a condo downtown.

He's never been this late before. And he's never been alone in the wilderness. A lightning bolt of something — *fear? anticipation? pain?* — ripples my skin and exits through the soles of my feet.

The funeral plans no longer seem a semi-morbid way to occupy my mind while I wait for the lights of his Jeep. Not pointless imaginings but preparation.

That sounds like a thought I should command to flee in the name of Jesus or some other holy incantation. But it stares at me with narrowed eyes as if to say, "I dare you."

Greg will give me grief over this when he gets home. "You worry too much, Libby. So I was a little late." He'll pinch my love handles, which I won't find endearing. "Okay, a lot late. Sometimes the wind whips up the waves on the larger lakes. We *voyageurs* have two choices — risk swamping the canoe so we can get home to our precious wives or find a sheltered spot on an island and stay put until the wind dies down."

I never liked how he used the word *precious* in that context. I should tell him so. I should tell him a lot of things. And I will.

If he ever comes home.

With sleep-deprived eyes, I trace the last ticks of the second hand. Seven o'clock. Too early to call Frank? Not likely.

I reach to punch the MEM 2 key sequence on the phone. Miss the first time. Try again.

One ring. Two. Three. If the answering machine kicks in —

"Frank's Franks. Frankly the best in all of Franklin County. Frank speaking. How can I help you?"

I bite back a retort. How does a retired grocery manager get away with that much *corny?* Consistently. One thing is still normal.

"Frank, it's Libby. I hate to call this early but —"

"Early?" he snorts. "Been up since four-thirty."

Figures. Spitting image of his son.

"Biked five miles," he says. "Had breakfast at the truck stop. Watered those blasted hostas of your mother-in-law's that just won't die. Believe me, I've done everything in my power to help them along toward that end."

I don't have the time or inclination to defend Pauline's hostas. "I called for a reason, Frank."

"Sorry. What's up?"

I'm breathing too rapidly. Little flashes of electricity hem my field of vision. "Have you heard from Greg?"

"He's back, right?"

"Not yet. I'm probably worried for nothing."

He expels a breath that I feel in the earpiece. "When did you expect him? Yesterday?"

"He planned to get back on Friday, but said Saturday at the latest. He hates to miss church now that he's into helping with the sound system."

"Might have had to take a wind day. Or two."

Why does it irritate me that he's playing the logic card? "I thought of that."

"Odd, though." His voice turns a corner.

"What do you mean?"

Through the receiver, I hear that grunt thing he does when he gets into or out of a chair. "I had one eye on the Weather Channel most of last week," he says.

What did you do with the other eye, Frank? The Weather Channel? Early retirement has turned him into a weather spectator. "And?"

"Says winds have been calm throughout the Quetico. It's a good thing too. Tinder-dry in Canada right now. One spark plus a stiff wind and you've got major forest fire potential. They've posted a ban on open campfires. Cook stoves only. Greg planned for that, didn't he?"

"How should I know?" Somewhere deep in my brain, I pop a blood vessel. Not my normal style — not with anyone but Greg. "Sorry, Frank. I'm . . . I'm overreacting. To everything. I'm sure he'll show up any minute. Or call."

From the background comes a sound like leather complaining. "Told my boy more than once he ought to invest in a satellite phone. The man's too cheap to throw away a bent nail."

"I know." I also know I would have thrown a newsworthy fit if he'd suggested spending that kind of money on a toy for his precious wilderness trips when I'm still waiting for the family budget to allow for new kitchen countertops. As it stands, they're not butcher block. They're butcher shop. And they've been that way since we moved in, since Greg first apologized for them and said we'd replace them "one of these first days."

How many "first days" pass in twenty-three years?

His *precious* wilderness trips? Is that what I said? Now *I'm* doing it.

Frank's voice urges me back to the scene of our conversation. "Hey, Libby, have him give me a call when he gets in, will you?" His emphasis of the word *when* rings artificial.

"He always does, Frank." My voice is a stream of air that overpowers the words.

"Still —"

"I'll have him call."

The phone's silent, as is the house. I never noticed before how loud is the absence of sound.

It's official. Greg's missing. That's what the police report says: Missing Person.

I don't remember filing a police report before now. We've never had obnoxious neighbors or a break-in. Not even a stolen

17

bike from the driveway. Yes, I know. A charmed life.

The desk sergeant is on the phone, debating with someone about who should talk to me. Is my case insignificant to them? Not worth the time? I take a step back from the scarred oak check-in desk to allow the sergeant a fraction more privacy.

With my husband gone, I have privacy to spare, I want to tell him. *You can have some of mine. You're welcome.*

I shift my purse to the other shoulder, as if that will help straighten my spine. Good posture seems irrelevant. Irreverent.

Everything I know about the inside of police stations I learned from Barney Fife, Barney Miller, and any number of *CSI*s. The perps lined up on benches along the wall, waiting to be processed, look more at ease than I feel.

The chair to which I've been directed near Officer Kentworth's desk boasts a mystery stain on the sitting-down part. Not a chair with my name on it. It's for women with viper tattoos and envelope-sized miniskirts. For guys named Vinnie who wake with horse heads in their beds. For pierced and bandanaed teens on their way to an illustrious petty-theft career.

"Please have a seat." The officer has said

that line how many times before?

Officer Kentworth peers through the untidy fringe of his unibrow and takes my statement, helping fill in the blanks on the Missing Person form. All the blanks but one — Where is he? The officer notes Greg's vehicle model and license plate number and asks all kinds of questions I can't answer. Kentworth is a veteran of Canadian trips like the one from which Greg has not returned. He knows the right questions to ask.

Did he choose the Thunder Bay or International Falls crossing into Canada? What was your husband's intended destination in the Quetico Provincial Park? Where did he arrange to enter and exit the park? Did he have a guide service drop him off? Where did he plan to camp on his way out of the park? How many portages?

I should have sent Frank to file the report. He'd know. Greg probably rambled on to me about some of those things on his way out the door seventeen days ago. My brain saw no need to retain any of it. It interested him, not me.

Kentworth leans toward me, exhales tuna breath — which seems especially unique at this hour of the morning — and asks, "How've things been at home between the two of you?"

I know the answer to this question. Instead I say, "Fine. What's that got to do with — ?"

"Had to ask, Mrs. Holden." He reaches across his desk and pats my hand. Rather, he patronizes my hand. "Many times, in these cases —"

Oh, just say it!

"— an unhappy husband takes advantage of an opportunity to walk away."

His smile ends at the border of his eyes. I resist the urge to smack him. I don't want to join the perps waiting to be processed. I want to go home and plow through Greg's office, searching for answers I should have known.

Greg? Walk away?

Not only is he too annoyingly faithful for that, but if anyone has a right to walk away, it's me.

I thought it would be a relief to get home again after the ordeal at the police station, which included a bizarre three-way conversation with the Canadian authorities asking me to tell them things I don't know. We won't even mention the trauma of the question, "And Mrs. Holden, just for the record, can you account for your own whereabouts since your husband left?"

Home? A relief? The answering machine light blinks like an ambulance. Mostly messages from neighbors, wondering if I've heard anything. A few friends and extended family — word is spreading — wondering if I've heard anything. Our pastor, wondering if I've heard anything.

I head for the bedroom to change clothes. The cotton sweater I wore to the station smells like tuna and handcuffs. Or is that my imagination?

Quick census. How many cells of my body don't ache? You'd think I'd find this king-sized bed and down comforter impossible to resist. But it's another symbol that something's missing. Something's wrong and has been for a long time. Moving from our old queen-sized mattress to this king represented distance rather than comfort. For me, anyway. I needed a few more inches between us. A few feet. I guess I got my wish.

I throw the sweater in the wicker hamper, which ironically does not reek of Greg's athletic socks today. On the way from the hamper to the closet, I clunk my shin on the corner of the bed frame. The bed takes up more of the room than it should. Old houses. Contractors in the 1950s couldn't envision couples in love needing that much elbow room. My shin throbs as it decides whether it wants to bruise. That corner's caught me more than once. I ought to know better. About a lot of things.

I pull open the bifold closet doors. Picking out something to wear shouldn't be this hard. But Greg's things are in here.

If he were planning to leave me, couldn't he have had the decency to tidy up after himself and clear out the closet? For the ever-popular "closure"? How long do I wait before packing up his suits and dress shirts?

One of his suit jackets is facing the wrong way on the hanger. Everyone knows buttons face left in the closet. Correcting it is life-or-death important to me at the moment. There. Order. As it should be. I smooth the collar of the jacket and stir up the scent of Aspen for Men. The boa constrictor around my throat flexes its muscles.

With its arms spread wide, the overstuffed chair in the corner mocks me. I bought it without clearing the expenditure with Greg. Mortal sin, right? He didn't holler. The man doesn't holler. He sighs and signs up for more overtime.

Maybe I'll find comfort in the kitchen. This bedroom creeps me out.

Greg has thrown us into an incident of international intrigue. Melodramatic wording, but true. We're dealing with the local authorities plus the Canadian police.

Staring out the kitchen window at the summer-rich backyard proves fruitless. It holds no answers for me. I'm alone in this. Almost.

Frank's my personal liaison with the Canadians — border patrol, Quetico Park rangers, and Ontario Provincial Police, the latter of which is blessed with an unfortunate acronym — OPP. Looks a lot like "Oops" on paper. I can't help but envision that adorable character from *Due North,* the Mountie transplanted into the heart and bowels of New York City. Sweetly naive as he was, he always got his man. Will these get mine?

Frank will be much better at pestering them for answers. My mother-in-law would be better still. Pestering. Pauline's gifted that way.

I'm no help. Big surprise. When I spoke with the north-of-the-border authorities, I either tripped over every word and expressed my regrets for bothering them or shouted into the phone, "Why aren't you doing something?"

They are, of course. They're trying. Analyzing tire tracks. Interviewing canoeists exiting the park. Looking for signs of a struggle. The search plane they promised is a nice touch. Under Frank's direction, they'll scan Greg's expected route to check for mayhem.

While I wait for yet another pot of coffee to brew, I brush toast crumbs — some forgotten breakfast — off the butcher shop counter into my hand. Now what? I can't think what to do with them.

The phone rings.

It's Greg's district manager again. He's the pasty-faced, chopstick-thin undertaker hovering just offstage in a lame Western movie.

No, no word from Greg yet. Yes, I'll let you know as soon as I hear something. Yes, I understand what a difficult position this has put you in, Mr. Sensitive, I mean, Mr. Stenner. Can we request a temporary leave of absence for Greg or . . . ? Of course, I understand. Not fair to the company, sure. Only have so much patience, uh huh. God bless you too.

Right.

Oh, and thanks for caring that my life is falling apart and my husband is either muerto *or*

24

just fine but not with me and either way he's a dead man.

I slam the phone into its base station, then apologize to it.

The sweat in my palm reconstituted the bread crumbs during the call. Wastebasket. That's what one does with crumbs.

How long will it take me to figure out what to do with the crumbs of my life?

And where will I find a basket large enough for the pieces?

2

Today's the day I call Dr. Palmer and ask for something to help me sleep. The over-the-counter varieties might work for pre-colonoscopy jitters or speeding-ticket insomnia or even the-mortgage-is-due-tomorrow woes. But they're no match for the knowledge that Greg found the escape hatch before I did.

I open the bedroom blinds to another sun-drenched day. Perfect for gardening or taking the bike path through the park or maybe an impromptu picnic. Antiquing. Another good choice.

No, I think I'll spend the day wringing my hands over my AWOL husband.

Did he even dip his canoe paddle into his beloved Canadian waters? The park rangers say he checked in or logged in or whatever wilderness adventurers do. He didn't log out. That's not required, apparently. Maybe someone should rethink that detail.

The view from our bedroom window is of a normal world. It stings my eyes. The neighborhood, green and flourishing, sounds noisy already with lawn mowers and kids on skateboards. I clamp one hand over my mouth to suppress my rant against normal.

Greg's Cherokee is gone from the remote lot near the Beaverhouse put-in point, according to reports. What does that mean?

Can't be a good sign.

I think it would be smart to make people check back in with the ranger station just to say, "Great trip. Caught lots of fish. Nasty portage on Half Mile Point, isn't it? Say, if the wife calls, tell her I'm on my way home."

I can't be the first woman to wonder.

If signing out were a requirement, would Greg have stopped to do so? Or would he have been in such a hurry he'd forget? What or who would make him neglect a thing like that?

Who? I should wash out my mouth with soap for voicing such slander. Greg Holden and another woman? Ridiculous. Not on his radar screen. He's the poster boy for faithfulness.

Why is that not enough for me?

I wander from bedroom to kitchen to family room, then open the sliding doors and slip out to the only place where I can breathe these days — the screen porch. Don't ask me why. Maybe I think this little slice of suburban nature anchors me closer to answers. Maybe I'm drawing some kind of warped comfort from the fact that if Greg's still alive but lost, he's looking into the same stratosphere. He's breathing this same mix of oxygen and carbon dioxide and whatever.

I drop into one of the swivel-rocker patio chairs and lean back as though I'm about to undergo a root canal. *If he's still alive.* Somebody stop me from thinking that line again.

It's not that I haven't prayed. I'm one of the prayer chain coordinators at church, for Pete's sake. I believe in the power of prayer. Well, you know what I mean. I believe God is powerful and moves mountains when we pray.

But this is different.

I can't put two sentences together that sound at all prayer-like. For three days now, all I've managed is *Oh, Lord God!* or *Jesus, Jesus, Jesus!* or *What am I going to do? What am I going to do?* repeated *ad nauseam.*

Mylanta helps the *nauseam* part. I'm smart enough to know that buckets of coffee on an empty stomach form an invitation for trouble. I don't want to know my blood pressure readings. The pounding at my temples and the ache in the back of my skull tell me the numbers aren't pretty.

A bird sings from one of the trees in the backyard. I want to shoot it from its sassy perch.

How does one go about inducing a therapeutic coma? Is it so wrong to want to sleep through this? I'll deal with it eventually, whatever the outcome. But could I skip this middle part? The not knowing. The wait-torture. The imagination that is so wildly fertile right now, Miracle-Gro has nothing on me.

I'm halfway out of my skin before I realize the apparition standing in the doorway from the family room to the screen porch is Jenika.

"Thought I might find you here," she says.

I can't even find me here. How can she?

She drops into the companion chair to mine, the one Greg prefers. "Any word?"

If she weren't more sister than friend, I'd shove those words back down her throat. She must read my nonanswer as a clear response. She's good at that. Without waiting for me to elaborate, Jenika slips out of her chair and kneels at my feet.

Taking my worthless hands in hers, she

29

rubs the back of them with her thumbs. Does she know some secret pressure point lodged under the skin? Will this ease the cramping in my belly that has nothing to do with coffee? Will it relieve the pain digging its claws into the mangled flesh of my heart?

A pressure point? Of sorts. It's the trigger for the tears that haven't fallen until now.

Jen could teach Greg a thing or two about friendship. I wanted him to be a friend. All he knew how to be was a loving, tenacious husband. And father. A prince of a guy . . . in everyone else's eyes.

Long ago I learned to hide my tears from Greg. They made his frustration meter peak. He wanted to fix the tears, or me.

"I'm crying for you, you big, dumb jerk!"

Jen looks up. "For me?"

The first words I produce in Jen's presence are harsh and ugly and not even directed to her. "Sorry."

"You okay, Libby?"

"Never . . . better." I hiccup the words.

She collects the tear-soaked tissues from my lap — now that's a true friend — deposits them on the pine TV tray disguised as a lamp table, and hands me a bottle of water. Where'd she get that? And where'd the tissues come from?

I take a sip of the icy water, surprised I

remember how to swallow, then hold the bottle against my forehead between my eyes. Jen waits.

I'm a wounded toddler, my normal breathing interrupted by sporadic sniff-sniffs. I may have ruined my sinuses forever. My eyes are hot hockey pucks stuck to the front of my face.

Still, Jen waits.

"Sorry about the waterworks."

"Are you kidding?" She scoots closer in the chair she's reclaimed. Our knees almost touch. "You needed to do that. It was an honor to be present when it happened."

I hold a degree from Self-Pity U. She's working on her master's from, well, the Master.

"Can I get you something to eat?" she asks. "I brought chicken salad in cream puff shells. Nothing too heavy." She digs into the soft-sided cooler she must have carried in with her. "And melon cubes."

"I'm not hungry."

"And my chocolate pudding cake."

"Okay." The speed with which I deliver that single word makes us both giggle. Just a little. Nothing dishonoring to the crisis.

Enough to take some pressure off the aneurysm forming in my brain.

"Jen?"

"What, hon?"

"Did Greg . . . did he say anything to you . . . or to Brent . . . about . . . about leaving me?"

"Don't be ridiculous."

"I mean, it's possible that he —"

"Are you out of your mind?" That's my Jen. Warm-hearted comforter one minute. Truth-teller the next. "I told the cops the same thing. It's a ridiculous notion from the pit of —"

"Wait a minute. You talked to the police?"

She stops uncovering plastic containers of food. "You didn't know that? Standard procedure, I suppose, to take statements from friends and neighbors."

"My neighbors?"

"That bothers you? Aren't you grateful the police are working on this?"

Since when does chocolate smell like handcuffs? "Jen, they questioned you?"

"Well, not *questioned* as in *interrogated.*" She's back to plating food as if her news is of no more consequence than the results of the local spelling bee.

I lick a smear of fudge frosting from the edge of the offered paper plate before I remember I'm not hungry and may never be hungry again. "What, then?"

"Libby, it's no big deal. They're trying to

get all the details they can and follow up on any leads."

"What leads?"

"They don't have any. That's what's so frustrating for everybody."

Grinding between my back teeth are the words you-and-the-whole-blessed-rest-of-the-world-have-no-idea-what-it-means-to-be-frustrated. I swallow that sour sentence and ask, "What kind of questions?"

"They asked, 'Did you notice anything unusual with Greg's demeanor before he left for his trip? How long have you known the two of them as a couple?' "

"How have they been getting along?" I offer.

"That too."

"What did you say?"

She sighs and turns from tending the food to face me. "I told the officer it wouldn't be fair to paint you as the perfect couple."

"That's a bit of an understatement."

Jen hands me a fork, as if I'll use it. "But I also told him that your troubles were survivable. Nothing serious."

Am I grateful or disturbed by that answer? Can a person be both? I wouldn't call our differences nothing serious. I'm having a hard time liking the man I'm supposed to love. I'm angry that he left me when I was about to leave him. That's not serious?

"So, I'm no longer a suspect?"

" 'Person of interest' is what they call it now."

When I drop my chin and throw my shoulders back, she adds, "Kidding, Libby! I'm just kidding. Sorry if that was tasteless."

"I'm not amused."

"I see that."

Neither of us speaks for a while. She takes a bite of chicken salad. I worry my cake into a puddle of moist crumbs.

"Are Zack and Alex coming home, Lib?"

"They just started their remote trek."

"Oh, no." She drops her hands into her lap, jostling the plate resting there.

"My sons couldn't have gotten summer jobs at the local Dairy Queen and Wal-Mart. Not my boys. The remote mountains of Chile. 'Great opportunity, Mom. Imagine how impressive this gig will look on our résumés. You can't beat an international experience, Mom.' And their dad and I said yes. What were we thinking?"

"You were thinking of affording your children opportunities of a lifetime."

I put down the cake plate. What's the point? "Now they're a trillion miles from home. And for the next week, they'll be so deep in the Chilean outback —"

"That's Australia."

"Whatever. They're beyond contact of any kind."

"Even for an emergency?"

"That was part of the allure. 'Cool, Mom. Research assistants so far from civilization, we have to cut our own trails. Ultimate adventure and college credit too. Sweet!' "

"Can we ask to have someone sent out to get them? Or at least get word to them?"

"What word? That their dad figured out a way to leave me and still save face? That Greg took a permanent detour on his way home? We don't know anything to tell them except that we don't know anything."

"Won't they want to come home?"

"They may have to, eventually. If we find —"

A body. If we find a body. The stuff of nightmares.

A bloated, gray body floating to the surface of crystal Canadian waters or careening like a log in a flume all the way to Lake Superior. No, wait. Hudson Bay, probably. A gap-toothed, cowlicked boy and his grandpa hook what they think is a trophy Arctic char only to discover it's my husband.

How much therapy would it take to get over a fishing trip like that?

Would I rather find Greg in a too-cheap-for-good-ad-copy motel in Saskatchewan? With a roommate named Trixie, a towel draped over the eyes of the Gideon Bible, and a smile on his face?

Yes.

No.

I don't know. I want to leave my husband, but I have to find him first.

The phone rings. I check the caller ID screen, expecting to see the French words for "No Tell Motel." Isn't the word *morgue* French already?

It's one of the other coordinators on the prayer chain. Lord, this better be more significant than Myrna's cat's digestive problems again or I may have to develop a swear language.

3

Apparently, I'm in the guilt stage. I try the bedroom armchair again, but it might as well be upholstered with razor blades.

This is all my fault. I'm not taking the blame for Greg's inattention or his failure to make me happy. I'm not ready to issue a pardon for his role in what happened to Lacey. But I do take responsibility for letting him go off without a companion. Not me, of course. A guy friend.

"I'd like to try it alone this time, Lib." That's what he said.

At the time, I hadn't noticed any twitch in the corner of his eye, any throbbing vein in his neck. I had no suspicions — no misgivings. But I do remember thinking, *I'd like to try it alone, too, Greg. And I don't mean a vacation.*

I can't even count how many of these trips he's taken in the past. At least one a year. Sometimes two — spring and fall — if he can swing time off from work. But always with someone else — another crazed fisherman who finds warped satisfaction in surviving for a week or two without the conveniences that make life worth living.

Frank serves as a companion paddler as often as he can. Greg's enlisted every male friend or potential friend from here to the Mississippi over the years. Old college buddies. Guys from church. His sons, the adventurers. Everyone but me. He couldn't sell me on the concept that the scenery and experience make up for the inconveniences. He's not that good of a salesman, which is why he's in the purchasing department at Greene's Grocery chain rather than sales.

The chair's not working. I cross the empty room, pull open a dresser drawer, grab the socks I came to the bedroom for in the first place, and sit on the edge of the bed. Gingerly. As if Greg is napping on the far side. I hope that's not prophetic. Napping on the "far side."

He's never gone on a solo trip. Never seemed to want to. Until now. What does that tell me?

I don't remember folding these socks without turning them right side out. I never skip that. As I look at the bumpy ridge of a seam that should be invisible, internal, I'm sympathetic to its plight.

"Poor thing. You don't get any respect, do you? Today, you will be visible."

I pull them onto my feet — left, then right, as always — proud of liberating an over-looked seam. If only life were that simple. What if I could redo the last three years but live them inside out?

What if I could push past whatever bony protrusion kept me from giving full birth to my grief over Lacey? What if I could do it again and presume — for the sake of argument — that Greg was on my side? What if I allowed him the grace I depend on?

What was I thinking, staying silent about Greg's solo trip? Of all times for me to clam up! Brilliant, Libby. Simply brilliant.

About as wise as having our boys fourteen months apart and teaching them self-reliance. Now not only are they so gloriously independent that their college experience is thousands of miles from Mommy, they're also not in need of a live-in dad. They'll be okay. Greg didn't leave them. He left me.

The muscles around my stomach spasm. Did he tell them? Did he take his sons into his confidence before he left?

"Here, guys."

"What's that, Dad?"

"My new address. Do me a favor, will you? Keep this just between us until I have a chance to tell your mom."

"When will that be?"

"I don't know. Soon."

Why wouldn't one of them snitch? I've kept their little-boy and hooky-playing-teen secrets and they know it. This is unfair. I should have a daughter with whom to share my own secrets. I should have a daughter.

I lift my body off the bed, groaning like a woman twice my age. Now that my feet are clad, it occurs to me I should shower. I skipped that phase earlier when the sun blinded me.

It's the Jeep. That's the thing. I've heard of cars careening off a steep mountain hairpin, staying lost in the brush for days before discovery. But there are no mountains between here and — what was that spot? Beaverhouse. With the highway patrols of two states and a Canadian province on the lookout, someone would have found it — him — if there'd been an accident. And neither of the typical border crossings have a record of his reentering the United States.

He's still in Canada . . . somewhere. Doesn't matter where. He's not with me. He's not here in this house: The House of Grief and Guilt.

I strip off the socks, undecided about seams and scars that show.

I can't even shower without guilt. Guilt pokes at the cellulite on my thighs and tells me that's the reason Greg's gone. It traces the spider veins on my legs and says, "Well, no wonder."

I'll wear jeans the rest of the day. It's too hot for jeans, but they cover more. Chambray shirt? No. Greg's favorite. Hardly seems appropriate. I'll wear the white tee with the hyacinth screen print. Or maybe not. I bought that in Ashland the year we celebrated our twentieth anniversary.

Our anniversary trip. Hope showed new buds on that trip to Lake Superior's southern shore. How had Greg found that particular bed-and-breakfast for us? Second Wind Country Inn's rustic charm was perfect for us.

I hadn't expected awe. I'd long since retired *awe* from my vocabulary. But perched on a high point overlooking Chequamegon Bay, the inn rose like an impressive log castle at the end of a long driveway meandering through close-cropped hayfields and long stretches of lawn.

The isolation of the inn offered a sense of safety. Was that it? Was that the reason I allowed myself to feel something other than

41

pain that weekend?

As I towel-dry my shower-damp hair, noting that before long I'll have to make friends with Miss Clairol, I wonder why I let down my guard on that trip. Was I starved for beauty? Is that why my heart relaxed into something akin to peace in that place?

Our room — our suite of rooms — lay at the top of a long flight of stairs. I questioned the location as we hauled our overnight bags up the steps. The questions ceased when the innkeeper opened the door and welcomed us into the sitting area. She pointed out the comfortable couch and fat, downy chairs. Who could pay attention with that breathtaking view staring us full in the face through a wall of twelve-foot-tall windows?

So much sky.

I pick up my wide-toothed comb and tackle the tangles in my hair. Working at them little by little, from the bottom up, the knots soon turn to wet but smooth silk. Where can I find a wide-toothed comb for marital tangles?

Was the inn and what it offered us an answer to that question?

We ate that night at a little bistro. Great ambiance. Not your typical franchise fare. Greg ordered brown sugar-smoked lake trout with wild mushrooms and dried cranberries over basmati rice. I had the grilled salmon with mango salsa and cilantro puree on a bed of fiddlehead ferns. Somehow the menu itself invited conversation. We talked as if we believed the map of our marriage led us into a quiet cove where we could lie naked on the beach and no one would know. We knew each other's warts and fleshy pockets well. That night, they seemed endearing.

I remember Greg waking me at three in the morning. He dragged my resistant body out of bed and invited me to join him in front of the castle windows.

"Isn't that something?" he breathed into space. His warm arm cupped my back at the waist.

As soul-igniting as had been the daytime view through those mammoth windows, it could not rival the night sky.

"Peppered with stars," he said, his voice low and reverent.

A simple moment of moonlit camaraderie led to some of the most authentic intimacy in recent history for us. He wanted to share the sky with me. And I let him.

When we finally peeled our bodies out of the luxurious log bed mid-morning, a divine Hand had changed the scene again. The windows revealed low-lying fog hovering in the brushy gullies and ravines.

Greg stood at the windows, nursing a cup of coffee left on a tray outside the suite door by a silent, no-missed-details hostess.

I hesitated to break whatever spell he was in. "Do you want to go down for breakfast, honey?" I'd asked, as best as I can remember. I think I called him *honey.*

"In a minute," he said.

I watched him move his head slowly, like a surveillance camera commissioned to take in the whole scene over the course of time.

"Fascinating," he said. "The world is shrouded in *mist*-ry. Wish I had my camera."

This from a man who spends his day swinging deals on potato chips and paper towels for Greene's. A man with a calculator, a laptop, and what I thought was no imagination.

Twenty years of marriage. In that moment, I feared I knew less about my husband than I ever had.

I vowed to pay more attention to the man who shared my marriage bed.

A few months later, Lacey died.

The hyacinth T-shirt? No.

Is there nothing in this closet that doesn't reek with memories?

I drain an ink cartridge printing out

MapQuest's version of the distance between where I am in an empty house in the heart of Wisconsin and where my husband was supposed to be three or four days ago. With the maps spread on the kitchen table around which we were once a family, I follow the main highway with my finger.

West or east? After he drove back to the Queen's Highway from the Quetico Provincial Park, did he turn toward Toronto or Winnipeg? Odds are he wouldn't have ventured farther north. Then again, who would have given odds he'd bail on his marriage and his career?

"Nice blouse. Is that new?" Jen may have knocked before entering. I can't swear to anything these days.

"You like it?"

"Great color," she says. "For me. Not so much for you."

"Oh, you flatter me."

"I'm just saying that it's not your best color," she comments as she deposits something foil-covered into my fridge. "Unless you were hoping to look even more tired and washed out than you are."

Remind me again why I love this person?

"It was supposed to be your birthday present, Jen."

"Well, thanks for test-driving it for me."

The lilt in her voice is a blessing. How lousy would I have to be to offend this woman?

I run my hands over the fabric where it covers my middle. "I just couldn't . . . I had to have . . . the closet was full of . . ."

Jen grabs a mug from the cupboard next to the sink and helps herself to a tea bag from the canister on the counter. "Don't explain. Nobody expects you to think rationally every minute of this thing, Libby."

"What did you sneak into my fridge?"

"Supper," she says.

"I'm still not hungry."

"Two things. Number one, so what? You have to eat or you'll be in worse shape than you are already. Number two, by suppertime, I will be."

"You're staying that long?"

"I'm staying *until,* Lib. Until."

I turn away from the table. I don't have a spare ink cartridge, so I can't afford tearstains on these maps.

A tissue floats over my shoulder, as do Jen's next words. "Get a grip, woman. We have work to do."

"Work?"

"The way I figure it, I'm the one to tackle the Internet because, truth be told, I'm better at it than you are."

"Sweet talker."

She doesn't skip a beat. "And if you man the phone, we can call every Best Western, Super 8, and Holiday Inn between here and Calgary before nightfall."

"Do they have Best Westerns in Canada?"

Jen slides into the chair across from me, the one Greg likes, and drops her head as if the hinge of her neck let go. Slowly, she raises up to look me in the eye. "Welcome to the computer age, Miss Little House on the Prairie. We will find out on the Internet, thanks to Al Gore."

"Do I want to find him?"

"Greg or Al Gore?"

I roll my eyes, surprised I have energy for it.

"You tell me," Jen says.

I want to know the answers, not have to figure them out. "Why would I want to fall at his feet and beg him to come home? He chose to leave me."

"You don't know that for sure."

"What else could it be? He's not much of a target for kidnappers, with his Swiss cheese bank account and lack of connections to anyone who does have money."

Neither one of us married for money. We have that going for us. Seems a pathetic tribute.

Jen teases the tag on her tea bag. "Another

possibility is that he's hurt."

"You don't think I know that? And for how long? What if he fell and broke his leg two days into the trip?"

"Libby."

"That would mean he's been lying in pain for more than two weeks by now! Out of his mind, maybe. I've seen the documentaries. He might have had to use his fillet knife to amputate an arm."

Jen sips her tea.

"Or what if he's had a stroke?" I add. "I know he's too young, but it happens. Or a heart attack. There's heart disease all over his mom's side of the family. His cholesterol's been creeping up these last couple of years. Or if a tree fell on him or he somehow passed out and tumbled out of the canoe or tried to make it through a rapids and hit his head on a rock and he's been unconscious all this time or —"

"Are you done?" Jen purses her lips like a school principal overseeing detention.

It may be time to advertise for a new best friend. "Any one of those scenes is a very real possibility."

"I know, hon. I've made a list of my own. But here's the deal. Dwelling on those what-ifs will drive us crazy."

"I'm halfway there. It'll be a short trip."

"What do we know for sure?" Jen asks, her face a portrait of concern.

"My life is over."

"Besides that." Concern morphs to chagrin.

"Look, Jen, if you're expecting me to say something trite like 'God is good all the time,' it might come out sounding slightly fake at the moment."

With both hands planted on the table, she pushes herself to standing, then paces the length of one counter. "We know God knows where Greg is."

"That much we can agree on."

She switches directions. "And we know that if Greg is intentionally AWOL, God is a much better seeker, finder, and avenger than we are."

"I'd like to take a stab at it."

Jen crosses her arms over her chest. "Sorry. Not your job." She's sensible to a fault sometimes. "And if Greg's injured or sick —"

"If not, he will be when I'm through with him."

She stops pacing and launches a balled-up paper towel at my head. "If . . . he's . . . sick . . ."

I fill in the blank she's left for me. "The Lord also knows that." It comes out sound-

49

ing like a sing-song Sunday school recitation, one I want with all my heart to believe.

Jen uncrosses her arms and reaches across the distance between us to lay a consoling hand on my arm. "Is Greg alone?"

"I sure hope so."

"No, I mean, if he's stranded in the wilderness somewhere, is he alone?"

"How can he still be alive? If he couldn't get word out to us, maybe he can't feed himself. Maybe he can't drink anything. And a person can only survive a couple of days without water. Maybe he's lying in a pool of —"

"Libby."

"Or at the bottom of —"

"I know you need to vent. And I know you might as well say these things out loud because the Lord knows your thoughts anyway. But it isn't helping to sit here paralyzed by fear about what may or may not have happened to your husband. I think God's given us a job to do."

"A job? I can't remember to brush my teeth."

She crouches at my feet again. Takes my worthless hands again. "Besides focusing on survival, Lib, I think God wants us to find Greg."

"Yeah, right." She must be sleep deprived too.

"I've been praying about this."

"Congratulations. I'm locked in a prayer cemetery. Ghosts and shadows but nothing that touches heaven."

The sympathetic woman squatting at my feet sighs like Jesus would if He heard me say that, which, of course, He did.

I'm a worm. If Greg is depending on my faith to conjure a divine rescue mission for him, he's a goner.

"It's time for us to get proactive, Libby."

Proactive. That's the advice she gave eight months ago when I finally confessed how empty this pseudomarriage makes me feel. *Get proactive, Lib. Don't let it die for lack of attention. Don't throw away a good man without a fight.*

Believe me, Greg and I are no strangers to the concept of fighting. We call our version the clam boil. I boil over. He clams up. Relational healing interaction of the highest quality.

Jen pounds the kitchen table pulpit. "Proactive, Lib. You and me. We can do something. Yes, we have to stay out of the way of the authorities and let them do their jobs. But don't you think two extremely intelligent women," she says, lifting her chin and affecting the timbre of an English professor, "can think of a dozen ways we can help this investigation along?"

"What do you want to do? Drain the boys' college funds and rent a float plane to cruise at treetop level over the whole Quetico?"

She leans back. "Now, see? You do still have a brain in that head of yours."

"Don't be ridiculous."

"And if not that idea, there are others. We can call motels. I suggested that before. We can call hospitals and resorts and . . . did you call your credit card company? Has there been any suspicious activity on your cards?"

It's a good thing one of us can think.

"Credit cards, Lib. That's a great place to start."

Jen conquered cancer five years ago. Now she thinks like a conqueror.

I suppose I should have expected this. I dragged her to concerts in between chemo sessions. I forced her to go to the cosmetology college for free eyebrow-drawing lessons. Some days she might not have gotten dressed if I hadn't insisted it would make her feel better. I would have been less pushy if I'd known she'd turn around and club me with it now.

I look at her pleading eyes and beautifully

arched reborn eyebrows and know the final dollop of excuses is about to meet the spatula of Jenika's insistence. But I'm nothing if not relentless, so I try one more.

"I don't have the energy to spit."

She rises, grabs the phone from its cradle, points it at me, and says, "It's a good thing you're not on your way to the dentist, then, isn't it? Dial."

I choke on the unspoken questions. What if we find him? What if we don't?

4

What is it called when computer screens get that bleached-out area if you don't use a screensaver? There's a word for it. It's the reason Bill Gates or somebody created screensavers. Whatever it's called, I think I have it. On my tongue. I've recited Greg's description, his Jeep's make and model and license plate number so many times the message is imprinted forever.

I wonder if God ever thought about creating a memory screensaver. A beach scene or mountain view or a vision of puppies to automatically flash in our minds when we've dwelt too long on something ugly. Good idea. I'll take it up with Him when this is over. We could share the patent.

Switching the phone to my right ear will mean writing with my left if I find a reason to take notes. So far it's not been necessary. A simple checkmark suffices. Is he here? No. Here? No. No. No. No sign of him.

I dial again. While I wait for the number to connect, I lean back in the kitchen chair. A knot at the base of my neck pops as if a vertebra rudely smacked its gum. One ring. Two. Three. Come on. Come on!

"Dew Drop Inn. Are you calling to make a reservation?"

"No. I'm —" I consider a smart-aleck answer. *No, miss. Thank you, but I have more than enough reservations. Among them are, how badly do I want my husband back? Am I absolutely, positively certain I'm not capable of homicide if he's done something reprehensible? If the wilderness became his grave, am I ready to be a widow?*

I swallow my sass acid and say, "I'm looking for my husband and thought he might have stopped there on his way home." Home.

"He's not here."

That was quick. I haven't even told the woman his name or vehicle model.

"Would you just check for me, please? This is important. A family emergency." That's not a fabrication. The arm Zack broke years ago might be acting up in the Chilean climate. Who's to know? My Zack — the only kid who's ever broken a limb in a marching band incident. That's one family emergency on record. Two? Lacey. Now this.

"Ma'am, I know for certain that your husband is not a guest here."

"But I haven't even told you his description." *Uno, dos, tres, quatro. . . .* Counting in Spanish is bound to be an even stronger stress-eliminator than in English.

"We got no guests registered."

I rub the prickled skin on the back of my neck. "None? Are you sure?"

"Only the four rooms. So, yeah, I'm sure."

The tiny little bubble of hope that appears with each number I dial dissipates faster than normal. Pop. Gone.

I'm developing a pressure sore on my tailbone. Time to get up and move. The sludge at the bottom of the coffee carafe looks like a science experiment gone bad. What happens if you drop crushed Oreos into a cup of Mississippi backwater? Compare and contrast.

I drink the sludge anyway. Something's wrong with me. Seriously.

When I bring the mug to my lips, I overshoot the angle. The vile liquid dribbles out both corners of my mouth and onto my shirt. It's going to stain. I don't care.

It's time to pick up the phone and resume the search.

I'm sure a counselor worth his salt would suggest there's something unhealthy about rehearsing the truth too often. "My husband's missing . . . missing . . . missing."

Any number of volunteers from church or the neighborhood would do this phone call research for me if I asked. But Jen's right. As acid-producing as it is to say the words, taking on a proactive role is better than sitting in a lump of festering concern.

Even considering the desk clerk at the Dew Drop Inn, I haven't met any unfriendlies on the phone. Privacy laws must be different north of the border. Everyone seems genuinely disappointed they can't help me. I have to believe they're telling the truth. Wish I could flush from my mind's eye the image of Greg slipping the motel managers a twenty and putting a finger to his lips to invoke their silence.

Every picture my imagination conjures rings false. None of these scenarios sounds like Gregory Michael Holden. But doesn't every neighbor of a serial killer or pipe bomber report, "He was such a nice, quiet man"? Could the same be true of good men who live lives of quiet desperation until given the opportunity to leave home and never return?

It catches me totally off guard when a

57

throaty voice on the other end of the line says, "Yeah. White Jeep Cherokee? Wisconsin plates? Sounds familiar. You'll hold for a moment? I'll go look."

What is this? He's there? My hand is shaking as my pen traces where I am on the list Jen printed out for me: Black Otter Inn — Whiskey Run, Ontario. I grab the MapQuest page for the area and scan for Whiskey Run. East? West? Where — ? There it is. It's not even a day's drive from Beaverhouse. Way to be clandestine, Greg. You'd never make it with the FBI or CIA.

"Jen!" I'm waving madly at her. Wonder what made her come back to the kitchen at this precise moment.

"What is it?" she whispers.

"A lead. We might have a lead." I drop her when the voice comes back on the line.

"Yep, he's here. Checked in last night. You want I should ring his room?"

I have no idea. Do I? Jen's ear is pressed close to mine, listening in like any good friend would. She pulls away and signals with hands, head, and eyes, "No!"

What? Of course, I want the guy to ring his room! Or wring his neck. Take your pick, mister. "Yes, please. I need to speak with him."

"Sure thing. Hang on."

Oh, I'm hanging on.

Jen's lovely eyebrows practically cross in the middle of her forehead. It's a new look for her. I wouldn't recommend she keep it.

"Hullo?" I hear through the receiver.

"Greg?"

A two-seconds-longer-than-eternity pause. "What?"

Is he drunk? That would be the first time ever. Unless this is more evidence I don't know him as well as I thought. "Do you want to explain what you're doing there?" No one will blame me for sounding less than gracious, right?

"What's this about, eh?"

I drop the phone. It hits the table, then the floor. The little plastic door to the battery compartment pops open and spills battery guts on the tile. My stomach contents will be next.

Breathe. Just breathe.

Jen's voice is oddly distant. My vision is shrinking. Full field. Tube. Pinhole.

"Libby! What's wrong?" Is she shaking me or am I doing that on my own? "Libby!"

"He's lived in the Midwest all his life," I drone through my zombie state.

"Yes? Sweetie, what is it?"

I cough out, "It's not him."

■ ■ ■ ■

I should have called the Canadian authorities before I talked to the guy with Greg's Cherokee but not his voice. If the imposter has a teaspoon of smarts in him, he's long gone already. But even half a teaspoon would have sent him to a motel considerably farther away from the scene of the crime, wouldn't it?

And what was his crime? "Offing" my husband so he could steal our high-mileage Cherokee? The villain is bound to regret that move, if he's caught. Which might not happen, thanks to my *faux pas.*

The driving need to talk to my husband exceeded my speed limit of wisdom. I should have let the authorities handle it, should have given them the information about the Jeep sighting and let them show up unannounced at the door of the motel room. No, I had to talk to him myself. I'll pay for this, won't I?

Jen uses her cell phone to dial the Ontario Provincial Police. She hands it to me to do the talking. As if I can.

With stretches of silence, the sergeant on the other end of the phone line expresses his disapproval of my techniques and poor

60

judgment.

"I'm sorry, Officer. I wasn't processing my thoughts. All I could think about was talking to my husband."

"Is it possible," the man ventured, "that it was your husband but his voice sounded strained?"

Do I need to detail how intimately I am acquainted with Greg's tummy-rumbling low voice?

Libby, I can't imagine my life without you. Will you marry me?

Deep, slow breaths, Lib. You can do it. One more good push, hon.

Libby. Oh, Libby, when you get this message, call me on my cell right away. It's Lacey. I've got to get to the hospital. Oh, Lib!

Lib, I don't know how to help anymore. What do you want me to do?

I return to the moment and reply, "I've heard my husband's voice when it's strained and that wasn't it." Strained. Every day for the last three years.

"The accent," I tell the officer. "I heard the Canadian accent, that way of pronouncing 'about.' A Peter Jennings accent. Not like my husband would say it, no matter how stressed. And the 'eh?' at the end."

No response.

"Okay, so it proves nothing except it

61

wasn't my Greg! If the desk clerk had his information correct and it was Greg's Jeep in the parking lot, then the person who drove it to the motel was not my husband, and any way you view that, something's not right."

"We'll look into it."

I drop my chin to my chest. "You will."

"I have someone in the area who will check it out."

And check out my story, he must be itching to say. How can he not want to investigate my there's-this-guy-in-a-cheesy-motel-and-he's-a-Jeep-thief story? I'm still a person of interest, aren't I? By some accounts, I can add obstruction of justice to my list of sins.

As Jen watches, I tell him, "Thank you. Please keep me informed if you discover anything?"

"Of course. But I must caution you not to let your own investigation sabotage the efforts of the professionals, Mrs. Holden."

Coffee. I need more coffee.

Jen may never forgive me for ignoring her warning. Oh, sure she will. Eventually. But for now she's letting me stew in the caldron of my error.

"What part of 'No, no, no!' do you not

understand, Libby?"

I pull open the junk drawer and paw through the refuse for the roll of duct tape. The battery compartment door on the portable phone won't stay latched. Duct tape. Why was that my first thought? It would have been Greg's — the Greg who may have been maliciously separated from his vehicle and his wife.

"Jen, I'm sorry, I'm sorry, I'm sorry. Put yourself in my shoes." It helps to focus on patching the phone while rationalizing. "If your husband were missing and you thought you were just a phone click away from finding out why, wouldn't you say, 'Sure. Be a doll and ring up his room for me'?"

"Not if my highly intelligent best friend were standing an inch away miming, 'No, no, no!' "

"My peripheral vision's not great."

"Uh-huh."

"I blacked out for a moment. Must be the heat."

"It's a cool seventy degrees in here."

The phone's fixed. A small but important victory in light of the recent string of defeats.

"Look, I can guarantee this won't be my last mistake."

"And it wasn't your first, either."

"Excuse me?"

I watch the skin around Jen's eyes and mouth soften from accusation to sympathy. "I know, it was a knee-jerk reaction. And who could blame you?"

"Besides you and the entire Canadian police force?"

"Hon, we're all on your side. We've got your best interests at heart. You know that, don't you?"

I put the phone on the table. Some would say I slammed it down. "Why are we debating this? You either forgive me or you don't. What's important is that we do have a clue. The Jeep is not in Greg's possession. Someone else has it. How did that slimeball get it?"

"Mr. Slime stole it?"

"Most likely."

"And that could mean —"

"I don't know." I grab fistfuls of my hair as if preparing to make tight pigtails. "Was Greg mugged in the parking lot? At a gas station? The authorities would have found evidence of a fight, wouldn't they? Or a . . . a body."

Jen reaches for a paper towel, wets it at the sink, then uses it to wipe something frown-producing from her elbow and the table on which she's been leaning.

"Maybe this guy you talked to swiped the Jeep while Greg was out in the wilderness somewhere. It doesn't necessarily mean Greg's hurt."

"If that's the case, why wouldn't Greg have made his way from the put-in point back to civilization by now and called home? He'd be fuming mad and maybe have worn out his walking shoes, but we would have heard from him."

"Ah."

A new thought dawns on me. "Unless Greg *sold* the Jeep to him."

"What?"

"We're exploring every possibility," I say, eyeing the call list I'm not eager to return to.

"It's also possible, and a lot more likely, that it wasn't Greg's Jeep at all. If the clerk read the license plate incorrectly —"

"It was a Wisconsin plate. He knew that much."

"And how many Jeep-driving guys from Wisconsin chose Canada for their vacation destination this year? Hundreds? Thousands?"

She's too smart for my own good. "Point well taken. But how many guys from Wisconsin sound like Peter Jennings used to and punctuate their sentences with 'eh'?"

65

"Point and counterpoint."

When it's all over, I should make an appointment to have this pain in my stomach checked out. When it's all over.

Where will I be when this is all over? Widowed? Divorced? Angry? Brokenhearted? Jilted? Relieved?

Did I just say *relieved?*

God help me. Is it an unpardonable sin to wonder what life would be like without the man I vowed to love and cherish and blah, blah, blah?

It looks like soup. Smells like soup. Feels like medicine going down.

Jen offers me another ladleful. I refuse her and use my spoon to point to what's left in my bowl — recalcitrant chunks of chicken floating in a cream-and-wild-rice sea with celery and mushroom flotsam. On an ordinary day, it would taste like a cooking contest entry. I'm not sure how long it will be before I see another ordinary day.

We're drinking cranberry juice with our meal and using Taco Doritos for crackers. Sooner or later, I'll have to get some groceries. Which means I'll have to leave the house. And see people. And answer questions. And pretend faith is enough. And that I have some.

Pastor asked if I'm planning to attend the prayer service at church tonight. Can you imagine? He's a good man, but he thinks like a male, no offense to the handful of sensitive men in the world who aren't gay.

I'm probably blacklisted from any future answers to prayer because I'm not attending the special prayer service *for my husband.* I can't do it.

All those naïve members of the congregation praying for Greg's return? Won't they blush if it turns out he's sharing a stateroom on a Mediterranean cruise with a woman he met on the Internet?

And that in order to bankroll his tryst he sold our Jeep to a Canadian somehow distantly related to Peter Jennings?

That should make an interesting bulletin announcement next Sunday.

Save your prayers for the funeral, folks. Either way, there's going to be a funeral.

5

And evening and morning were the fourth day.

I know by the rhythm of the knocks that Frank is at my back door. No standard tap-tap-tap for him. Or even a lighthearted tap-tap-tuh-tap-tap . . . tap . . . tap. No, Frank announces his arrival with something that sounds like a cavalry bugle cry right before the word, "Charge!"

"Door's open, Frank." I don't move from my place at the sink. Dishes and laundry aren't honoring the fact that Greg's gone. Why can't they hold a moratorium on household chores out of respect for the man who paid for them? Every time I look out the window, the lawn tugs at my sleeve. *A little attention here?* How rude. Brent offered to mow it for me. Remind me again why I turned him down?

I sent Jen home to tuck her girls into bed last night. They need her. A little girl needs her mama. I'm living proof. Jen probably sang to them, read to them, brushed their hair and their My Little Ponies' manes. She snuggled their warm bodies into hers and assured them of her love. She prayed with and for them and promised to protect them always. I should warn her not to make promises that might prove impossible to keep.

Jen returned around ten after receiving Brent's blessing to stay as long as needed. Brent's parents are coming to take over childcare for the duration so Brent can get back to work. To how many people will I be indebted when this is over?

Frank knows better than to ask if there's any word. We called him about the Jeep and talking to the imposter. I appreciate his silence on that subject. He nods to Jen, who's reentered the kitchen from returning pre-sympathy phone calls in Greg's office.

"What does Greg usually keep on that middle shelf above his computer?" she asks after wiggling her fingers at Frank as a symbol of greeting and solidarity.

"Middle shelf? I don't know." What do I care if a book or computer disk is out of place? What's missing from my life right now is decidedly bigger. "Why?"

"Just curious. It's dusty."

"You know where I keep the furniture polish." I don't even fake courtesy these days, which draws a frown and narrowed eyes from Frank.

Like a toddler forced to apologize to a sibling, I mutter, "Sorry," and return to the limp suds in the sink.

Jen rattles on. "The space is about eight inches wide, but only the outer inch along each side is dusty. Something usually occupies that spot, but it's gone."

I mentally trek back to the office and scan my memory for an image of how that room looks in its normal state. Greg's meticulous about his workspace. Not regarding dust, but clutter. Says he can't focus in chaos. Maybe that explains why our marriage isn't working. The chaos of unmet needs overwhelms him, so he checks out. But the unmet needs are mine, not his.

For the most part.

The office is Greg's personal space. I haven't crossed that threshold except out of necessity in a long time.

"Coffee, Frank?" I'm already pouring.

"Thanks. None of that flavored garbage, is it?"

"Mr. Holden, you're no hazelnut fan?" Jenika probably knows the answer to that, but I'm grateful she's shouldering the load of conversation.

"Me?" he asks, sniffing the brew I hand him. "Give me full octane, please. Nothing fancy." He slurps a scalding mouthful, then smacks. "Ah. Now, this is the real thing."

"It's decaf." Why did I insist on interjecting that unimportant piece of information? I know what his response will be.

"Get me a bucket! I'm about to spew!" The family drama king strikes again. He doubles over and holds his hand over his puff-cheeked mouth. Corny can be endearing sometimes.

I can see Jen struggling to suppress a laugh. She glances my way as if seeking permission to let it out, as if the circumstances demand she obtain a warrant before smiling or enjoying a joke. I appreciate Jen's thoughtfulness, but I am far from the boss of this situation.

"Libby, I've been thinking," Frank begins, after growing up about fifty years.

"What's that, Frank?"

"I'd like to take a look around the Quetico for myself."

I catch Jen's facial expression. Is she surprised he suggested it or surprised all three of us considered the same insane chess move?

Frank shrugs. "Maybe I wouldn't find

71

anything that would make us any smarter than we already are about Greg's disappearance."

No smarter? We're in the negative column at the moment.

"Then again, maybe I'll see something others overlooked. Or find my boy." He clears his throat. Sniffs. Sends his gaze and his private thoughts out the window.

Is his pain greater than mine? Is that possible? He lost someone he's loved longer than I've known him. I lost someone I contemplated leaving.

Greg hasn't always thought in sync with his dad, especially not on faith issues. But Greg managed to respect him all these years. That's impressive, now that I think about it.

My boy. Frank still calls him *my boy*. At his age.

Have you asked my boy if he's going golfing with me on Saturday?

Is my boy home?

I was thinking about taking my boy to the stock-car races this weekend.

Greg almost always says yes. I wonder if he ever told Frank how much he dislikes stock-car races.

Halfway down the hall to Greg's office, I

stop, lean against the wall, and press a thumb and forefinger to either side of the bridge of my nose. Will this be the setting for my total collapse?

I'm lost. In some ways, more lost than Greg is at the moment.

It's not that I haven't paid any attention all these years. Just not enough. Is it ever enough?

I know Greg made lists, computerized printouts of his menu ideas for wilderness living. Every time a new product appeared on the shelves at Greene's, he analyzed it for wilderness-worthiness — ease of cooking, minmum of additional ingredients required, not a lot of bulk to add to the weight of his pack, and proper packaging. No glass or cans allowed in the Quetico region, according to Greg. So any dried, dehydrated, or envelope-packaged product became a candidate for the menu plan of a guy with a pioneer spirit toward both canoe and frying pan.

Entering Greg's office feels like walking into a morgue to identify a body. The room is a lifeless shell lying on a metal gurney. *Is this him? Is this your husband?* the air asks.

It's a bright day. Despite the natural light, I flip on the ceiling fixture and desk lamp, chasing out the morgue references.

Where are Greg's lists of equipment and other supplies? Didn't he always carry around a clipboard and check off items in the weeks before his trips? Sleeping bag, camp stove, candle lantern, ground cloth, matches, iodine water tablets — which in recent years he exchanged for a filtration system — reading material for rain days, tent, extra stakes, toilet paper, paddles, life vests, tackle box, flashlight . . .

Knowing him, I imagine the list alphabetized. But I can't imagine where he kept it. *Keeps* it.

We need that list. Yes, we. Frank lost the battle to insist Jen and I stay here. After explaining that Alex and Zack — the natural choices — will be out of reach for at least another week or more and that Brent's job situation is too tenuous at the moment to risk leaving, we watched Frank's resistance suddenly give way, as if we were arm wrestling and he let us win at the last second, his arm and arguments slammed to the table.

I swivel Greg's high-backed office chair until it faces me and allows me to lower myself into it. It seems an act of intimacy I'm not prepared to process. I force myself to relax into the fabric as if lowering myself slowly into a Jacuzzi that promises comfort but requires a few moments of acclimation.

Frank's at his house, informing my mother-in-law he's about to haul two inexperienced, outdoors-challenged women miles away from civilization and indoor plumbing for the purpose of a north-of-the-border Canadian wild goose chase. She'll flip. Then she'll call me and demand I talk him out of it.

"You can't let him do this, Libby."

"Pauline, I obviously have no control over my own husband, much less yours."

"Yes, well, you don't have to feed his hare-brained ideas."

"Greg is your son. Aren't you as worried as we are? Don't you have half a mind to join us?"

She'll pause a moment and say the words that will remind me why we've never grown close. *"Stepson, Libby. He's my stepson."*

Right.

A stepson who's been a part of your life since he was a toddler. And you still can't look at him as anything but a foreigner to you, a young man who belongs to your husband — *his boy* — but not to you.

Oh, Greg! Did you finally find a woman who would embrace you with her whole heart, nothing held back? You don't have a great track record for that, do you?

I don't want Pauline's caustic, cold voice — liquid nitrogen — talking us out of searching for him, or reminding me of myself.

If Jen and I find that list, maybe we can get on the road before Pauline dials the phone.

I pull open a file cabinet drawer.

Not having Zack and Alex here at Search Central is wrong on so many levels. When they find out what's happened and realize that while they were dancing on mountaintops — as happy as little boys with a new tree fort — their father was in trouble and their mother planned to join him, they'll freak.

If they were here, they could use their techno-machetes to hack into Greg's laptop for me. Maybe he told them his password. I'm not privileged to that information. As it is, I hope Greg left a paper trail.

"Any progress?" Jen asks, entering the office with more energy than ought to be legal. She presses an apple into my hand. She's more my mother than the woman who gave birth to me. What is it about the matriarchs in our lives? Great role models.

"Nothing yet."

"Did you look in here?" She pulls open the top drawer of the four-tiered filing cabinet next to Greg's desk. "Whoa!"

The color-coordinated, carefully labeled folders — as tidy and symmetrical as rake marks in a Japanese garden — can't help but impress.

"Tried the top drawer already," I tell her. "All work related. Second drawer is too. Third is household stuff. Maintenance records. Receipts. Bank statements."

She reaches for the handle as she asks, "What's in the fourth?"

"It's marked 'Personal.' "

"You don't think that at a time like this, rules of courtesy might need to be jettisoned in favor of finding your husband?"

My thoughts exactly. That's not what keeps me from opening that drawer. Searching in vain for words to explain what I most fear discovering, I feign interest in a stray piece of paper from Greg's in-basket. "You can look if you want."

Jen moves quickly, punctuating her search with a peppering of "hmm" and "aha" and "well, isn't that interesting?"

How can I not respond? "What's so interesting?"

"Looks as if he's kept every card or note you've ever written him."

"He did not. He's not into cards."

Jen pulls a bulging folder from the bottom

77

file drawer. "Then what do you call this?"

Does it surprise me that the cards are chronologically organized? No. It surprises me that he kept them.

Touching them lightly, as would a detective sifting carefully through the ashes of a burnt-out home, I glance through a few cards, fighting that familiar constriction in my throat.

"This isn't . . . helping," I say. "We're looking for his equipment list. And clues."

"You don't think these are clues, Libby?" Her voice drips with meaning.

I close the folder and aim to slide it back into the drawer, reaching in front of my friend like an uncouth uncle at a family dinner.

"Try that one." I point to a folder marked "Canadian Adventures."

"I was getting to it." Jen springs to her feet, folder in hand, without the groans customary to my rising from a squatting position. A few seconds into the folder's contents, she says, "This is great stuff."

"What? Did you find it? The supplies list?"

"No." Her voice barely registers on my internal decibel meter.

With thoughts of Pauline's idea-squelching voice in my ear, I let my exasperation show. "Jen, will you please focus?

We don't have much time. We're looking for
—"

"This could be genuinely helpful," she says, refusing to mirror the edge in my voice.

"What is it?"

"Greg's journals."

"He kept a diary?"

"His trip journals," she said, flipping through pages of a pocket-sized spiral memo pad. "These are rich."

I grab the little book out of her hands and toss it onto the desk. I'll probably have to apologize later for my roughness. Right now, I'm driven to get our vehicle and canoes pointed north.

"Jenika, find me that list or get out of the way."

She purses her lips.

"Sorry," I tell her. "It's that important."

She stares me down, but her facial features soften like a stick of butter on the kitchen counter in July. Turning back to the bottom drawer, she pulls out the next folder, opens it, and slaps it on the desktop.

"There."

The list.

Ten or twelve photocopies of it. As if he had more trips in mind for the future.

Was this the work of a man who planned to leave home?

I grab one copy and bolt for the door. We have work to do. After two steps into the hall, I stop and retrace my steps. Wrapping my fingers around the spiral notebook, I yank it off the desk and motion for Jen to follow me. We are, after all, in this together.

Between Greg's, Frank's, and Brent's garage and basement stashes, we round up enough equipment for the three of us. How many times did I throw a frown or snide comment Greg's way because he wanted to purchase a second cooking stove or a better-quality sleeping bag? Now I'm grateful for the excesses.

Brent's kelly green canoe hasn't been road- or water-tested yet. I find it remarkable he's willing to let us take it on its maiden voyage. Maybe Frank will use that one, and we women will commandeer Frank's banged-up, dented tin can with pointy ends. An echo of Greg's complaints about how heavy it was to haul it — much less all their supplies and equipment — over the portages when he was a kid makes my back ache.

It finally hits me what I'm about to do. Portaging over rugged trails that connect one navigable stretch of water to another. Canoeing. Sleeping under the stars. Drinking water with pine needles and microscopic who-knows-what floating in it. Using a log for a toilet seat.

I am in so much trouble.

Frank insists we take fishing equipment — not for pleasure, but for survival. The word *survival* scares me. It's hard not knowing exactly how long we'll be gone. We've told our loved ones no more than a week. Jen says she has an appointment a week from Tuesday that would be tough to reschedule. It's quite a lot already asking her to leave her girls for as long as we'll be gone. And Brent. What a guy!

Pauline laid down the law for Frank. She is not going to miss their vacation to Branson over Labor Day weekend, whether we know anything about Greg by then or not. Sweet woman. The other couples sharing the RV with Frank and Pauline are depending on their third of the rent for the unit and their third of the gas money.

Give or take a day, we three have one week to conduct our search. I can't dwell too long on the idea that finding anything more than a corpse would be a miracle after this much time anyway.

So, we have a week. We grab loaves of bread, Ziploc bags stuffed with peanut butter, sticks of summer sausage, pancake mix, slab bacon, string cheese, boxes of hash brown potatoes. We have no way of knowing if it'll be enough, or if we'll find a stranded man who'll be grateful for a crumb of our leftovers.

"We need the freedom to supplement with fish," Frank says.

I can see it now. Three adventurers, our pant legs rolled up Huck Finn style, watching fat little red and white bobbers dance on the waters of a crystal clear lake. The sun is in our faces. Frank's chewing on a piece of straw that he got from — where? Jen and I are hoping we catch something edible without having to impale another worm on a hook or handle one of those slimy artificial nightcrawlers Greg claims are lunker killers.

"Anything?" Jen will ask.

"Got a nibble," I'll answer.

"Play it cool, Libby," Frank will add. "Set the hook good before you start to reel him in. And keep that rod tip up."

"This is the life, huh?" Jen will add.

"Ideal day," I'll say, "except for the fact that my husband is missing and may be dying and we're wasting our time filling our frying pan!"

The garage feels crowded. Too many people. Too many thoughts. With Frank looking over my shoulder and continuing his rationale for the need for rods and reels and tackle boxes, I pull open the storage door behind which Greg keeps his fishing poles. What could possibly be left in here? Won't he have taken most of it with him?

My stomach flips end to end. Shouldn't there be blank places, at least a couple of them, where his fishing poles normally rest? But they're all here. Every rod holder embraces its mate.

"Curious," Frank says from behind me.

"He probably bought a couple of new rods and just didn't tell me."

Jen asks, "Do you think he would do that?"

"Doesn't explain this," Frank says, dragging a sewing machine-sized tackle box out from the floor of the storage unit. The scraping sound of plastic on concrete sets my nerve endings on edge.

"Would he have taken a smaller tackle box in his canoe?" Jen offers, stuffing sleeping bags into a garbage bag-lined pack. "That big one's probably too heavy for a solo trip, right?"

"Maybe." Frank seems absorbed in something along the far wall of the garage. "Both of his telescoping fishing nets are still here. What was my boy thinking?"

As we gather our own needs from the

more than ample supply of fishing tackle left to us, some emotion between anger and fear returns and churns within me.

You didn't intend on fishing at all, did you, Greg? You lied to me. To your father. To the boys. Coward! Why couldn't you tell me to my face that you were leaving me?

I'll have to forgive him for that. He could accuse me of plotting my departure with the same level of cowardice.

6

When Frank said, "We'll get an early start in the morning," I didn't know he considered anything after midnight morning. The garage door is open. As I stare into the comfortless night, a rogue breeze tickles a handful of leaves in the driveway. They skate out of the shadows into the garage to escape its teasing.

I don't dare look too far past the Blazer parked just outside the doorway. If a crowd of onlookers is forming, I don't want to know. This process is private. Personal.

Silence accompanies us as we pack Frank's Blazer. We should talk about the trip. Plan. Strategize. All the words are locked in some internal dungeon of pain.

Greg, what have you done?

We have a long trip ahead of us with little elbow room for our bodies or our minds. We secured everything we could under the overturned canoes now lashed to the top of the canoe carrier on the Blazer roof. Fishing nets, life vests, canoe paddles, and a few other items are tucked up, strapped in, and ready to go. The final tie-down of the canoes must wait until we close the back end of the vehicle for the last time, which won't happen until we've shoehorned in the rest of our equipment.

My fellow travelers leave companions behind. Pauline and Brent will hold down the fort while their mates are gone. Frank and Jen will be missed. Other than a message on the boys' voice mail services, I have no contacts to make.

Brent's a gem. I know he must worry about letting Jen take off like this. She's as inexperienced as I am in these things. But he trusts her.

What he actually said was that he trusts the Lord in her.

Brent promised to pick up my mail and field any can't-wait phone calls. I am free to leave home and no one will notice. Or care. Not this time.

Before that thought's reverberation dies, the phone rings. Pastor heard from the church secretary, who heard from one of our neighbors, that lights are on at our house. At this hour. I wonder if Mrs. Hensley mentioned the canoes.

Assured there is no emergency other than the one he already knows about, Pastor asks how I'm holding up and tells me the elder board is planning another prayer vigil. Can I help it if I'm distracted? Every minute spent celebrating the wonder of "the family of God" is another minute Greg is in trouble.

"Did I call at a bad time? It's three in the morning. Of course it's a bad time."

"What? No. Well, yes. We're . . . um, Greg's dad and Jen and I are . . . we're packing to head north. We hope to retrace Greg's trip."

No immediate answer. He's probably searching his brain for a way to tell me God loves the mentally ill.

"Libby?"

"Yes?" I feign innocence, though I know his next words are bound to be an exhortation of biblical proportions.

"If that's what you believe the Lord is calling you to do, then you can be confident He'll go ahead of you."

Those words would comfort me if I'd thought to ask Him first.

It's almost time to take our final bathroom breaks prior to buckling ourselves into the Blazer when Pastor jogs up the driveway and into the garage. How did he get here so fast?

"Looks like you're all set," he says, eyeing the overloaded gypsy wagon for the outdoorsman. And women.

"It'll have to do," Frank says.

Pastor and Frank have met several times on multiple Easter Sundays and Christmases.

"You be careful up there," Pastor says, his eyes sweeping the lot of us. "And keep in touch as able. Do you have cell phones with you?"

Jen jumps in to explain that there is no cellular service where we're headed. She might want to dive into an explanation of the wonders of satellite phones, but we have a full day's drive and an unknown future ahead of us. So I pull away from the communication curb faster than she can and tell him, "Thanks for coming to see us off, Pastor. That means a lot. We hope to be back before the week is out."

"I came to pray God's blessings on your trip."

So he does. Then he presses two hundred dollars from the church's benevolent fund into my hand to help cover the cost of the trip. Before he can say *bon voyage* or *vaya con Dios* — either of which would sound a little strange coming from a tall Swede — I thank him and open the passenger door.

"Well," he says, "we won't stop praying for you three and Greg. Can't wait to hear the miracle stories."

Yeah. Me, either.

I watch the familiar fade from my field of vision. Riding shotgun isn't all it's cracked up to be when the road leads away from the comfort of home and toward an unknown that promises nothing but the likelihood of an unhappy ending.

The first miles of our trip seem innocuous enough. If it weren't for the twin-peaked canoe "awning" visible through the windshield and my father-in-law behind the wheel, this could be a trip to the antique mall — if it weren't for the awning, my father-in-law, and the tightness in my chest.

Dawn was tardy but eventually showed up. The corn looks good. Both sweet and field. Subtle difference in tassel color. Even those of us who don't farm can appreciate the sight of healthy cornstalks along the highway followed by close-cropped hayfields followed by pastures of healthy-looking Holsteins.

Greg always sees these scenes through the spectrum of a grocery store: cases of creamed corn, gallons of milk, a cooler full of meat, ingots of cheese.

I see them as artwork. Green on green. Shadows and light. The delicate symmetry in the height of the cornstalks and the pattern of enormous round hay bales waiting for hungry heifers.

What have he and I ever observed through the same eyes?

Our children.

I turn in my seat to see if Jen has anything to talk about. I need a diversion stronger than corn. She's napping. Good idea. Would if I could.

"You okay?" Frank asks from the cockpit of this adventure ride.

I face forward again and search the view through the windshield for an answer to his question. "Fine."

"How is that possible?" He tosses me a smile full of empathy.

"Frank, thank you."

"For what?"

"Making this trip. Allowing us to come."

His hands grip the steering wheel at eleven o'clock and six o'clock. Now ten and two. Now five and seven. "Did I have a choice?"

"Sure you did. You could have told us what we already know — that we're crazy."

"And if I hadn't given in to you two, what

would have happened next?"

The turkey farm to my right draws my attention but offers no words for me. I'm on my own. "We probably would have pestered you until your eardrums bled."

"Figured as much. Get a steady diet of that at home."

He's never before admitted anything of a personal nature. What am I supposed to do with the confession? "Well, thanks anyway."

"You're welcome. I'm no saint, though."

I know. Me, either.

He continues, "I don't mind telling you I have my doubts you two can stick this out more than a couple of days at the pace we'll have to keep. No offense."

I want to respond with a reminder of how many years it's been since he took a trip like this, how rusty he might be, how much older he is, how it's dangerous to underestimate the power of a woman scorned or grieving. But I have more confidence that he's right than that I am.

"You know we'll try our hardest, Frank."

"I know. You always have. On almost everything."

Almost? I don't need to ask what he means. The whole world knows I could have tried harder to keep Greg from wanting to leave me.

Frank reaches to turn on the radio, another move for which I'm grateful. Until the music starts.

Elvis. He's so lonely, he could die.

"Could we change the channel?"

Frank flinches. "I guess. None of that 'Rock of Ages' stuff. Okay?"

Punching the "seek" button four times lands us on an oldies-but-not-as-old-as-Elvis station. Safe for now.

I lean my head against the side window. Closing my eyes against the blast of air conditioning, I disappear into the sound of yesterday's troubles seeming so far away.

Not true.

7

We've been on the road for nine hours, and we're still more than a hundred miles from our first Canadian destination — the ranger station where we'll check in. We could have been well on our way toward a vacation on a white-sand beach in Florida by this time.

Instead, we're bumping along narrow highways with a great variety of roadkill littering the shoulders. Bloated porcupines, whole families of raccoons, mangled white-tailed deer pulverized by passing semis, a rare coyote — or was that a wolf once upon a time? — and something big and brown with a long, flat tail. I thought it was a beaver, but Jen thinks she saw tire tracks on the tail, which means the tail may not have started out flat.

I let down my grief-guard long enough to appreciate the wildflowers along the road. Despite their weedy heritage, the periwinkle-blue chicory blossoms are an elegant adornment against a sun-scorched, windblown late-summer landscape. The newspapers are full of complaints about the purple loosestrife that's reproducing like rabbits without consciences, but I find its color a relief from endless miles of green and brown and tan in the ditches. Indian paintbrush, black-eyed Susans, and Queen Anne's lace complete the long, narrow bouquets.

"Did you notice," Jen asks between bites of granola bar, "that the farther north we venture, the wimpier the pine trees get?"

I'm driving. Jen's navigating. Frank's supposed to be sleeping in the backseat in preparation for his next stint behind the wheel. But he mumbles, "It'll get worse. Where we're headed, the topsoil, if you can call it that, is as thin as my wife slices cheese. Solid rock underneath. Nothing can put down traditional roots. That's one of the reasons you won't find many oaks and other taproot trees this far north. The thin topsoil changes the ecostructure."

Ecostructure? When did he start using words like that?

"Tree roots," he says with a yawn, "like cedars and pines, spread out rather than reach downward. Makes them . . . unstable . . . in high . . . winds."

Jen and I glance at each other and smile. He's snoring before he finishes the word "winds."

The burger we grabbed at a drive-through hours ago sits like wet plaster in my stomach. As we bounce over yet another bump the highway department neglected to announce, I note that the wet plaster is tumbling in a cement mixer. I should be starting this trip much stronger than I am.

Physically too.

Jen's experimenting with the satellite phone Frank rented from Northern Rent-All for more money than we'll inherit when he passes. She has to roll down the window and point its antennae halfway to the Twin Cities to get it to work, but she manages to make a test call. Her beloved. How sweet. She reports our progress, lets him know she's fine, and says she misses him and their girls already. Tell me about it. Then she asks Brent to call Pastor and make sure he put our trip on the prayer chain.

Something wrinkles inside my chest. Is that what I want? For this misadventure to be broadcast all over the church? Less than a day into this crisis, church friends were showing up at my door with casseroles, Bundt cakes, and Jell-O salads with fruit cocktail and marshmallows. Pastel-colored marshmallows. If God had wanted marsh-mallows to come in pastel colors, He would have —

Never mind.

It's not that I don't appreciate the gestures. But as I packed more food into my fridge, it became more evident that I was the only one at home to eat it. I suppose I'll have to write thank-you notes when I get home. If I'm not knee-deep in funeral preparations or searching for a cheap but determined "marriage eraser" lawyer. People with Bibles on their coffee tables don't use the "D" word.

In the confines of the Blazer, it's impossible not to overhear Jen on the phone. She reassures Brent that we all understand how much he wishes he could have joined us. I would have gladly let him take my place. He would serve this team well with his experience and strength and the fact that he can care deeply without falling apart like I do.

His work wouldn't allow his accompanying us. Plus we would need the space in that second canoe to . . . to bring Greg home.

"That's a little weird to get used to," Jen says after finishing her test-run with the SAT phone.

"What is?"

"The time delay. We both can't speak at the same time or the voices cancel each other out. I suppose it would work better if we did that thing they do in the movies."

I check my rearview mirror and pull into the left lane to pass yet another logging truck. The canoes strapped to the top of Frank's Blazer whistle and sing with the increased speed.

That could get annoying.

"What thing?"

"Next time I use the phone," Jen persists, "I'll finish my sentence, then I'll say 'over.' That'll let Brent know it's okay to talk."

"How much battery life does it have?" I'd love for us to have to use it our first day out to tell the boys and Greg's stepmom and Pastor and the prayer chain that we found Greg, safe and sound, and are coming home. That's what I want, right?

A week. We have a week to find our answers before life and its appointments force us to return home. If Greg is out there somewhere in the wilderness, how could he last that long? If he's on his way to a new life in Aruba with a woman who — unlike me — could afford a plastic surgeon for her imperfections, why are we doing this?

We pull into the gas station/convenience

store/Subway restaurant combo in International Falls for a much-needed bathroom break. We're running on fumes in the gas tank, but Frank insists we need to wait to fill up until we cross into Canada. He wants to maximize our ability to stretch our gas supply for the Canadian side of our trip, noting the infrequency of gas stations there compared to the U.S. side.

Frank danced in his seat when we crossed from Wisconsin into Minnesota at Duluth and discovered a significant drop in gas prices between the two states. I half expected him to call Pauline on the SAT phone and talk her into moving to Minnesota.

Frank nods toward the restaurant half of the convenience store as he checks the straps holding down the canoes. "Better take advantage of the opportunity for some hot food."

"Hot food? Does that mean I can't have a cold smoked turkey sub with provolone and cucumber?" Jenika teases.

"Mark my words," he says. We wait for what those mark-worthy words will be. Nothing.

"I just want a Diet Pepsi," I tell Jenika as I lean against the side of the Blazer to stretch my back muscles.

"Ask for extra ice," Frank says.

"Why?"

"A week from now, you'll think ice is a gift from heaven."

So he's assuming this will take all week. That's not a good sign.

It's always a little nerve-racking with Frank behind the wheel. He was one of the reasons someone invented cruise control, which wouldn't be a problem if the cruise control worked on the Blazer.

We don't need to worry about his speed behind the wheel as we approach the border crossing, though. We crawl in a line of forty or more vehicles waiting to pass through the Canadian customs checkpoint in the heart of International Falls.

I should have brought a book to read. Jen occupies herself by talking sign language to the little boy who signs back from the rear window of his family's RV in line ahead of us. Did I know she knew sign language? Oh, that's right. Her niece is deaf.

We're forty-five-minute veterans of the crawling line now. Frank slips the Blazer into "park" and turns off the ignition. What is he doing? He undoes his seatbelt latch and opens the door. Right here on the highway!

When I hear him fiddling with the gas cap, I understand. He's using the spare gas can to pour a little American gas into the tank so we can make it as far as a Canadian gas station. Before the vehicles behind us have a chance to grow impatient, he's back in the driver's seat, catching us up the five feet the line has moved since he turned off the engine.

Ontario is less than a block away now. The customs office looks like an enormous, glorified toll booth. In just a few minutes it will be our turn.

"Let me do the talking, girls," Frank says, as if we're smuggling contraband or something. We're not, are we?

Jen reaches over the back seat toward me. "Hand me your passport."

I dig though my purse for the document I've needed only once in my forty-five years, when a short-term missions trip to Belize with the boys' youth group two years ago convinced me I was allergic to orphanages.

I remember Greg's incredulity when the U.S.-Canada border crossing rules changed and a driver's license was no longer adequate proof of identity or citizenship. How had I kept my wits about me to remind the others to include their passports in our warp-speed packing?

While the customs officer scans the interior of our vehicle and looks over our documents, I scan the interior of my purse. I'm about to embark on a leg of this journey for which I won't need my purse or anything in it. I remove a lip gloss and slip it into the breast pocket of my denim shirt. From my wallet, I grab pictures of Zack and Alex. They join the lip gloss. I dig into the depths of my bag again.

My fingers brush against a long, thin, paper-wrapped cardboard tube at the bottom of my purse. Oh, no! I didn't even think about —

While Frank answers the border patrol's questions about explosive materials and firearms, I clutch the neck rest on Jen's passenger seat and pull myself toward her ear.

"Jen!"

"What?"

"Tampons!"

"Not to worry. I packed extra. Stuffed them in the foot of my sleeping bag, just in case."

"Thank the Lord."

"At least," she adds, "I think that's the bag I'll be using."

We both eye the man in the driver's seat. It could be an interesting first night in the wilderness.

■ ■ ■ ■

"Lib?" Jen's whisper slides out of the side of her mouth. We're both in the backseat now. Somehow that's where we landed after the stop for gas.

"What?" I counter with my own sideswipe.

"You sighed just now. Something new? It almost looked as if you held your breath until we cleared customs."

I angle my body farther toward the back of the vehicle, hoping my words will dissipate in the air and not reach Frank's ears. His thick fingers tap the steering wheel to the rhythm of something twangy burping its way out of the radio speakers. The danger of his hearing us over that noise is parchment thin.

I begin, "Frank's got it in his head that rules and regulations are more challenge than guide."

"I've noticed."

"You have?"

"When he's driving, we don't have to worry about whiplash at intersections with a light or sign. He's yet to come to a complete stop. And isn't there some well-publicized rule about not passing on the right of a slow-moving vehicle?"

I stifle a chuckle. Greg didn't inherit those habits from his father. I always feel safe with Greg behind the wheel. That's a blessing, I guess. One I haven't thought about for a while.

Safe. I wonder if Greg's computer thesaurus lists *dispassionate* as a synonym for *safe.*

Was I always a half-empty thinker? How far back would I have to trace to find the point at which I lost hope? It wasn't an episode. My bucket of hope for us — Greg and me — sported a mere pinhole. That's why it's taken so long for me to run dry — the reason I didn't walk away three years ago.

The honeymoon. Did it start then? Would the pinhole have sealed itself over if Greg hadn't flipped on the television in the motel when we were done?

If I'd spoken up rather than pouted, what might have happened? What if I'd told him, "Greg, honey, could we just hold each other until we fall asleep?" I can't imagine he would have refused me. Not his style. Maybe he didn't know how much I needed the comfort of his steady breathing, the re-assuring weight of his arm across my middle, the coordination of our pulses.

Somewhere along the line, I stopped expecting what I needed. Now I expect I'll be disappointed. And I am. That's an easy expectation to meet. And then, of course, Lacey.

Jen's voice breaks through. "Are you asleep?"

"What?"

"You sleeping or thinking?"

"Thinking."

"Is that wise?"

Jen deserves her own talk show. Or radio counseling program.

"You're missing some great scenery," she says. "We're through Fort Frances and heading into the true North."

I lift my head and glance out the window. The road isn't a four-lane ribbon of asphalt anymore. It's a thread. One lane each way. Smooth enough, but almost absent of shoulders. Road, rock, water. Nothing much between. A glacier-thrown pottery "fence" of gray, lichen-covered rocks keeps Rainy River and Rainy Lake from washing over the road.

Four hundred miles south, the pine trees are thick-necked linebackers. Here, many of the pines that cling to the rocks are more like pool cues with shaved chenille pipe-cleaner arms. Their branches start high on their trunks, as if their arms extend from narrow chins. No necks.

Did you notice that, Greg? When you passed this place, did you notice the skeletal trees? What was on your mind? Did you know already you weren't coming home? How long ago did you decide?

One of these days, I'll know.

One of these days, the truth will come out. He'll call home, say he's sorry but he couldn't take it anymore and hopes the boys and I will forgive him. Or he'll slip up and get caught on film — convenience store or ATM surveillance footage, in the crowd at a high school football game in his new hometown, on the video phone of Greg's new neighbor — a computer geek — who stumbles onto the "My Dad's Missing" website Alex will create.

One of these days I'll know if I have penance to pay for thinking such thoughts, for wasting time on anger when I should have spent it on worry. Or grief.

I can't begin to process this until I know what happened. *Should I feel sorry for you, Greg? Or sorry for me?*

Frank powers down his driver's side window and spits into the wind.

"Frank!"

"It was just chewing gum. Lighten up."

Jen presses her lips into a thin line. Or are they zippered shut? I, on the other hand, can't make mine stick together. "No doubt Canada has rules against littering."

"It's biodegradable." The rearview mirror captures his expression. Deadpan.

Biodegradable? That's his reasoning? Number one, are we so sure? And number two —

Jen puts a hand on my knee, as if holding me back from jumping over the seat in front of me. Not that I would.

She's right. I can't let irritation over Frank's habits override my gratitude.

She taught me that lesson the first time years ago, when her every morning began with a prayer of gratitude for the breath of life.

8

As the hash marks on the road register our progress like ticks on a stopwatch, I fight with a voice that seems to rise from the moan of tires on asphalt.

What do you think you're doing? And how dare you involve these innocents?

I need Frank and his expertise. I could do without his creative driving practices, but so far we've avoided blue-and-red bubble lights, sirens, and a need for airbags. I stare at the back of his head, with his loved-on baseball cap firmly settled on top. Little tufts of wiry gray hair poke out from under the cap near his ears and along his collar.

What would he do today if he weren't here on this misadventure? Get a haircut? Wander down to Hardee's for coffee with his buddies? Tag along with Pauline to her weekly visit to the herbologist in whose hands she trusts everything from her skin care to her digestive function? I'm sure Pauline has good qualities. Thinking I'd find them in the mere two dozen years I've known her must have been rushing it.

Lord, bless Frank for putting up with her.

I wonder if Frank looks at me and asks God to bless Greg.

Dangerous thoughts. I shift my daydreaming to Jen, who tugs the seatbelt away from her throat.

"So, what do you think?" she says. " 'Ninety-nine Bottles of Beer on the Wall' or 'Ten Little Monkeys' or 'The Song That Never Ends'? Your choice."

"We're not singing."

"Not even 'It's a Small World After All'? That would make the time fly."

I've heard of people who need to seek a therapist's help to get that song out of their head following a trip to Disney World. It's playing catch-me-if-you-can in my brain tunnels already.

"Jen, if you start, be prepared to thumb a ride home on a logging truck."

"Then quit touching me."

"I'm not."

"Are too. Frank, she's on my side."

He doesn't respond to our child's play. With feigned disgust, I snatch the hem of my denim shirt back onto my half of the seat and make a show of plastering myself against the door on my side. "Happy?"

"Always."

And she is.

As challenging as they were for her, her cancer years merely made the sound of her life more musical as the water bubbled and bounced and sparkled over and around the rocks thrown in her stream's path.

Mine? Sluggish water doesn't gurgle and sing. It lies there, breeding mosquitoes and dull scum. Was that depression? Should I have listened to Greg when he suggested I might need the help of a professional to conquer it? Instead, I resented the implication. What if I'd found a way — through whatever means — to make magnificent waves over the obstacles rather than allow them to form impenetrable dams?

Jen had been looking for a whiskey barrel and a home church the day we met in the garden center. A whiskey barrel in which to grow flowers, and a home church in which to grow her young but exuberant faith.

What made her think she could ask me a question about church? In faith matters, she was bold as a Magic Marker. Still is. Some days I feel as if I'm writing the story of mine in chalk.

"Your tote bag," she'd explained that first day. "It's what gave me the confidence to ask. 'Women of Faith.' Pretty clear advertisement."

A better advertisement than my life at the time.

I wrote our church's web address on a corner of my grocery list, tore it off, and handed it to her. Jenika thanked me and clocked me. That's the phrase, isn't it? *Clocked me* means she knocked me flat, right? She said, "Do you mind if I pray for you?"

The newcomer, a stranger five minutes earlier, wanted to pray for me? Maybe she'd find our church a tad mild-mannered for her tastes.

What could I say? "Sure."

"Lord, please bless Libby today. Clear the path ahead of her. Fill her with Your presence and Your joy. And may she find answers waiting where she thought there were only questions. In Jesus' Name, amen."

"Amen," I agreed more deeply than I thought I could.

I brought years of faith experience to the table. She brought life. Joy. Exuberance. I like to think I offered our friendship the benefit of wisdom, but somewhere along the line — remarkably close to the time my marriage grew stale — that shifted to her camp.

I mentored her — isn't that a laugh? — for the first couple of years. We met weekly for Bible study and prayer. I knew my stuff. She infused it with life.

Then, the invasion. A small but powerful army of cancer cells invaded her left breast. We cried together. She stopped crying before I did.

Somewhere in the process, we switched roles. I blame cancer. That's an easy option. Who would side with cancer? It made her stronger. Her spiritual growth spurt outdistanced me.

I shrank. She thrived, disease and all.

I might have caught up with her, but Lacey died that year.

Jen is tugging at her seatbelt again and trying a different position for her legs. It's my fault she's uncomfortable. No one has to tell me that.

"Thank you for doing this, Jen."

"Doing what? Backing off on the singing idea?"

Always the comedian. "For coming on the trip. For sacrificing so much."

"Don't make me nobler than I am. Only part of this is for you. And Greg, of course. The rest of it is for me."

She already won her lifetime membership in the Courage Club. What more could she need to gain?

I'm the one who's starting at square one.

9

As we fly along the last few miles of Canadian asphalt, I finger my sons'. photos — candid shots from their senior year in high school. Their hairstyles have changed radically since these were taken. Not their smiles, though, or their Greg Holden eyes.

I used to carry a picture of Lacey in my wallet. But I created too many scenes in checkout lines. When asked to produce my driver's license for identification, I'd flip open my wallet and there — in her electric blue gymnastics leotard — was my darling daughter.

Ma'am, are you okay? Can I help you? Ma'am? Someone call the manager!

Too many times. Too many tears.

It's better for everyone if her pictures stay tucked away in my lingerie drawer.

Greg couldn't have known sending her to school that day was the wrong thing to do. He thought he was being a good dad. Isn't he famous for that? Good dads don't cave in to their preteen daughters' mood fluctuations, right?

I wish I'd been home. I would have let her skip school that once. Ginger tea sometimes helped me. We would have talked about the glories of heating pads and Midol and marked a butterfly or something on the calendar to remind us of her first sign of approaching womanhood.

How would Greg have known to do something like that?

I can't blame him. But the truth of the matter is that she'd still be alive if he'd been a little more sympathetic to a girl's cramps.

My mind never listens to me. Against my better judgment, it thrusts me back three decades. I'm eleven and in agony.

"Libby, unlock that door and get out of the bathroom."

"I can't, Mom."

"Are you mouthing off again? I told you to get out here this minute."

"Something's wrong with me."

"Save it for someone who cares. I have a date and I need my hot rollers."

The smell of stale nicotine slithers under the bathroom door. I'm already close to barfing. That doesn't help.

The gruesome pamphlet from sex-ed class told me this was coming. I thought it spewed way too much information. Now I wish it had told me more, the kinds of details a regular mom might tell her daughter.

"Lib-by!"

Sure, Mom. I'll just go pass out in my room.

I should have grabbed Lacey's picture before we left. That's what good moms do. Jen and Frank would have waited. I don't have two children. I have three. One I can't hold, even if I could afford the airfare.

"Libby?"

"What?"

"Did you hear what Frank said?" Jen's question bears no edge.

How should I answer her? I heard rumbling. I didn't hear words. "No."

"He says this gas station up ahead is our last chance before the ranger station."

"Last chance for — ?"

Frank chimes in. "Indoor plumbing. Soft drinks. Cheetos. Floors. Walls. Doors."

"Okay, I get it." I'd kicked off my shoes while reliving junior high. Time to put them on again and face the current crisis. As I open the door on my side of the Blazer,

115

warm air rushes in. Warm bordering on stifling. In Canada? Who would have thought?

I can't help wonder if a few days ago Greg walked over the gravel now crunching beneath my feet. Did his hand touch this door handle? Did he talk to the flannel-clad clerk behind the counter? As Frank heads for the men's room, I'm tempted to tell him, "Watch for clues."

But we're not likely to find hints if Greg purposed not to leave any.

"Anything appeal to you?" Jen asks. She's rifling through cellophane packets of gumdrops, fried pork rinds, and beef jerky.

"Not really."

Sunflower seeds. Greg would have gone for the sunflower seeds. Lacey too. They shared that. In the shell. When they indulged, popping open the salty shells and extracting the tiny little seeds, they left piles of empties. If I hadn't insisted they drop the shells into a paper cup, I might have found the family room floor looking like the ground under the bird feeder.

Lacey on her Daddy's lap sharing sunflower seeds. That's the snapshot I should have with me.

Greg and I held each other like a good Christian couple after she died. We cried onto each other's shoulders at her funeral. We prayed together for the family of the young man who turned a rabbit gun on the school janitor, our daughter, and himself. We led a support group for grieving parents, counseling others with words we could not absorb.

No one could have imagined that Greg's simple words — "You're going to school, Lacey" — would carry a bullet impact. Or that the ricochet would wound the whole community and destroy our marriage.

To be fair, his decision didn't destroy our marriage. It stretched a pinhole to the size of a pencil eraser, through which all the life drained out.

And now I'm the mother of two sons whom I trained not to need me. I'm the wife of a man who grew tired of waiting for my heart to heal enough to let him back in.

How will I explain it to our church friends if we discover that Greg bailed on what was left of our marriage? We've covered so well, haven't we? Until now, I wasn't sure even Greg knew how thin and brittle was the ice on which we skated.

He knew I was sad too much of the time — in private. That I was stuck on stage four of a six-stage grieving process.

I didn't know he'd figured out I gave him

full credit for that.

When some people lose a child, they grieve most deeply over future events they'll never share with that child. High school graduation. Wedding. Grandchildren.

I most miss the child as she was. I don't mourn the loss of an opportunity to shop for a prom dress. Prom has never been my idea of a good time. I don't lie awake at night wishing it were possible for Lacey and me to spend a weekend in Madison or Green Bay or the Twin Cities searching for the perfect wedding gown.

I miss the twelve-year-old who hadn't lost her little-girl desire to sit as close to me as possible during lightning storms. I miss her wide-eyed devotion to her big brothers. I miss her spidery legs entwined with mine when we camped at opposite ends of the couch with a bowl of popcorn and the DVD remote between us.

What keeps me awake at night are mental snapshots of her personality. Such a charmer.

"Mamacita?"

She started calling me by that endearment after befriending the daughter of a family of Mexicans who worked at the cranberry processing plant near us.

"Mamacita, don't you think it's time for a

girl day?" She scheduled girl days with the finesse of a professional event planner and had done so since she was six or seven. "We'll have lunch at McDonald's because you got to choose last time. Then we'll go to Goodwill because Tatiana says they just got in some vintage stuff that's to die for."

Vintage? A twelve-year-old?

"Then the mall because frankly, Mama (she put the emphasis on the second syllable), you could use a haircut. And while we're there, we might as well stop at the gift shop in case they happened to get in the new Ginny Gymnast figurine I've been waiting all my life to add to my collection."

All her life.

"Are you planning to use your birthday money for it, Lacey?"

"That's already spoken for."

"Oh?"

"I plan to give all my birthday money to help the missionaries build that hospital for AIDS victims in Africa. You know, Mamacita. We heard about it in church on Sunday. Seems like the least I can do."

Did I have any other choice but to shell out the money for a ceramic Ginny Gymnast?

The last-chance store is many miles behind

us now. As is the ranger station check-in point. The shadowed thoughts are still with me.

Jen spares me from further introspection and my penchant for picking at emotional scabs by asking, "Are you ready for this?"

I'm not sure to which of my crises she's referring until I note that Frank is swinging the Jeep in a tight curve into a wide spot between rocks. This must be it. We're here.

Checking in at the ranger station an hour ago gave me a false sense of security, I see now. It had a real parking lot. An actual building. People. Not many, granted, but people nonetheless. People and moose heads and flattened beaver pelts and samples of tents made into shredded wheat by "nosey and normally harmless" black bears. Too many descriptors. "Harmless" would have been enough.

The sound of our footsteps had bounced off the cavernous ceiling of the ranger station and made us sound like an army. If only. Frank logged us in, while Jen and I used the refreshingly modern restrooms and then perused the racks full of brochures.

Contrast that scene with where we are now.

We emerge from the Blazer and stretch muscles and limbs that are sure to sport bruises tomorrow morning, considering the condition of the back road we just traversed. Frank disappears into the undergrowth just beyond the parking area. I'm tempted to put "parking area" in mental quote marks. He's gone less than two minutes, which means he wasn't exploring but relieving himself.

Though my bladder's been bounced and shaken, I'll wait until we reach our first campsite, thank you.

"Canoes first," Frank says, as he tucks his shirt back into his pants and assumes command of the launch process.

"Where's the water?" I ask.

He smiles. Smirks. Something. "A quarter of a mile that way." He points to a slight opening in the woods. No wider than, say, a canoe.

That man and his sense of humor. A quarter of a mile before we even reach the edge of the water?

I offer to hoist one end of the canoe he's released from its car-top perch, but he's already shouldered it and is starting down the trail, bouncing it a little to adjust its position like a woman would fuss with her bra.

"Frank? What should we do while you're gone?"

"Bring the other canoe," he calls back, and then laughs in a way that reminds me of Bela Lugosi, the horror film star. The sound wrinkles my spine.

Jen and I look at each other. The second canoe is still strapped down on top of the Blazer. We shrug in unison, mirror images of each other's ignorance, and set to work undoing the straps.

I have to open the passenger door and step up on the running board to reach the clasp on the front strap. The two canoes were lashed down separately. Probably a smart move, considering the jostling they've just endured along with us. But that means removing the first canoe didn't simplify the process in which we are now engaged.

Jen works on the back tie-down.

A wave of doubt overwhelms me. This is crazy. Nuts. Insane. We're not outdoorswomen. Not only will we not be a help to the investigation, we'll probably kill ourselves or one another while we're at it.

I wish I'd said yes one of the times Greg asked me to experience this adventure with him. Imagine the advantage I'd have right now. I'd know how to get a canoe off the top of a Blazer without ramming it through the windshield or dropping it onto the rocks.

"What do you think?" I ask Jen. "Slide it

off the side or end to end?"

"Side. Isn't that what Frank did with the other one?"

I wasn't paying attention. I was swatting mosquitoes. One good thing — they're so thick in the air up here that when you swat your arm, you can kill half a dozen at once. We did pack insect repellent, didn't we? And I thought Greg said the bugs aren't bad late in the summer.

Jen and I are both in shorts. Frank warned against it, but I thought he just didn't understand how uncomfortable we'd be in long pants. Along about swat number sixteen, we decide to abandon the canoe project and find the insect dope.

And long pants.

We relinquish our grip on modesty and change right beside the Blazer. It feels roughly like the open locker room in gym class. But we're so far from civilization there's no reason to fear pimple-faced Peeping Toms or girls who like to make fun of underdeveloped or overdeveloped body parts.

Slathered with insect repellent, we dig through the packs for the hats Frank insisted we bring, despite my protests about hat hair.

One sniff reveals we smell like a chemical that is surely outlawed somewhere. But our legs are covered, our arms sport long-sleeved shirts, and we've neatly lined the packs along the Blazer's flanks.

A state-of-the-art but incredibly heavy backpack for each of us, plus a Duluth pack for the food, a light but bulky pack that holds the sleeping bags, and another, smaller pack for miscellaneous supplies. Our ensemble is completed with tackle box, fishing rods broken down into short sections and stuffed into a rod case, a net, five canoe paddles — Frank insists one each is not enough — and our life vests.

I've just donned my life vest when Frank reenters the scene. How long has he been gone on his two-way trek down the portage trail and back? Forty-five minutes? That does not bode well for me.

Splatters of mud halfway to his knees tell us this portage is not going to be a walk in the park, or the old but tame roadbed Frank claimed.

"Took a little longer than you thought, Frank?" I ask, not sure I'm ready for the answer.

He removes his cap and swipes perspiration from where it rested moments ago. "Water level's down. What used to be a quarter of a mile stroll is now a half mile. Hope you women are fond of slogging through reed beds. Fond or not, that's what you got."

Frank eyes my life vest and asks, "Afraid you might drown in a mud puddle on the portage, Libby?"

"I thought I might as well wear my life vest rather than carry it," I answer. Do I have to tell him I'm hoping it will serve as mosquito protection for my back and chest? A bite-proof vest?

He shakes his head. He may need to save his strength for head shaking and tsk-tsking. I'm sure he'll use both actions frequently on this trip.

"Do you still want us to take this canoe, Frank?" Jen asks.

"No, I've got it."

And he does. He leans one end on the ground, walks underneath it until his shoulders rest under the padded yoke, then with one smooth motion stands fully upright, balancing the beast on his shoulders.

"Meet you on the other side," he says as he jogs toward the trailhead. Jogs. Show-off.

I turn to the only other person in the vicinity who understands my apprehension. "Where's the satellite phone, Jen?"

"Here, in the waterproof bag."

"Good. We need to keep an eye on that thing."

"Do you think checking in with Brent once a day is going to be enough?"

"It'll have to be." I reach for my backpack, then realize I'm going to need help putting it on. Jen notices and holds it for me to slip into like a gentleman would hold a coat for his wife — a gentleman like Greg. The only times he failed to do so were when I beat him to the punch. Did I rob him or rob me?

"The batteries?" Jen asks.

"What?" I must have lost track of the discussion. Happens a lot lately.

"Is that why we shouldn't use the phone more often? To save the battery life?"

I'm pleasantly surprised at how well-designed this backpack is. The majority of the weight rests on my hip bones. I may be able to carry something in each hand, too, and save a trip back and forth on the trail. Distraction averted, I respond, "That's what I understand. If the OPP find Greg and call back home, we need to know. A couple of minutes on the phone with Brent will tell us the bare facts. Then we'll book it out of here and connect through a land line at the ranger station to get the details."

"Let's hope and pray that's how it happens."

"Tonight wouldn't be too soon."

"Do you have a *feeling?*"

"You mean, from God?" I don't have that kind of relationship with the Lord anymore. I don't *hear* from Him. He doesn't promise me things like He does some others. Feeling? I haven't felt anything for longer than I can remember. "No. Wishful thinking."

I help her don her own backpack, surprised at how clumsy I am with all those pounds on my back. Like the weight of grief, it makes me stumble on simple motions. It throws off my normal balance. I can't move gracefully. I don't glide. I waddle. What I need is a gymnastics class and some of Lacey's agility.

Jen and I hit the trail, wobbling and bent too far forward, which we soon realize is a hazard.

"You take the lead," I tell Jen. "You'll be quicker on your feet."

"Don't count on it."

I lean my backpack bustle against a tree and let her slide past me in the narrow corridor of the forest. It takes a surge of courage to push off from the leaning tree and start after her. A large part of me wants to wait in the Blazer. For days, if necessary. Until they find him. Or don't.

10

Like a boxer boasting about the bruises he gained during his last match, Greg regaled me with stories about these portage trails.

Portage. A French word synonymous with torture.

On a good day, walking a rugged portage trail with the aid of two sturdy stabilizing poles would be challenge enough. Today, parts of the path are as slick as yogurt because of the recent rain. And we're carrying who knows how much weight on our backs. I don't know about Jen, but I feel as if my back is nine months pregnant and at least as awkward.

I used to watch "Survivor" on TV and pity the contestants who scratch their poxlike bug bites during the personal interviews at their jungle camps. Now I want to tell them, "Try strapping half a house to your back and itching at the same time."

"Ahk!" Jen cries out.

"What?"

"I just swallowed something! I think it's still flying!"

"Don't worry," I assure her. "It won't live long."

Jen sends me a dark look. "You should consider a career in professional comforting."

She coughs. So do I. Sympathy cough.

Certain sections of this portage are downright impossible. I stand on a fallen log that's split open. Surveying the next twenty feet of the trail offers me no viable options. All I see is what appears to be a path made of ankle-deep mud. We'll never know how deep unless we step into it, and I'm not volunteering. Conjoined trees on the left of the trail. Something that resembles moss but could be cleverly disguised quicksand to the right.

I'm grateful I let Jen lead.

She tiptoes along the left edge of the mud pit, hugging trees like a woman who suddenly thought better of the idea of jumping off the ledge of a tall building.

I don't tiptoe well. The ooze into which I slide threatens to suck my hiking boots off my feet and take my socks with them. I spread my toes inside my boots and lumber out of the muck onto a stretch of trail that descends like steps with tree roots as treads.

So much for the hiking boots. We're all of fifteen minutes into the wilderness, and I've ruined one of the two pairs of shoes I brought.

With the caking of mud, my feet seem as heavy as the load on my back. Because the mud on my shoes is as slick as that on the trail, my boots are like fresh-waxed skis on sheet ice. I have to be all the more cautious where I step.

"The rocks are our friends," I chant. "The rocks are our friends."

I lose Jen. She's no doubt in the next province by now, as slowly as I'm taking the so-called path.

Marathon runners say they reach a point they call "the wall," when their minds tell them they can't go on, not another step. By my calculations, I hit three invisible walls on this first portage. As I emerge into the light and joy of the shoreline at the edge of Beaverhouse Lake, I promise myself I won't ask how many more of these portages we'll face before the trip is over. I don't really want to know.

"Frank, that was no half a mile," I complain as I drop my backpack on the shore near the two canoes and a breathless Jenika.

"Yeah. May have underestimated. Tell you

what. I'll make the last trip back up the trail solo. I'll haul the last of the equipment while you women recuperate."

I'm drowning in the words "last trip solo."

Jen answers for both of us. "Thanks, Frank. That's big of you. But I think there are two packs and a couple of hand-carried items still back there."

"Don't think I'm gonna go soft on you girls more than this once," he calls over his shoulder as he heads back into the north-woods version of the Trail of Tears.

Soft? I close my eyes. We just experienced the soft part of this trip?

Most of the mud slips off my hiking boots when I wade into the water. My assignment is to get the now-loaded canoe far enough from shore that it won't drag on the rocky bottom once we push off. Jen's in the back, steering, supposedly. Frank's out on the water, halfway to the Atlantic Ocean. I'm working on getting into the canoe more gracefully than I emerged from the woods. Not to worry. I'll have other chances.

"Don't swamp us before we get a good start," Jen chides.

Still maneuvering my body into the tri-angle reserved for me, I glance back at the equipment crammed into the bottom of the canoe. Most of it shows mud or water-spot evidence that testifies to my lack of grace. I'm grateful the SAT phone is tucked in the waterproof bag. We can't afford to let that thing get as soaked as I am.

"There's a trick to this," I say as I settle my bottom onto the canoe seat that's only a hair more comfortable than aluminum bleachers. "I haven't figured it out yet."

Jen and I experiment with the wilderness equivalent of parallel parking. We're backing the canoe out of the cove, turning it around to face the direction Frank's going, and — in his words — *starting to fix to commence to begin* to follow him.

I imagine Jen's grateful for her summer camp experience with a canoe. I now wish I'd chosen canoeing over basket-weaving for my elective. What are the odds I'll need to pull out my basket-weaving or pot holder-making talents up here?

Lord, please tell me I won't need to use my CPR training.

In his dented tin can canoe, Frank looks like he's jogging in place or treading water, waiting for us to catch up to him.

My heart spasms. "Jen! We have to go back!"

"What?"

Frank's too far away to catch every word,

but I can tell from his posture that he's not happy with my announcement.

"How could we have done that?"

"Done what?"

"I was in such a hurry to get on the water, so concerned about pulling my own weight on the trail, that I didn't look around the parking area for clues. The Blazer might be resting on top of an important piece of evidence! We have to go back."

I stop paddling. That alone will fuel Frank's ire, I'm sure.

I'm more convinced than ever that this is a bad idea — this whole trip. Great detectives, aren't we? Greg could have been lying in the underbrush along the edge of the parking area, and we would have missed him.

"What's she yapping about?" Frank asks Jen.

"She's worried that we should have combed the put-in point for evidence, Frank."

"I did that. Thoroughly," he says.

"You did?" I want to believe him.

"When?" Jen asks.

"When I went back for the last load, while you girls were taking your sweet time resting at the end of the portage trail."

I would have argued, but the only point

on which I could hold any ground was changing *sweet* to *sweat*.

Frank investigated. He took care of it. "Anything turn up?" I ask, reining in my galloping hopes.

His agitation carries well across the water between us. "Would I have kept something like that to myself?"

I'm beginning to wonder if I'll ever regain full brain function. It must be the lack of sleep. I take a breath to fuel an apology, but Frank interrupts my self-loathing.

"We're not," he says with finality, "going back. Not until we find him. Get those paddles back into the water and try to keep up."

"Lib." Jen's voice sounds parental.

"What?"

"Start paddling. We're moving forward."

So we are.

After a million, I stop counting paddle strokes and grunting like a tennis star with each one. It's all about rhythm and efficiency of effort. No wasted motion.

I haven't even begun to conquer the proper method when Frank uses his canoe paddle to point toward a spot along the far shore and mouths the word "portage."

I've been in labor three times. The second was fourteen short months after the first.

Not nearly long enough for my body to bounce back as it should have before tackling such a monumental project again. With Alex, I saw six shift changes in the nursing staff while on the maternity floor, if that says anything about duration.

Piece of cake compared to this.

When I was in labor, I had the option of calling for an epidural. I didn't, but I could have, and I drew enormous comfort from that knowledge.

No epidurals exist for the pain I'm in now. It's not all physical. I don't need a psychologist to tell me that.

But in addition to the contractions my heart endures as we cross the water, my arms ache, my hands are cramped, my back screams its protests, and I've lost all feeling in the part of me that's glued to the canoe seat. I guess that's an epidural of sorts — the numbness.

The packs in the bottom of our canoe look more and more like pillows. How often does Frank turn around to check on us? Could I sneak in a nap? Stretch out my legs? Stop the endless rhythm of paddle strokes?

"You doing all right?" Jen asks from her perch behind me.

"Peachy. Why do you ask?"

"I've never seen a canoeist pull off a limp before."

"Limp?"

"Your strokes are slowing, and they're not as even as they were before. Should we ask Frank to let us take a break?"

"Us?"

"I'm significantly younger than you are."

"Great time to rub that in."

"But this is more physical exertion than I've put out since I ran cross country in high school."

"You ran cross country? Did you ever tell me that?"

"One season."

"Just the one?"

"I quit for my parents' sake."

"Why?"

"To save them from the embarrassment. It didn't bother me to come in last every race."

Memories of all the ways I unintentionally embarrassed my mother — according to her — slide through my mind.

"It earned me a special trophy during the sports awards ceremony," Jen rambles. " 'Heart of a Champion,' which I think meant 'Least Likely to Place, Much Less Win.' "

I've found another excuse not to paddle.

Overwhelming empathy. "Oh, Jen."

"Like I said, it didn't bother me. It probably should have, but I joined the cross country team for all the wrong reasons. Boys. Track and cross country guys didn't have the swelled egos of guys on the other sports teams. Made some great friends. And please keep paddling."

"Yes, ma'am." My arm strokes resume with false vigor.

"After that first season, I could no longer imagine forcing my parents to wait at the finish line long after the other parents packed their lawn chairs and coolers and headed home."

"You're exaggerating."

"Not by much. I wonder now how much stronger I'd be if I'd stayed in sports throughout high school and college, and if I ever found an exercise program I liked in adulthood."

"I hear you."

"You're watching for blisters, aren't you, Lib?"

"Blisters?" I'm watching the shoreline for a snatch of fabric from Greg's shirt. I'm watching the water for a floating clue. I'm watching the horizon — what we can see of it through breaks in the trees — for signs. I'm watching the sun sink too close to the horizon. But no, I'm not watching for blisters.

"Did you bring gloves?" she asks. "If we're paddling this many hours every day, we'll either have to toughen up fast or wear gloves."

I don't feel tough. I'm beaten down by the effort it takes to do anything up here, and by the fact that I didn't get my wish. Dusk will soon be upon us. When we pull out the SAT phone tonight, we won't report victory. Greg's still missing. Over and out.

11

Seven quadrillion nautical miles after launch, we nose the canoes onto the shore at the base of a picturesque humpbacked island. I assume Frank intends for us to take one of our disturbingly frequent bathroom breaks. The island seems little larger than the swim raft at camp.

"Start hauling gear, ladies," Frank barks as he uncoils his legs and sprints out of his canoe.

"Where?" Jen asks before I can.

Frank points with his forehead and chin. "Up there." He hoists the rough canvas Duluth pack, the tackle box, and the waterproof container for the SAT phone, and takes the rock climb two-at-a-time like a teen bounds upstairs to his room after school.

"Jen?"

"What?"

"Do you suppose he means we'll camp here tonight?"

"Looks like it." She keeps her voice low as she unstraps the cord securing our packs to the safe interior of the canoe. Sound carries too well here.

I roll my shoulders, preparing to switch from paddling mode to hauling. "Isn't this the ultimate in inefficiency?"

"What?"

"We unload the Blazer, then load it all into our canoes, paddle untold hours past bays and pine trees I know I've seen before, then pull into a portage location, haul it all out of the canoe, pick up the canoe, carry it over the trail, go back for the equipment, haul it over the trail, load it all back into the canoe, paddle another hour or two, pull into another portage location, start all over again."

Jen turns her back to me so I can lift her pack onto her shoulders. She adjusts the weight against her hips and adds, "And now we're hauling all that same stuff up Mount Everest so we can camp on its desolate peak and wake in the morning to load our gear into the canoes and begin the process again."

I slip my arms through the straps of my pack with Jen's help, and we turn to face our Everest.

"Reminds me of laundry," she says.

Laundry?

"Or grocery shopping."

I entertain the idea of letting that go, but instead say, "Huh?"

Jen punctuates her words with huffs and puffs as she climbs. "What do the *Guinness Book of World Records* people say is the longest a clean sink has gone without a dirty dish or glass?"

"Ah."

"And has a laundry basket or hamper ever been truly empty more than a few milliseconds? What's the world record?"

Focused on planting my feet on flat, dry rock pseudo-steps, all I can think of at the moment is how much Greg appreciates it when I take the time to dry the sheets outside in the sunshine rather than in the Maytag. How many men would notice?

And how seldom did I offer that simple gift?

"Put a little hustle in your bustle, ladies." Frank stands on the plateau at the peak and wiggles his behind. He has to wait to make another trip for gear until we reach the top, our campsite. It's a single-file climb and descent.

"Shall we show him what we're made of?" Jen calls over her shoulder.

"Marshmallow crème and pillow stuffing?"

Her sigh carries well. "Rawhide and pure muscle!" she grunts out as she takes the rest of the climb in double time.

It's not that I don't have the energy for it . . . exactly. It's that I don't have the heart. If Greg had been here when we reached this island, he'd have taken the pack from my back and carried both his and mine. I know he would.

If Greg had been here, we wouldn't be.

Frank's attitude would win him an early vote off the island if Jen and I were allowed to vote. He's bossy . . . for good reason. He's the only one who knows what he's doing. Jen and I need direction for every step of the process of setting up camp. He tells us where to put the tent, where to stash our equipment, where we'll construct a makeshift kitchen. Then he tells us *how* to put up the tent, *why* we're stashing our equipment where we do, and *how* to make a meal with no table, no counter, no cutting board, and no microwave or fridge.

He's a decent teacher . . . except for the bossiness. His instructions are worded simply enough so we don't end up impaling anyone while pitching the tent or strangling ourselves while hanging the food pack in a tree.

Success.

Exhaustion. Is it bedtime yet?

Location, location, location. If I were into real estate, I'd have no trouble selling this island property for the view alone. Frank had us position the tents and the "kitchen" area in consideration of the wind direction and flat ground. Serendipity positioned our temporary dwellings with stunning views of woods and water.

The view intoxicates me. I guess this is what intoxication feels like — a heady distancing from reality. As dusk lays its kind, calming hand over the scene before me, the water stills completely. The fire we've built in the rock-hemmed circle comes alive against the darkening sky. Worry never leaves my side, but it graciously retreats to a spot a few feet away while I plant myself on a log to watch the fire.

The air chilled noticeably when day decided it had enough. The part of me facing away from the fire feels the chill, as if I have backed into an open refrigerator.

Jen is inside our tent, arranging things by flashlight. I half expect her to poke her head through the zippered opening to ask if I prefer minimalist, art deco, shabby chic, or mid-century modern. Seems to me the only real decision is whether our sleeping bags will face north-south or east-west.

Frank must have decided already. From his tent wafts the music of air pushing through his throat and nasal cavities.

The aroma of the fire reminds me of times I've pressed my face into Greg's chest when he returned from one of these trips. His shirt always smelled of fresh air and flame-broiled wood. He always came home. Before this past week, I'd never seriously considered that one day he wouldn't. Why did I draw such lopsided comfort from his campfire-scented embrace? The last several years, I think burying my face in his smoky shirt might have been equivalent to grabbing for a thread of hope. *He's home. Good. Maybe I'll feel differently now.*

But though he always came home, Lacey never did.

How did King David do it? How did he learn of his child's death, then rise out of his grief, reenter life, and abandon himself to the God who refused to answer his prayers?

I should study up on that when we get back home. Wish I'd thought to bring my Bible.

Pressing my hand to my heart as if that

will keep the cracks from widening, I feel the thin notebook nestled in my pocket — the journal from Greg's office. It seems fitting to read his words by firelight, with wood smoke embracing me as he would if he were here.

I refrain from removing it from my breast pocket until I've stoked the fire to give more light and heat. As I bend over to position a couple of sausage-thick logs among the flames, I hold the pocket closed with my other hand to keep the words from slipping out. I can't afford to lose them.

"Beautiful night, isn't it?"

I didn't hear Jen exit our tent. How did she do that so quietly? "It is."

"Frank's out for the night, huh?"

"He plays the tough guy, but this has to take a toll on him."

"Don't forget how long all three of us spent bent like pretzels into the Blazer before we even hit the water. And Frank did more than his share of the driving."

"And yet we're still alive," I add, brushing bark crumbs off my hands and onto my pants.

Jen draws a log of her own next to mine. I tap my shirt pocket with a promise to make the connection with Greg's words when we're alone.

"How are you doing?"

"Better than I thought," I say.

She considers my answer for a few beats. "I . . . I have a favor to ask."

"What is it?" I poke at the base of the fire with a two-foot-long stick. Sparks wake from their slumber and dance upward into the night sky. *Man is born to trouble as the sparks fly upward.* Of all the scriptures for my mind to retain! Where is the cranial folder of comfort verses?

"I need to make a pit stop. In the woods."

"Not surprising. Happens to the best of us."

"I'd like not to have to go out there alone."

I hadn't thought that far ahead. A wall-less bathroom is hard enough to take in broad daylight. But at night?

"I'll hold the flashlight for you," I offer, "if you'll return the favor for me."

"Sounds like a plan."

She rises from her log and does a Jenika version of a River Dance number.

"Now?" I ask.

"Now."

On our way past the tents and into the suffocating blackness of the woods, Jen asks, "Did I ever lend you my copy of the novel that talks about moments like this?"

"Moments like this?" We're looking for

restroom in the middle of the wilderness. A small branch crackles underfoot.

"The necessary circle."

Neither of us can read facial expressions with the flashlight trained on the ground in front of us, but Jen must know by my lack of a response that it doesn't ring a bell.

Jen slows her pace as the darkness overwhelms any light the campfire behind us offered. "Pioneer women showed their respect for one another by forming an outward-facing circle so one by one the women could take care of 'necessaries' in the center while the others formed a privacy curtain with their bodies."

A one-woman circle. Big help I am.

Jen's a mother with two young daughters. She's used to limiting her time in the bathroom. When it's my turn, I let the cold night air and the threat of whatever lurks in the dark beyond press me to hurry.

Tomorrow, I will make my "necessary" trips with gratitude for the glare of revealing sunshine.

12

I sincerely hope I don't regret how much Maglite battery power I used up reading Greg's journal under the covers last night. When I was certain Jen was asleep, I buried my head as deep into the sleeping bag as I could without suffocating and flicked on the mini flashlight. It illuminated his penmanship and his soul.

The notebook I'd grabbed off his desk registered his thoughts about — of all things — the first trip he took to this wilderness area after Lacey died. Nine months later. Long enough to have another child. Long enough for him to have nurtured a seed of grief deep within his spirit, tended it, fed it his own lifeblood, brought it to maturity, and birthed it as I'd wished I could have. During those same nine months, and for the three years since, my version of grief miscarried a dozen times.

He didn't overanalyze his grief on the

pages like I do. But it threw shadows on the journal. Inescapable. That's mourning for you. He wrote:

The mayfly hatch yesterday completely killed the lake trout fishing. What self-respecting lake trout would pass up a mayfly for one of our artificial lures? Denny grew irritated by the hatch. He counted on digging into that wild pink flesh with his fork tonight for dinner. Granted, the swarms and the debris of the larvae stage they shed form the closest thing to litter we've seen in this human-deprived territory. But nothing's worth getting irritated over. Certainly not an insect.

I watched a few dance on the surface of the lake water, their wings fluttering, their bodies gyrating to a music neither Denny nor I could hear. Reminded me of Lacey. What doesn't? She often danced when the rest of us were unaware of any music. She too fluttered the wings of her indomitable spirit just for the joy of flapping. I suppose I should have known we wouldn't have her long enough, a child like that. I thought Libby's heart and mine would stop ticking for eternity the day four-year-old Lacey looked up from her chicken nuggets to tell us; "I really miss the angels."

149

We should have known.

Denny's making beef stroganoff for supper with a little sprinkling of whining that it's not lake trout fillets. Maybe the bass will hit in the waters under the painted rocks tomorrow. Might lift his mood.

The notebook is back in my pocket. I intend to return it to Greg when we find him.

The morning drags my attention from last night's private interlude with my husband. Will the day hold any hope?

The smell of coffee hits the sensors in my nose. What is it about this northwoods atmosphere that rarefies the simple, everyday things? This isn't even the good stuff — hazelnut or Cinnastik or caramel-pecan French roast. Frank did the food shopping. His tastes gravitate toward store brands and anything for which he has a coupon.

Generic coffee?

Here, it smells like a corner Starbucks in heaven.

Maybe it's because I'm one ceaseless shiver. Frank warned it might get cold overnight, even in summer. How close are we to the Arctic Circle?

The sleeping bag zipper leaks air. Sometime in the night, during my attempts to flip and flop and find a rock-free pocket of ground for my hips, the zipper's teeth chattered, clamped down hard, and then opened wide in an expression of horror. "Oh, no!" it and I screamed as the night air rushed in to challenge my body heat to a duel in the darkness.

First order of business this morning? Fix the zipper, if possible. Right after another cup of coffee.

Frank's bent over the cookstove, attempting to coax a steady flame out of the current spurt. I lift the coffeepot from the nest of rocks within the fire circle.

Another campfire. How blessed are we? Two days of solid rain before we arrived in addition to the dousing the area received from the thunderstorm sometime last week nullified the previous fire ban. It made the portages a study in mud. But we are free to warm ourselves — one side at a time — at the firepit.

I raise the mug to my lips and sip too-strong coffee. It fights the obstacles in my throat on its way to my stomach.

"Bacon and pancakes for breakfast?" Frank asks.

"Bad for my cholesterol and my waistline, Frank."

"Bacon and pancakes it is, then."

No one asked him to serve as camp cook. He assumed the role as if born to it. Standing around staring at him as he works makes me feel more useless than ever. "What can I do?"

"Filter some water for us."

He shows me the filtration bag and how to load it.

"Where do I get the water?"

His expression reminds me of a toddler's first taste of dill pickles. "Oh, I don't know," he says. "There must be some around here somewhere." His right arm sweeps a wide arc, the spatula in his hand serving as his laser pointer to the lake that surrounds us on all sides.

"We just use the water from the lake?"

"You did catch the *filtered* part, didn't you?"

How many ways can this trip force me out of my comfort zone?

I grab the handle of the aluminum cook pot he offers and head down to the water's edge. There's a song in my heart. Not a pleasant one. *Parasites and germs and fish gunk — oh my! Parasites and germs and fish gunk — oh my!*

As I stoop to scoop a potful of lake water, I discover a second verse. *Water bugs, sand,*

and pine needles — oh my! And what are those little black things? They're moving.

Vile insects. The list of threats against Greg's life mounts. If he is lost or hurt or stuck here in the wilderness somewhere, is he able to get water for drinking? Does he have a filter or those foul-tasting iodine tablets we tucked into our packs as backup?

Silly questions. By this time, parasites would be the least of his concerns.

For a moment, I almost hope he's not lost out here but drinking champagne from someone's slipper at the Ramada Inn in Toronto. Saw that in a movie once.

It's a trick keeping the water from sloshing out of the pot as I climb back up to the campsite. The pot's still three-quarters full, though, when I reach the top. I set it down carefully on a pad of pine needles and dance a Rocky Balboa jig to celebrate the victory.

One corner of Frank's mouth curls up. It reminds me so much of an expression I've seen on Greg's face that I have to turn my back.

Jen's awake. I vow not to tell her that the Mary Kay lady was right — she looks more "natural" with makeup. Makeup is a luxury forbidden on this trip. No room in the packs. No sense carrying extra weight.

"And I thought *I* needed a kitchen makeover," she says, nodding toward Frank, who crouches over the low rock on which the camp stove sits. Our food pack rests in the triangle formed by a cedar's exposed roots. Last night, it hung twenty feet in the air and six feet away from the trunk of a mammoth pine, suspended like a giant ham from a thick nylon rope.

"Bears," Frank explained as he'd maneuvered the pack higher and higher off the ground shortly after we'd finished our summer sausage sandwich supper.

"Bears?"

"Precaution. Just a precaution."

"But we're safe on an island, right, Frank? Bears can't swim, can they?" It was Jen's voice, but my thought.

"Oh, they can swim if they smell summer sausage and cheese waiting on the other side."

Great. Bears. Jen and I looked at each other as if to say, "And just how are we supposed to get any sleep now?"

But we did sleep. Exhaustion helped. And Frank's presence in the other tent. Although, as tough as Jen is, I would have much preferred Greg in the sleeping bag next to me rather than her.

Greg — the man who a month ago grated on my nerves when he flossed.

154

My standards are changing. No doubt about that. The pancakes are as thick as folded towels and at least as dry. The bacon is black along the edges. I don't care. We have to use an enormous amount of syrup to wash down the pancakes, but the crisp air and the promise that the less food in our pack, the less appealing it is to wildlife spur us on to eat like lumberjacks.

"What do we do now, Frank? What's our plan?" I choke down the dregs in the bottom of my mug and try to sound determined, not desperate.

"You tell me," Frank answers. He lifts the ever-present Chicago Cubs baseball cap off his head, scratches his scalp with his other hand, then repositions the worn cap.

"Me?"

"What do you think we should do, Libby? How should we proceed?"

I look to Jen for support, but see only raised eyebrows and yet another person waiting for me to decide.

It surprises me to hear myself saying, "I think we should pray." Where did that come from? Good idea, but I haven't had many of them in the last several days. Or years.

Frank doesn't budge from the log he claimed as his chair. Jen's already on her feet with hands outstretched as if this is one of those times we need the prayer-boost that comes with holding hands while we talk to the Lord. She extends one toward Frank. I do too. But he develops a sudden cough and waves us to "go ahead without me."

The hush of this place penetrates my skin and travels deep into my soul. Only when the breeze picks up do the pines whisper at all. Only when a mother loon calls to her children or her wandering mate are we reminded that others share this space with us. The silence is a character in our play, walking with us through all its scenes.

Silence is when reruns on TV Land are so lame Greg and I turn off the television. But always underneath that faux quiet pulses the hum of the furnace or the rattle of the ceiling fan or the growl of the air conditioner. Traffic still rumbles past our house and makes the loose windows shiver. As we settle into what I think of as quiet, the phone rings or the beep of the microwave announces that our bag of popcorn is done.

Until now, I did not know a silence this deep. It both frightens and calms me. How can that be?

"Lord, what Your world must have been like before we filled it with noise!"

Jen squeezes my hand at those opening words of my prayer and whispers a soft,

"Amen."

More silence. I keep my eyes closed but can hear the friction of fabric on wood. As unused as Frank is to communing with God, he's squirming enough to rub a smooth spot in the bark of his log-chair.

I know there are more words to be said, a petition that sounds like a real prayer eager to be given voice. But my mind lands on a single thought that pushes its way up from somewhere near my toes. "Oh, Lord God! We don't know what to do, but our eyes are upon You."

"Jumpin' Jehoshaphat!" Frank cries.

He tears across the camp and flies down the approach to the water.

"What is it?" I call after him. "What's wrong?" Fear doesn't need an engraved invitation to flood back into my mind.

Jen and I follow him, sliding and slipping where he is surefooted.

He doesn't answer us, but in a flash bends to unlace his hiking boots, fling off his socks, and wade into the just-shy-of-icy water.

"Biting ants!" he shouts as he dances in the lake, lifting his pant legs higher on his white calves.

Our larger mission postponed for the moment, Jen and I convulse with laughter. God must have known we'd need this endorphin boost to tear down camp, load our canoes, and pick up our paddles.

Frank's scowls fail to discourage our laughter. Were the tables turned, he'd guffaw like a vaudeville audience.

A tiny intruder can create a great deal of turmoil.

Under the microscope, the small choices in my marriage might have seemed insignificant too.

Jen gave me a teaching tape a year ago. A CD. Did I ever return it? Jen bugged me — Pauline style — until I stuck it in my car stereo system one day while making my annual trek to the apple orchards just over the state line in LaCrescent.

Despite my resistance to "teaching" at the time, I was impressed by the way the speaker took the heartbreaking story of David and Bathsheba and walked us through all the points along the way where David might have made small but wiser choices that could have changed the outcome.

"In the spring of the year, when kings go off to war, David stayed back at the palace . . ." is how the biblical account begins. And it all went downhill from there. Why did he stay home that time? Why did he need a nap? Why did he not avert his eyes when he first spied Bathsheba bathing on her roof? Why wasn't his first reaction to call for the palace maintenance guys to build a privacy fence?

How would the story of his life have changed if he'd made a different choice at one of those crossroads?

In the spring of the year when Lacey's life ended, so did mine.

A small choice. Two roads diverged in the dark forest of my grief. And I? I took the one that distanced me from the one man, the one person who understood better than any other human being what it was like to lose a daughter like Lacey.

13

Out comes the sun and dries up all the mud.
That's the hope. But the shade on the portages weakens the sun's power to dry anything. Frank says that if the maps are accurate we have only one portage today, though. I'm almost giddy with joy over that prospect.

As I climb into my narrow canoe cockpit, I'm conscious of muscle groups long dormant. I didn't realize muscles have voices, but when I pick up my paddle and make the first of a quadrillion strokes through the water's resistance, I distinctly hear a small, strained voice screaming, "Please don't do this to us again! What have we ever done to you?"

I apologize to the voice . . . without sincerity. Greg deserves far more than the sacrifice of my discomfort.

He does?

Yes. Far more.

"Are you as sore as I am?" Jen asks.

"Remember how many years I have on you. And pounds. Whatever you feel, multiply that by ten for me."

A breeze skirts across the surface of the lake, wrinkling its skin. We do not need a headwind today. We need to make time.

Jen and I slip into a familiar rhythm. Frank still outdistances us. I blame that on my lack of upper body strength, which he has in abundance.

Every paddle stroke stirs a whiff of me. It's a strong smell of wood smoke, perspiration, and damp socks. The socks I swished through the lake water late yesterday were not completely dry this morning. But it somehow seemed important to save my one other pair — Frank only allowed two pairs for each of us — for a time when having dry socks might save my sanity.

As the breeze stiffens, I note that my odor now wafts Jen's way.

"Sorry you have to sit downwind of me, girl."

"Want to trade places?" she asks.

"You'd trust my ability to steer?"

"Not for a minute."

Lord God, how did You know that Jen is the kind of friend I'd need beside me to survive

*this? If I couldn't have Greg here to support
me —*

Time to redirect my thoughts. "Think it
will warm up enough for a swim later today?
A swim masquerading as a soapless bath?"

"I miss my curling wand already."

"Me too. And microwave popcorn."

"And my girls."

I can't paddle through the new wave of
pain.

"Oh, Libby. I'm sorry."

I can feel Jen's sympathetic gaze boring
through my back.

"It's okay," I say, as I plunge my paddle
deep into the crystal water. "I'd miss mine,
too, if I had a daughter waiting for me at
home."

"Lib—"

"I'm happy for you. They're wonderful.
You're wonderful. Brent's wonderful. You
deserve one another."

"And you and Greg don't deserve joy?"

"I had a chance."

"Had?"

I need my energy for moving this canoe
forward. "Can we talk about something
else?"

"I want to respect when you need space,
or whatever you want to call it."

"You always have," I say. "And I thank

you for that."

"But would you consider the possibility, please, that we might have been drawn to this place for more reasons than finding answers about what happened to Greg?"

I have no response to that. Of course I've considered the possibility. Right now, all I can manage to swallow is the lump that says my husband's missing. Discovering what's wrong with me lodges sideways in my throat.

"What's that?" Jen asks, her voice more strained than a moment ago.

"I didn't say anything."

"No. That."

I twist my body and find she's pointing toward the left shore ahead of us. At ten o'clock.

"Frank!" she hollers across the water. "What *is* that?"

The color palette is limited here. Shades of green, brown, gray, blue, white. A flash of red stands out against that backdrop like a single red pepper in a bin of green ones. It's small but real.

We paddle toward it with a speed I didn't know we had in us.

If we'd had more time to prepare for this trip, we might have been able to secure special permission for motors. Would the authorities allow that, in an area where motors of any kind are banned? Probably not. Even under the circumstances. Too bad. That would have sped our trip. But if we'd been traveling faster, would a small flash of red have caught our eye?

I lean forward to gain more leverage in my strokes. I dig deep, forcing the water out of my way, propelling our canoe closer. We pull even with Frank. Are we stronger than we were a few minutes ago, or is there something to the link between adrenaline and superhuman strength?

The shoreline is rocky. No level place to pull in. The object of our attention is wedged between rocks about five feet from the water's edge. It's cloth. Beet red, not scarlet. What clothing item of Greg's is beet red?

Frank directs the rescue operation. "Libby, if Jen and I stabilize the two canoes, can you climb out and see what it is?"

Stabilize is a strong word for what they attempt to do. Frank uses his paddle like a mock anchor, planting it in the lake bed and hanging on. He asks Jen to loop one leg over the side of his canoe to form a bizarre catamaran. I've felt more secure standing on a rocking chair to change a light bulb, but I manage to crawl out and onto the shore.

By the time I can touch the fabric, I already know it isn't a clue.

It's a ball cap — red with gold lettering. Washington Redskins. Not Greg's team. We still have no sign that my husband ever passed this way. But I'll have a dandy bruise on my knee from falling back into the "stabilized" canoe.

Why is it any harder to push off from this shore than the others we've touched? Why does the water feel even more resistant than normal? Is it any wonder none of us can think of anything suitable to say?

We're back on track, paddling mindlessly toward an unknown emptiness for all we know.

Lord, is it too much for me to ask for a clue? Doesn't have to be a big one. Some evidence that Greg was here. Is here.

No answer.

I don't blame Him. If I were God, I wouldn't want to talk to me, either.

Jen and I are well into our practiced stroke rhythm when Frank noses his canoe toward the right-hand shore: starboard. Left equals port. Right equals starboard. I can't remember what movie taught me that bit of information.

I scan the area ahead. Did he see a sign? I

just put in my request!

Within minutes, it's obvious we're approaching land because we've reached our one and only portage — *please, Lord?* — for the day. Let's get this over with.

"Frank," Jen asks, as she and I begin the routine of unloading the canoe onto the shore, "did you tell us how long this one is?"

"Nope."

The look on Jen's face reminds me of a little girl who's heard the nurse say, "It won't hurt for long. A little pin prick. That's all."

If Jen isn't going to press him, I will. "How far is it, Frank?"

"It's a hike of some magnitude."

"Meaning?"

"Magnitudinous. Lacey would call it giant-NOR-mous."

"That's GI-nor-mous, Frank." Lacey. I can hear her voice in my ears. Or heart. Everything in her life was ginormous. If childhood is a ray of light for most, hers was a laser. She danced through her days and drew others to the rhythm. Me. She drew *me* into its rhythm.

Once she learned the truth about God, Lacey embraced it in a ginormous way. If she'd lived to adulthood, she would have had the influence and energy of Beth Moore and the compassion of Mother Teresa.

"Libby?" Jen's voice breaks through the fog of fantasyland.

"Yeah?"

"We'd better get moving. Portaging." When her voice is soft like that, I know she's aware of where my thoughts have wandered.

"You go ahead, if you're ready."

"I don't think so."

"You don't trust me to pull my weight?"

Jenika holds my pack, waiting for me to slide my arms into its constraints. "I think it's wise for us to stick together. No matter how rough it is, it's easier if we're facing it together, isn't it?"

Is that a veiled reference to my failure to lean on Greg and let him lean on me? She might as well have said so out loud. I'm already thinking it. I breathe deeply and silently decide to consider the idea later. After we've found him.

"Time to prove we're stronger than we were yesterday, huh?"

Jen lifts the weight of my pack off my shoulders so I can untwist one of the straps.

"That's the spirit," she says.

We start down the path at a pace I know we can't sustain. But we'll try.

One foot in front of the other — again and again and again and again — with the weight of a small desk strapped to my back and a heavy sadness still camped in my heart.

Am I grateful that there are no mile markers on the trail? Would I appreciate a sign that tells me *Next rest stop: unbelievably far away?* Jen takes the lead. I watch her body language for a signal that she's sighted water up ahead. We're forty minutes into our trek with no end in sight. I am not comforted by the fact that Frank hasn't jogged past us on his way back for another load. How ridiculously long is this portage if Frank hasn't made the U-turn yet?

Jen stops and leans her extended arm and hand against a tree. Her body registers what mine feels. She's carrying this empathy thing beyond the call of duty.

"You okay?" I ask.

"This one's a beast."

"Agreed."

"Where's Frank?"

"I wonder the same thing. We have to be more than halfway, don't we? Please don't tell me different."

Jen shrugs out of her pack straps. "I need a break. Sorry."

"Don't be sorry. I needed one twenty minutes ago but was afraid you'd razz me about my age."

"I'm too tired to razz anybody." She pulls her shirt away from her body in front.

"You're not coming down with something, are you?"

"You mean, in addition to sore shoulders, sore feet, sore arms, sore legs, sore back — ?"

"Don't forget the hunger, thirst, and bug bites." We should write travel brochures for the Quetico Bureau of Tourism.

"Maybe I'm just dehydrated," she says. "It's hard to remember to drink enough when drinking means straining bugs through our teeth."

I slip out of my own pack and aim it toward a flat rock. I don't know why I need to brush off the rock's surface first. It's not as if there's an inch of anything we brought that isn't dirty already. But I bend to sweep away a handful of seeds.

Sunflower seeds. Shells, rather. Empties. Something genuinely biodegradable and with the power of a fully charged defibrillator.

Greg may have stopped at that convenience store and decided to tuck a packet of sunflower seeds into his food pack. I know he's not the only Quetico traveler partial to sunflower seeds. But I also know that sunflowers don't grow here naturally.

"Jen?"

"What?"

"Do you have an extra plastic bag on you?"

"What for?"

"Collecting evidence." Saliva has DNA, right? When we get home, if we haven't found Greg, we can haul a couple of empty sunflower seed shells to the crime lab and request a stat DNA test. What a cruel consolation prize! I might discover he was once here.

"Evidence?" Jen stands over my shoulder, looking at the contents of my outstretched palm. "Sunflower seeds? Do you think they could be Greg's?"

I consider the ridiculous conclusion I've just drawn. "You're right. It's just silly. I thought . . . I thought we might have our first clue."

I toss the seed shells toward the deep woods, away from the trail.

"What are you doing?" Jen screams.

I thought I was the crazy one. She's chasing snack garbage, tiptoeing through moss as if she doesn't want to leave footprints on a freshly vacuumed carpet.

"Here," she says, breathing hard and depositing four shells in my hand. "We're keeping these."

What's she not saying? That these little things might be the only clues we'll ever find?

I think my gall bladder just dumped a pail of acid into my stomach.

"Well?" Jen says, wriggling her arms into the straps of her pack.

Yeah. I don't feel like resting anymore either. Time to hit the path. With her help, I don the my own northwoods bustle.

"I'm ready. Let's go." As we point our noses toward the elusive shore we hope is not far down the way, I follow a spotty Hansel-and-Gretel trail of empty sunflower seed shells.

Lord, if these aren't Greg's, if they aren't clues, don't You think this might be overdoing it in the cruelty department?

Two here. Four there. Each sighting messes with the electrical system in my heart.

We clear the woods and find Frank sitting by the water, stroking something lying across his lap like an old man might stroke a lethargic cat.

"Frank? What's up?"

He doesn't turn toward Jen's voice or answer us. As we step closer to him, he stiffens. The look on his face tells us he's back on this planet, in the current century, with us.

"I found something," he says simply.

Jen asks what it is. I don't have to. I can see. It's part of a broken canoe paddle. It's handleless and splintered lengthwise. Where is the rest of it? And where's the person who last used it? Needed it?

"This isn't — ?" I begin.

"Greg's," he says. His eyes are wild. Or misting. Sometimes it's hard to tell.

"It can't be." Don't ask me why I think it can't.

Frank lays the broken paddle on the ground at his feet and squeezes lake water from his pant legs. He waded somewhere to find it.

"That's the one Greg made in woodworking class."

Jen joins the discussion. "How can you possibly know that for sure?"

"He got a B minus," Frank mumbles.

We're all tired. Does that explain his answer or my inability to understand him?

"What, Frank?" I ask.

"See this ridge of epoxy?"

"No."

"Run your hand over it. You'll feel it."

I don't want to touch it. But I do. Yes. There's a definite ridge of hard glue or something.

"It cost him in his final grade," Frank said. "He was in a hurry to finish, to get started with the layers of spar varnish. Didn't take time to sand down that ridge like I suggested. Teacher gave him a B minus."

I have a sudden urge to find that teacher and slice him off a piece of my mind.

Frank smiles. He smiles?

"Greg loved that thing, though. He always said it cut a wicked stroke through the water because of that ridge."

The hush engulfs us again. A Canadian jay breaks the stillness with its raw call.

Jen huddles near me and reaches to touch the wood. "It's splintered. What can that mean?"

"Means one thing for certain."

I finish his point. "Greg was here."

14

Sounds float around me. Jen and Frank, setting up camp. I should help them, but I can't move.

I'm huddled on a rocky point, high above the water. Greg made it this far, or nearly this far. A trip into the wilderness was at least part of his plan, if not its whole.

And that means?

Maybe nothing. But it narrows down the field of possibilities.

We now know that Greg did not cross the border on pretense and take an immediate left, right, or U-turn. He intended to, and came to these waters.

We know he was — or is — here.

We don't know if he left or how long ago or with whom.

And we know that something splintered his paddle. Storm? Capsize on the rocks? Angry fit? A or B. Definitely not C — angry fit.

If we'd found the paddle whole, we'd still wonder how it was separated from its owner. But the fact that it is damaged adds more questions to our endless litany.

I'm afraid to watch the water, to trace its surface with my eyes. I'm afraid but can't help myself. A few hours ago, a splinter changed everything. Was it carried from a distance on the current that flows in this unique interconnection of lakes and rivers? Pushed by a wave-making wind? I don't want to see a body floating in its wake.

"Libby? Some help here?" Jen struggles to unfold the plastic ground cloth that is now not only huge and bulky but damp and plastered with pine needles and other debris.

I leave my perch and rejoin the world. After shaking off all the debris we can, we decide which of the two sides is filthiest and lay that one on the ground so we can pitch our tent on top of it.

Frank issues no instructions. Maybe we're learning a few things. Maybe we're not as incompetent as he thought. Maybe he has a lot on his mind.

The broken paddle rests against our food-pack tree. We'll haul it with us, useless as it is for its intended purpose. It might serve as evidence for the authorities. Or a memorial.

By the depth of darkness and silence, I'd guess it's two or three in the morning. Worry's witching hour. For days I've begged the Lord for clues. Now that we have one, sleep is even harder to find. New scenarios swirl through my head. Most of them involve a canoe folded in half by a wicked stretch of rapids and one of several versions of drowning. I pray for relief from the video playing in my mind.

Thank You, Lord. But I suppose I was thinking of a longer period of relief than half a second. Is that so wrong?

Something pokes me in the back. A tree root. Or rock. Shifting to my side invites pain to a new area of my body. What am I saying? There isn't a cell within me that doesn't scream in protest. Some of it is physical.

My nose itches. I wiggle my left arm and hand free from the sleeping-bag cocoon. That's a regrettable move. Cold front's living up to its name. The night air feels like the interior of a meat cooler at Greene's. The nose sensation wasn't an itch. It was frostbite! Or a close facsimile.

How can I be this miserable — inside and

out — and yet in awe? The difference between hearing Greg's recitations about this place and experiencing it is like radio versus HDTV.

The moss fascinates me. It's thick and lush and everywhere. It reads like a plush carpet tucked among the tree roots. But when I bend close to it or lift a piece to my eyes, I can see that it's composed of delicate filaments of green. Incredible.

The landscape's artistry seems intentionally composed for maximum eye appeal. I picture God's hand reaching down to move a rock a little to the left or drag His finger through the dirt to create a rivulet that links two light-reflecting lakes.

My tailbone connects with something unforgiving under the tent floor. I shift to lie on my side. Air mattresses would have been a good addition to the weight in our packs. Air mattresses? What am I saying? God bless the guy who invented memory foam.

The downy feather I found earlier today while sweeping debris from the square of ground now underneath me wouldn't go far in creating something soft to sleep on. Little except for moss is soft in this environment.

A soft place to land. That's what the relationship experts claim we humans need.

Greg tried to cushion my landing after Lacey died. A caretaker of the paralyzed, he stroked my hair and put his arm around me whether I could feel it or not. I couldn't.

The search for a position conducive to sleep reaches critical mass. Should I blame the pebbles and roots underneath or the internal thorns?

Before climbing into the tent for the night, I watched the sparks of our campfire climb heavenward against the black backdrop. An orange glow of life inhabited each one. Higher. Higher. Knocking on heaven's door. And gone. Then my eyes traced the path of others fighting to stay alive. Some died sooner. Some later. All glowed while they could.

Lacey glowed while she could, with a light so bright I can still see its image behind my closed eyelids.

If Greg is in serious trouble, or if his spark is knocking on heaven's door, he'll see Lacey again before I do. That's wrong on so many levels.

The cry of a distant wolf ripples my skin like the surface of the water responds to a sudden wind gust. The animal doesn't want me. He's crying for his mate.

So am I.

Something stands between the moon and our tent, casting its shadow on my already dark existence.

It snorts. Do bears snort?

I can hear it scratching on something. Sounds like fabric. Fabric? Our tent? Frank's? Bears have no business being close enough to fondle fabric.

I whisper into the darkness, "Jen! Jen!" She's completely comatose. Great.

"You trying to wake the dead?" I hear through the tent wall.

"Frank?"

"Who else did you expect? It's late. Go to sleep. Big day tomorrow."

Frank made a trip to the undergrowth in the middle of the night? That man needs to see a urologist when we get back.

I flip onto my right side, hoping that's the magic position to encourage sleep. My hip bones act as if they have no padding whatsoever. The seam on my blue jeans digs impressions into my cellulite. I feel the impressions now. I'll see them when I make my own latrine trips. Getting used to sleeping fully clothed will not happen while we're here. If I could get over that mental hurdle,

I might be able to fall sleep.

Or not.

Frank's right. Every day of paddling and searching is a big day. I need my rest.

Some people go to bed clutching a stuffed animal or silky piece of fabric for comfort. My hand is tightened around the mini flashlight. I click it on now just to make sure Jen is breathing and we're alone. We are. When I click off the light, the darkness rushes back in like spilled ink and smothers the oxygen.

The stranded FedEx employee in the movie *Cast Away* spent his flashlight batteries the same way, clicking the light on and off for a split second of reassurance. Soon after the batteries died, he slipped dangerously close to insanity.

The faint, filtered light from the moon ought to be enough of a nightlight. But it isn't.

I bury my head under the sleeping bag "comforter," pull Greg's journal out of my pocket, and click on the light. Reading offers a good excuse to leave the light on.

I finger the pages I've already read and slowly flip through to new territory — uncharted pages. He writes about his friend Denny's pyromaniac attitude toward campfires, flirting with setting his pant leg, their tent, and the surrounding forest on fire. Greg expounds for half a page on the merits of using a fly rod with a Dahlberg Diver — a lure or fly or something, I assume — for smallmouth bass.

Then this. This entry.

Saw a commercial for paper towels the other day, one of those dumb lumberjack commercials. The man in a red-and-black flannel shirt, jeans, and suspenders leaned on a tree, looked into the camera, and said, "A real man knows if you can navigate nature, you can navigate a woman's heart."

I might have believed him a few years ago. I've never lost my way up here. Not for long. But the maze of rivers that wind and twist through Libby's heart should be marked on the maps "unnavigable." Or is it just my pathetic lack of wisdom?

No, Greg! No.

Shouldn't love count for something?

Yes. It does.

God, I don't care if I go home without a trophy fish again. I don't even care if I go home without arms or legs! Just please give me a clue! Send me home with a clue about how to reach her, how to reconnect, how to help us heal.

And please forgive me. I've failed her when she needed me most.

Is that what Greg's been laboring under all this time? I thought he was quiet and unresponsive because he didn't feel our grief as deeply as he should.

Our grief.

Until now, I've always called it mine.

15

Frank and I are the first ones up again. I'm pushing bacon around a skillet with a fork to keep it from sticking. Frank is filtering water. The air's thick with the smell of bacon, coffee, sun-warmed pine needles, and cedar. The Bath & Body Works research and development team should consider a new fragrance line. I can see the display in my mind's eye. It looks a lot like our camp, only tidier.

For some reason, Frank thinks powdered Tang is a fitting substitute for orange juice. I don't argue when he stirs a batch, though. It camouflages the floating things in the water.

Pancakes again. The complete pancake mix makes up fast and easy. I make the batter thinner than Frank's version and succeed in producing enough skillet-sized cakes for the three of us. I turn off the camp stove and leave the pancakes stacked in the hot skillet. No sign of Jen yet. I'll have to wake her. We have no microwave to warm the food later.

Not wanting to startle her, I choose not to holler through the tent wall. Bending to the base of the tent door, I reach to pull the zipper slowly, politely.

Jen's not asleep. She's sitting cross-legged on her sleeping bag, reading.

"Sorry to disturb you. Breakfast is ready. We'd better eat while it's hot."

"I'll be there in a minute."

"What are you reading?"

"My Bible."

"Oh."

God, forgive me. How can I expect Your help if I neglect the book in which You store so much of it?

I wait while she finishes whatever passage she's reading. Maybe I'll gain something by osmosis.

"Find anything worth sharing?"

She shoots me a look that says, "You're kidding, right?" When she opens her mouth, honey flows out. "I needed a reminder that finding Greg isn't up to us."

"We're all he has at the moment," I counter.

"You know that's not true," Jen says, her

voice that of a loving parent in comfort mode.

What I know is that I'm choosing a path that may lead to something I don't want to hear. But I'm drawn to the hope of healing in God's words like the bugs are drawn to our lantern at night.

"What did you read?"

"Joshua." She crawls off her sleeping bag, smoothes it, and works at rolling it tighter than sushi. "God told Joshua, 'Remember that I commanded you to be strong and brave. Don't be afraid, because the LORD your God will be with you everywhere you go.' "

"Even here." I'm in awe that I actually believe it.

"Yes. Even here. Especially here."

"I wonder —"

"What?"

I stop rolling my own sleeping bag, not caring that when I let up on the tension of rolling, the down in its baffles swells and plumps.

"I wonder if Greg hears that promise ringing in his ears."

"I'd guess yes," Jen says. "If he's —"

"Yeah . . . if."

As we have so many times since the day I realized Greg wasn't coming home, Jen and

I shift gears, choosing not to dwell on the ugly side of truth, the unnerving side of imagination. It's not denial. When we close the pantry door on the mental pictures of pools of blood or wolf-ravaged leftovers, we know they're still there as surely as we remember the peanut butter, rice noodles, and three cans of tomato soup in the pantry at home.

This isn't denial. It's survival.

So we finish rolling our sleeping bags, eat breakfast as if we care, and dismantle the camp with an energy we don't feel.

Peanut butter, rice noodles, and tomato soup in the pantry.

I watch Frank tuck Greg's splintered paddle securely alongside the packs in his canoe.

"What do you think it means, Frank?" Our canoes are still close enough in the bay of the island for us to talk.

My stroke is much smoother than it was yesterday or the day before. Our first several hours on the water, the pattern I traced with my paddle looked like that of a first grader trying to master calligraphy when she hasn't yet learned cursive.

Frank draws his paddle through the water — once on the right, twice on the left — before he answers.

"Greg's paddle? Wish we'd found some other evidence near that spot."

We'd fanned out and combed the area as if searching for lice nits in a kindergartner's hair. Nothing. Not a footprint or fabric swatch or what we most feared — a broken canoe.

I paddle forward but keep my eyes trained on Frank. "I wish we'd found —" I can't choke out the end of that sentence.

Frank fills the gap. "I think finding Greg's paddle means there's hope."

I turn to catch Jen's expression. She doesn't speak, but her eyebrows disappear into the fringe of bangs that haven't seen a curling wand in three days. Is that a sign of agreement or doubt?

"Hope?" I shove the word across the water with my paddle. "How do you figure that?" *Please, Lord. Please make his explanation sound logical.*

Frank's sigh ends with the shudder of a loon song's final notes. "At least now we know not to look in Mexico. Or France. Or the Ukraine. Narrows our search."

From behind me comes laughter that echoes across the water. I wonder if Greg can detect its sound waves where he is. Will we joke about it later? Will we use this moment as one of the story points when telling our grandchildren about the trip, this rescue operation?

Frank is married to the laminated maps he carries. It's a good thing. It's not like a person could go by landmarks around here. "Turn left at the pine tree. Then look for a cluster of three small islands and hang a right."

All the shorelines look alike. All the pines are siblings, apparently. A series of three small islands is sure to be followed by another clump just like it.

Now that we're out of the cove and into more open water, Frank's canoe takes a strong lead. It doesn't matter that we don't know where we're going. He does. If Jen and I stay focused on keeping up with his seasoned strokes, we'll be okay.

A few years ago, when I was more sensitive to these things, I would have turned that observation into a lesson for the women in my Bible study.

"We don't have to know where we're going," I would have told them, "if the guy in the lead — the Lord — not only has the map, but *wrote* the map."

And one of the women — maybe even Jen — would have said, "Oh, that's good! You always come up with the best illustrations. Thanks for helping me understand that concept better."

It's the kind of thing a person like me would want to tell her daughter. Or her husband. But I can't share it with either of them.

The cold front is back. Or its cousin. The sun is shining, but it has the warming effect of a lightbulb in a refrigerator. What would we do if the wind were blowing? God must know we need calm waters today if we are to make any headway through this tangled labyrinth of lakes and rivers.

"Crystal clear water" is the expression I've heard Greg use. It fits. No matter how deep I dip my paddle, I can see to the end of it. I've been focused on conquering the wilderness since we got here, but even I can't deny the beauty. It soaks into a person. The majesty. Light and shadow. Textures as rough as, well, tree bark and as glassy as the pool-of-mercury water at night. A morning mist with the color and fire of opals. Seventy shades of green in the verdant trees and underbrush lining the shore.

"I've stood in some mighty-mouthed hollow," I recite, "that's plumb-full of hush to the brim."

"What's that?" Jen asks.

"A line from a poem Greg used to quote. Not exactly Shakespeare. Certainly not

Robert Browning or Emily Dickinson."

"It fits, though. *Plumb-full of hush.* If it weren't for the noise we're making, would there be any other sound than the lap of waves or bird song or soft rustle of pine needles?"

I draw in a deep breath and refill my lungs with the closest thing to pure air this planet offers.

Jen and I settle into a comfortable rhythm. We're roughly the same height, so our stroke lengths match. Periodically, one of us will call out "switch" and we'll change from paddling on the right to paddling on the left or vice versa. Our arms move all the time while we're on the water, but switching sides temporarily redirects the muscle strain.

Frank should be slower on the water than the two of us, considering we have two paddlers. But even with his salvage-yard canoe — the one he wouldn't trust to us — he slices through the water as if riding a razor.

Splat! A spray of cold slaps across my back with the shock of the first rude burst from a shower head. "Hey!"

"Sorry," Jen says. "Unintentional, I assure you."

When I turn from scowling at her to face forward again, something snaps mid-spine. I freeze, afraid to breathe, afraid to move.

"What's up?" The concern in Jen's voice reveals she's aware I'm not refusing to paddle in protest.

The snap and lightning bolt of pain that traveled farther in a split second than we'd managed in two days fades like a struggling flame on wet wood. Gone. I inch my arms down to my sides. *Smooth motions, girl. No sudden movements.*

"What is it? What happened?" Jen waits for an answer.

"Nothing. I think I'm okay."

"Your back?"

"Just a little pop. It's all right now."

"You sure? We can get Frank to let us take a break, if you want."

My feet are crammed into the nose of the canoe — it's probably called the stern section or the bow or something similarly nautical — as if I'm wearing one giant pointy-toed shoe. I reposition them and my entire body, hoping to choose something back-friendly.

"Let's keep going. I'm over it, whatever it was."

Did Greg think about what might happen to him on a solo trip if his back went out like it did at the company picnic years ago? What would he have done if he couldn't paddle himself out of here? Is that the explanation? Is that all it is? His back went out? Did he put us through all this trauma because of a simple herniated disc?

Why would that make me angry? It would be a blessed relief, wouldn't it?

Lord, I hope I like myself better before we find him.

A prayer with more than two words in it. What do you know?

Frank motions toward the shoreline to the right about fifty yards from us. I see nothing of significance there except a small sandy beach. We follow, nosing our canoe with a whoosh of sound onto the sand. He's already out of his canoe, heading into the underbrush for another of his bathroom breaks. He really should get his prostate checked. It's not something you want to tell your father-in-law, though.

Jen and I take turns heading in a different direction of underbrush. We know better than to pass up a wayside moment. One of the least appealing aspects of the wilderness. Fresh air bathrooms. Frank says there's talk of making it mandatory to haul out all used toilet paper. Haul it out of the wilderness. Can you imagine? The bears don't have to haul out their waste. We've seen plenty of it. And moose droppings. Interesting-looking nuggets the size of those small chocolate Easter eggs.

I bury the evidence of my presence in this wilderness with leaves and pine needles. Picking my way over tree roots and around moss pillows, always on the alert for sure footing, I see a tiny indigo gem flash its dusty face at me from low on the ground. Low-bush blueberries.

I nudge a berry until it rolls off its stem into my hand, then pop it into my mouth before I stop to think that my ignorance of this area might have made that simple act a death knell. There's no such thing as poisonous blueberries, right?

"Frank. Jen. Come here."

"We need to get a move on, Lib," Frank calls with a huff. "What is it?"

"Wild blueberries. I think. Check it out."

In minutes, they've joined me. I hold out a handful of the tiny berries with bluish-purple tufts at their crown. Jen uses her pointer finger to roll them around. They lose a little of the dull blush in the warmth of my hand.

"Looks like wild blueberries to me," she says. "What's your opinion, Frank?"

We don't have to ask if they're okay to eat. Frank pops them like M&Ms from the candy dish on his wife's antique sideboard.

"Can we spare the time to harvest a few?"

I ask, bent to the task already.

"Up here, a person knows better than to ignore free food. And nothing tastes quite as good as something that didn't make a layover in a grocery store."

That sounds odd coming from him, since he worked as a grocer until he retired. I wonder if Greg feels the same way. Would he have stumbled onto a patch of wild blueberries up here and found joy in the fact that they didn't need a middleman like him?

"You girls pick if you want," Frank says. "I'll stand guard."

Stand guard?

"We're not the only ones who like blueberries in our pancakes," Frank explains without invitation. "These little bits of heaven make mighty fine bear dessert, if you know what I mean."

Strangely confident with a close-to-elderly man as our watchman, I suggest to Jen that we consolidate our individual rolls of toilet paper into one plastic zip bag so we can collect blueberries in the other.

"What I wouldn't give to grow a crop like this at home." Jen's hands make quick work of stripping mature berries without disturbing the white infants and pale adolescents clinging to the bushes. "Isn't God good?"

Where did that come from? Oh. Creation and all. Abundance. Tiny berries of provision in the middle of nowhere.

"Not that we need them," Jen continues. "But that makes them more of a treat, right?" She looks up at me from her berry-picking crouch.

She wants me to draw my own conclusion, doesn't she? Something about God lavishing things on us that we don't deserve. Something about His intimate care of us and that He's interested in the tiniest details of our lives. Something I've too-long forgotten.

Does Frank see it that way? Sometimes I think Greg mourns his father's lack of faith more than he mourns the loss of our daughter. I can't put those thoughts in the past tense — mourned. I have to believe Greg still has the capacity to feel.

Do I?

For him? Yes. Warts and all. Especially the warts.

Another handful of berries finds my mouth rather than the collection bag.

"Your appetite's back?" Jen asks.

"About time," Frank adds.

I'm hungry. I never saw that as a gift.

"Ladies," Frank says, adjusting his hat, "we best be going."

Jen and I are upright immediately, our eyes scanning the perimeter of our berry patch for signs of black bear fur or beady, greedy eyes.

"Don't look there," he says. "Look up."

Up? Through the lacy-armed cedars and anorexic pine boughs?

"Dark clouds and aching joints. A sure sign of rain. This isn't the best spot for us to hunker down. Not much open space to set up a shelter of any kind."

We're following him to the canoes like baby ducks behind an all-wise mother. Jen slides quickly into the back of our canoe again. I'm more skilled at lookout than I am at steering, so I don't object. With one leg backward in our pointy-toed canoe, I push off from shore with the other, dragging my Nike in the lake water. My hiking boots are still drying, along with my pant leg. The hem of my khakis is soaked. From the looks of the changing sky, it won't be the only thing that would soon be wet.

16

By the time we find a spot suitable for sitting out a thunderstorm, the surface of the water is pimpled with droplets. We grab the necessities, haul them to high ground, then invert the canoes over the rest of our packs and equipment.

Rain drips down the back of my neck and the valley of my spine while we work to follow Frank's orders. He thinks we can get by with just the lean-to tarp rather than go to all the effort of setting up the tents. But the rain rode in on waves of a fickle wind — first one direction, then the opposite. An angled, one-sided lean-to is no protection at all.

I don't recommend pitching a tent in the rain. It's no small feat when what the tent pegs have to work with is a dusting of soil no deeper than the powdered sugar on a donut — damp powdered sugar. Damp on its way to muddy.

We work as a team, motivated by a strong drive to hide from the now pelting rain. Midway through putting up the first tent, we agree that one is enough. We'll huddle together until the storm passes.

The illustrators for L.L. Bean or Eddie Bauer might get a chuckle out of our shelter, but we're out of the elements, listening to the rain rather than soaking in it.

We strip off what we can and still retain some modesty in the presence of one another. Our wet outer clothes land in a pile near the tent door, while we congregate in the middle of the tight space.

Frank takes off his boots. I wish he hadn't. Jen scrunches her nose. She agrees.

He reaches as if to remove his wet, well-used socks. Jen and I both sigh with relief when he merely scratches his foot.

"Hope the rain lets up enough for us to move farther before nightfall, or at least get that second tent raised," he says. "We smell like a pack of sour wolves."

We do? And how does he know what sour wolves smell like?

Before I have time to ask him for more details about the wildlife population in this area of the Quetico, he's pulling his boots back on and digging through the pile for his wet flannel shirt.

"Where are you going, Frank?"

"Nature calls," he says as he unzips the tent and unlatches his belt simultaneously.

He's been gone too long for our tastes. No one back home would believe us if we told them we lost *two* men in the wilderness.

Jen and I keep our voices low. Why?

"Do you think we should go look for him?" Jen ventures.

"Frank? He can take care of himself." That's what I want to lean on.

"What if he had a heart attack or something? At his age —"

"He's in better physical shape than either one of us."

"Yes, but —"

"Jenika, will you quit imagining the worst? He's fine. He has to be fine." I don't like being the boss of the Take Courage patrol.

How long do we sit in a damp lump, waiting for that welcome sound of footfalls on rock or the zip of the tent opening? The wind slaps the nylon sides of our shelter like dish towels on a clothesline in a hurricane. The staccato of the rain keeps up its annoying rhythm.

Did we sabotage Greg's chances of survival by waiting as long as we did to act? Are we now pressing a similar fate on the only man who knows how to get us where we're headed and back home again?

If Greg weren't missing, these morbid thoughts wouldn't enter our minds. We're raw right now when it comes to rescue operations. Jen's closed eyes and moving lips suggest it's not just me. It's us. She's praying.

Her faith registers more sanguine than my choleric relationship with the Lord. Even when a cloud passes overhead — a cloud, a crisis, cancer — she bounces back quickly. She mouths "amen" and takes a granola bar from her pocket. I do the same. Not from hunger, but from wanting to follow in her footsteps.

It's amazing how misshapen a granola bar can get when tucked into the breast pocket of a denim shirt. Frank insists we carry granola bars in an accessible place for quick energy on the water, or if we're delayed finding a place to stop for lunch.

A place to stop for lunch. *Applebee's or Perkins today? Or Olive Garden? Let's do Wendy's. I'm hungry for their Southwest Taco Salad.*

I nibble on the end of the granola bar I've exposed. It could be a while before our next hot meal. We'll give Frank five more minutes, then we'll hunt him down.

A loud crack somewhere just beyond the tent sends a jolt through my nervous system. Jen beats me in the high jump, though.

"What on earth?"

"You gonna hide in there forever?" Frank's voice pours healing oil on my nerves.

We scramble to the tent door, tripping over one another in our haste.

"Frank? Where were you?" Whose voice asked those questions? Jen's or mine? Does it matter? We're thinking the same homicidal thoughts.

"Exploring," he says, his back to us.

"You can't be serious!" That voice is mine for sure. It hurts my throat when I growl out the sentence.

"What? You think I've got that Old Timer's disease?" Frank turns to face his trembling little ducklings. His shirt is bulging as if he's near full-term.

Alzheimer's, Frank. But no.

"Had a little run-in with a fallen log." He cradles his pregnant belly with one arm and hand and points toward his left shin and torn pant leg with the other.

"Frank, you're bleeding!" Jen rushes toward him and kneels to take a peek at what he's done to himself.

"It's not as bad as it looks. I pushed the bone back in."

"Frank!" I join Jen, not sure I want to see what fascinates her.

He backs away from the two of us. "I'm kidding. Lighten up, women. It's just a scratch."

Jen's tsk shows her exasperation. "This is more than a little scratch, Frank. It needs attention. Do we have a first-aid kit?"

"It's in my pack," I volunteer. On my way to the spot on shore where we inverted the canoes, it dawns on me that the rain had stopped. When did that happen?

I flip the canoe upright and move it out of the way so I can dig in the pack. Buckles and zippers. Flaps and pockets. Where did I see that thing?

Jen has Frank's pant leg torn open the rest of the way to the knee by the time I reach them with the kit. The blood soaked into his sock ribbing seems significant to me. Jen blots at the wound with a piece of cloth. It looks like the T-shirt she wore under her outer layer a few minutes ago.

"Frank, sit down," I urge. "Give Jen a better look at your leg."

"Can't do that very well at the moment," he says, massaging his overgrown belly.

"What is that? What have you got in there?" I unbutton his flannel shirt, chuckling at the oddity our trio makes at the moment. A pregnant old man. A young woman kneeling in front of his hairy, naked, bloody leg. And me . . . helpless, as usual.

He bats my hands away. "Careful, there," he says. "Dry kindling is worth its weight in government bonds on a day like today."

Kindling? He stuffed his shirt with kindling?

Sure enough. At my promise to handle with care, he opens his shirt and unloads his bundle of joy into my waiting arms. Crisp-dry pine needles, small cedar bows, and bits of bark.

"Where'd you find this in a rainstorm, Frank?"

"Hold still, Frank!" Jen's and my comments hit him in an unintentionally coordinated effort.

"I tripped over a stupid log that had no business being there. Landed face first at the base of a big old cedar. I suppose I should thank the Lord the downed branches I landed in didn't poke my eyes out."

Thank the Lord, Frank? Bravo.

His shirt now empty of its contents, Frank leans toward the ottoman-sized boulder to his left. Jen follows as he sits and elevates his leg to give her easier access to his wound.

"The kindling, Frank?" I'm nothing if not persistent.

"Under the young branches. Never would have discovered it if I hadn't fallen."

You'd think he'd found a new route to China.

"I bent myself over the branches and stuffed my shirt as full as I could."

"Can you hold this, Libby?" Jen extends a roll of adhesive tape toward me. My arms bulge with the kindling. I hesitate to drop it on the damp ground, so I sidle closer to her and offer a pinkie finger. She slips the roll onto my finger, smiles, and returns to her paramedic tasks.

"I still don't understand what took you so long, Frank." Now that the fear is gone, my interrogation softens to the level of normal conversation.

"I guess, maybe, I might have lost consciousness for a minute or two."

What?

"Frank!" Jen grabs the tape from me and slaps it over the gauze now cradling Frank's leg wound. She turns her attention to his head.

"Frank, you have a goose egg the size of . . . of . . ."

"Of a goose egg?" he offers.

"What did you do?"

"Oh, I almost forgot," he adds without missing a beat. "Picked up some of these beauties too." He digs into his shirt pocket and fishes out a handful of things that look like arthritic fingers. Dead ones. Long dead.

Can a concussion make someone fall in love with woodland refuse?

His eyes search ours for the appreciation he must expect to find. "You know what these are, don't you?"

We city girls shake our heads no.

"Pieces of cedar root. Full of resin. Better than lighter fluid for starting a fire."

Okay, then. He still has a few marbles left. That's a relief.

I survey the mess we've made. A listing tent. A wounded soldier. A concern-weary makeshift paramedic with mud where her knees used to be. And me, my arms full of kindling I'm protecting as if it holds the potential to save our lives.

I think I know the answer, but ask anyway, "Are we staying here for the night, Frank?"

"Probably best," he says. His speech seems slurred. That can't be, can it?

"I'm feeling . . . a little . . . lightheaded," he says and topples off the boulder backwards into another nest of cedar boughs.

The cloth label sewn into the nylon of the tent flap says it's a four-person tent. If they sleep standing up, I suppose. Or crouch.

None of us can stand up in here.

Jen and I somehow maneuvered Frank's limp body into the tent, where he now rests comfortably, if we can believe the words of a guy with a knot on both the front and back of his head. I retrieve the sleeping bags from our packs near the water's edge. Sooner or later, Jen and I will need to haul it here to the campsite. Right now, Frank's health is our main concern.

I stuff dry clothes into one of my sweatshirts and make him a pillow for his neck. Jen swivels from checking for blood seepage through the dressing on his leg to watching his pupils and taking his pulse. How does she know this stuff?

I ask her. She reminds me her mom was a nurse. Good enough for me.

Frank falls asleep, evidenced by his rumbling, deeply comforting snores. Is it an old wives' tale or are you not supposed to let a concussion victim fall asleep? As if we could stop him.

Would it do me any good to look at the maps in his pocket? We can't find our way out of here without Frank's help. And even if we could, it would mean giving up our search for Greg. The thought slices through my heart with dagger-like efficiency, severing blood vessels and fleshy pockets of hope.

We need a hero. I need my husband.

It's taken most of the late afternoon to set up camp without Frank's help. We're grateful for the smallest favors — a flat rock on which to put the camp stove, a windless respite after the storm, air temperatures cool enough to make the bugs sluggish and less aggressive against the new flesh we offered them by invading their northwoods territory.

I'm grateful, too, that we had a couple of days under Frank's leadership before we were thrust out on our own. Getting our food pack hoisted into a tall-enough tree will be a trick without Frank's throwing arm to toss the rope over a tree branch. I wonder if Jen participated in women's softball in college. We could use an ex-pitcher about now.

I dig in the food pack for our cooking utensils while Jen heads into the woods with a plastic bag of toilet paper. That reminds me of blueberries. What happened to them? It seems a shame to waste the very things that cost us precious time earlier in the day.

I look toward our canoe parking spots, trying to imagine where I might have tucked the bag of berries among the few remaining things we left at the water's edge. The shore is less crowded than it should be. The pounding in my head matches that in the veins in my neck. Where's the other canoe?

"Jen?"

"Give me a minute," she says from somewhere deep in the trees.

"Jen, one of the canoes is missing."

She must not have heard me. The fact that I choked on the words might explain why.

What did I do? In my efforts to truck everything to the campsite, did I dislodge it from its snug resting place? Was it not as snug as I assumed?

The thoughts accompany me to the water. I shield my eyes against the sun that is too close to setting. Frantic to see that familiar green canoe, I search the water, close to shore at first, then in widening circles.

Oh, Lord! This is my fault. It's all my fault! Everything! I'm probably somehow to blame for Frank's leg and his lumpy head and — for all I know — global warming! Please bail me out again! Please help me. I have to find that canoe. Oh, God Almighty! You know where it is. Would you kindly . . . if You don't mind . . . share that information?

I'm running along the shore now, stumbling from my own stupidity as much as the unevenness of the rocks.

How fast is the current here? Is there a

current? Are we still on a lake or is this a wide section of river? If it caught the current, it could be halfway home by now, like a dog bent on reaching its own yard before nightfall. The shoreline juts in and out of the water, as jagged as the torn edge of handmade paper.

And there it is. Our canoe. Bumping along the uneven edge, the length of a football field away from me. What's beyond that far arm of land that curves toward me? Open water? Hopelessness? If I follow the shore, the canoe could be long gone. We can't survive one more disadvantage like this one.

I fling off the hooded sweatshirt that's kept me warm all afternoon and kick off my shoes. This is no Bahamian beach. My stocking-clad feet rebel against the cobbled lake floor as I wade in until the water's deep enough for me to swim.

My water aerobics instructor from a decade ago would be embarrassed by my form. I know I'm flailing. Panic is never smooth. I try to remember to breathe, but I can't lose sight of that green lifeboat.

How can water be this cold in the middle of summer? My lungs scream, "Unfair!" My legs grow numb after a few minutes of wave-pounding. And the green slice of life retreats farther from me. How can that be?

I'm moving, aren't I?

God, help me!

That familiar cry.

Lord, You promised! my mind shouts to the heavens above me. *You promised to help those who cry out to You!*

My foot slams against something hard and unmoving, sending waves of pain up a leg I thought was numb. Is it shallow this far out into the little bay? I stumble to my feet, favoring the one that throbs. Knee-deep now. Not good. The water holds me back as I slog toward the canoe. Resistance is the last thing I need. Is this water or cold honey?

But I'm making progress at last. Slipping. Lunging. Grabbing an edge of kelly green.

"Libby, are you okay?" Jen's shout is loud enough to alert the Toronto police half a province away. Why didn't we think of that before?

I can't answer or breathe. But I think I know what a stroke feels like. I grab the canoe by the scruff of its neck like I would a naughty puppy and proceed to walk it home.

I know Jen will sympathize. She'll make me something hot to drink and listen to the story. But what I really want is Greg's embrace. I want to snuggle into his chest and feel the beat of his heart reminding me of the pace at which mine should pulse.

And I don't want to warm my blue lips on hot cocoa, but on his. How long has it been since a thought like that crossed my mind?

What will I do if we don't find him? What if we find him but his lips are forever blue?

17

A sleeping bag makes a pretty decent shawl when you need to warm up fast. The current cold front may be good for discouraging mosquitoes and black flies, but my teeth chatter so much I'm afraid I'll crack a crown.

We're Scrooge-frugal with our pirated kindling but manage to start a fire. Jen scrambles for more dry wood. It's rare to find a log too large for a campfire up here. Most of the fallen limbs or downed trees are thin enough to catch fire quickly. The trick today is finding something that escaped the rain under an umbrella of other fallen logs or thick undergrowth.

I check on Frank. That's one thing I can do while my blood thaws. He's awake, complaining of a headache. Big surprise, the poor guy. I find a spare gallon-sized plastic zip bag in the food pack and lay it near his head. Seems to me concussions and vomiting go together, if I remember from the boys' short-lived football experiences.

My boys. I may have let them go too soon. I may have forced open the bud of their independence. Why was it so important to me to make sure they didn't need me? Did I fear letting them down if they depended on me, like I let down Lacey? People get paid to figure out things like that. I probably should have paid someone to tell me.

It's not that I resent their aliveness. I don't want my daughter back *in place of* my sons. A family can still be a family if it's missing one of its key members, can't it? The sparkling member. The one who helped balance all the male-dominated décor and activities and sports babble. The one who had me by the heart.

"Jen?"

"It's me, Frank."

"Oh, good."

"Do you need something?"

"Pit stop."

"Ah."

I can't imagine successfully helping him into the woods in his current state of weakness. We just found another use for the "air sickness" bag.

"Do you think we should call Brent to send

help?" Jen's voice holds a thread of uncertainty atypical for her.

"I haven't earned a reputation for wisdom the last few years, but I think we should see how the night goes. Frank's tough. If you ask for the tour, he'll show you scars from any number of wars. He may bounce back by morning."

"Do you think so? Deep in your heart?"

I don't dare dig that deeply right now. But I tell her, "What can it hurt to wait until morning? Unless Frank takes a turn for the worse. I think he's a little more with it already, don't you? He was able to eat a little at supper. Great job with the dehydrated chili, by the way."

"The fresh air's made you delirious. It tasted like cardboard soaked in tomato sauce."

"With a hint of cilantro," I add.

"When we get home," she says, "I'm going to hug my spices and kiss my microwave."

When we get home. How many of us will make the return trip? Just the three of us? Will I have something more than kitchen appliances to hug?

I should be sleeping. No matter how you look at it, tomorrow promises to be a rough one. But I'm mesmerized by the dance of flames in the fire and stars overhead. This wilderness is a civilization vacuum. Suck all the people, all the commotion, all the busyness out of a place, and all you have is the pure Presence. All the hindrances retreat like grim-faced armed guards who once lined the entrance to the throne but now step back to allow me access to the King I've ignored too long. A King whose voice called through the crowd and I missed it.

This is it. This is why you came, isn't it, Greg? Because of the vacuum. The wilderness drew you because of its absence of people like me demanding things of you that you couldn't deliver. You sat on nights like this and saw the heavens opened to you, didn't you? You walked the surface of the water to the Jesus waiting for you to come to Him.

I always thought the light dancing in your eyes when you returned from these trips was due to the fish stories you collected and the vacation from the daily routine of your job. Now I know it was more likely a reflection of the Light with whom you came in contact while sitting here with nothing in the way.

"Libby?"

Jen has volunteered to camp out in the Tent of Snore tonight so she can listen for changes in Frank. I'll be alone in the second tent.

The call comes with a hand on my shoulder this time. "Libby? You okay?"

"Listen."

"What?" She plants herself on a log that resembles an Adirondack chair if you squint and don't think about it too hard.

"Did you hear that?"

"I don't hear anything other than your father-in-law."

"I've been sitting here waiting for the Lord to tell me everything's going to be all right."

"Oh, hon."

"No, you're right. We don't have any guarantees. This could all end very poorly by our way of thinking."

"And if it does?"

I look out across the water and above the treetops on the far shore to the place of the moon's crooked grin.

"Since the beginning of time, there has never been a night that has not been followed by a dawn."

"Some days are birthed in gray clouds." She's baiting me, I know. She's the optimistic one.

"Trace back through history and find me a gap, an empty space in the records, a day when dawn refused to come."

"And you're okay with it if the sun doesn't shine all day and suddenly it's night again?"

"No, not okay. But more confident than before that the sun isn't gone forever just because it's hidden from my view."

Jen's eyes reflect starlight, moonlight, firelight, and the light of God. "This is huge, Libby."

"I know."

A low growl interrupts us. We snap to attention. I don't know about Jen, but I'm wishing Frank had smuggled firearms over the border.

Another growl . . . with words this time. "You women going to stop talking any time soon so a guy can get some sleep?"

He's back.

18

Two or three days ago, hurry was our goal. We can't hurry anymore. That scares me, I admit. It's almost laughable to think we could find Greg alive at this point. Not rational, certainly. And we've already blown our hope of getting back within a week if we keep going deeper into the wilderness.

But we press on, sluggish as bears six weeks into hibernation. I wish they were in hibernation. It would save us fussing with that food pack and fighting off the panic of night sounds. Scratching and snapping twigs. Huffs we hope are wind exhalations. Grunts we attribute to Frank because any other option is unacceptable.

We haven't seen any real evidence of bears other than their fertilizer. But the danger hovers like stink on a skunk. Jen's more an animal person, but she likes them smaller than she is.

I'm cooking breakfast. The chill air keeps

our food so close to refrigeration temperatures that I'm not nervous about frying up
the slab bacon we haven't used yet. The
powdered eggs Frank brought hold no appeal. So it's pancakes again. We wouldn't
take time to cook a hot breakfast, but we
have to carb-load, as the marathoners would
say. We have vast stretches of water to cover
today, if Frank's energy holds out. We'll
need our strength.

The pancakes are thinner than Frank's
version but far from pretty. I pray we're not
in this wilderness long enough to learn how
to regulate the cookstove.

"Does he look all right to you?" Jen stage-
whispers as I flip the last pancake onto her
plate.

I eye him for the dozenth time since he
emerged from the tent an hour ago. "Seems
a lot more steady on his feet."

"I hope we're doing the right thing by
moving on."

"Me too."

"Me, three." He's sneaky, that man.

I put my hands on my hips, grandmalike,
flicking stray pancake crumbs onto the
ground as I do.

"I'll be fine, you old mother hens," he
says. "Look. See? I can bend my leg. I know
who the president is. What year it is. And

my mother's maiden name: Finkelmasterson. Bet she's glad she married a Holden."

Something brushes against my pant leg. I hurdle over logs and rocks in my effort to distance myself from whatever it is before my eyes can focus on the beast.

"Chipmunk," Jen calls across the miles. "You should see him. He's so cute."

Pancake crumbs. That's what lured him. It wouldn't have been so bad if he hadn't startled me.

I remember thinking that same thing on an ocean-deep level after the coroner told us Lacey was gone. It startled the life out of us. We didn't have time to prepare — no time to say good-bye.

Initially, stupidly, I thought how much better we could have coped if we'd just known our time with her was short. Who expects to lose a twelve-year-old daughter?

If I'd known what was coming, I would have put off getting a part-time job until she was away at college or something. If I hadn't been working that day, I would have been home. And so would she.

"Libby!" Jen calls. "It's safe. You can come back. He won't hurt you."

Frank's laughter carries to where my panic took me. That's a good sign, but I'd better rejoin them before his chuckles turn to spasms.

Jen feeds the furry offender bits of pancake she tosses from her plate as if feeding pigeons or squirrels at the park.

The sun is too high in the sky by the time we have the camp dismantled and the canoes loaded. Jen offers to paddle Frank's canoe and allow him the so-called benefit of my paddling assistance. He turns her down, insisting that if we slow our pace a tad, he'll manage. I'm guessing the cold wave is over, judging from the sweat puddling in my bra.

I'm beginning to think Frank's enlarged prostate is a gift from God. We know he'll have to stop frequently for breaks. Maybe we can talk him into stretching the break times to include cat naps.

According to Frank, we're tracing the most likely path Greg took. We're all conscious, though, that so much of what Greg told any of us ahead of time doesn't jibe with the evidence. How could he have left home without his fishing equipment? What was on his mind?

Right now, the only confirmation we have is a broken paddle and a handful of sunflower seeds that may or may not have been his. He was here — somewhere in this vast expanse of hiding places.

Jen hums something familiar.

"What is that?"

"Me."

"I mean, what song?"

"An oldie. 'Guide Me, O Thou Great Jehovah.' Seems appropriate."

It occurs to me that I miss music more than my microwave. I misplaced music three years ago, right after the funeral.

Jen's moved onto another song — a worship song. I recognize it from church and entertain a moment of shame that it's lived there but not in my heart. Her effortless soprano voice floats skyward. I hum an alto harmony part I didn't know was in me. By the second verse, I'm using words too. I can't imagine any other kind of music that would fit this setting.

The sun's reflection on the water is strong today. Less than twenty feet ahead of us, Frank lays his paddle across his lap, removes his glare-blocking sunglasses, and wipes a fleck of dust or something out of his eye.

Dust.

I can't think about Frank's spiritual needs right now. Searching for Greg is a consuming task. Survival consumes us.

Lord, can it wait until we're back on terra firma?

No.

Of course not. I let Jen's voice solo for a while and turn my attention to praying for the man with his back to us and to Him.

Another portage. Not a good day for it, but it's the only link from this lake to the next lake in the chain. The droop of Frank's shoulders tells us he's fading. Will he take our suggestion that he let the two of us women bear the brunt of the effort for this portage?

"Jen," I begin after we've straightened our bent knees and stomped out the prickles in our sleeping feet, "you know what I'd like to try sometime?"

"What's that?" The innocence in her voice tells me she's unaware of the plot hatching in my mind.

"Don't you think you and I could haul a canoe across a portage? We're stronger now than a few days ago."

"Speak for yourself, lady." She rubs a spot on her left shoulder, but at the glare I shoot her way she changes her tune. "Stronger. That's right. Regular Amazon women. I'm considering signing us up for *The Amazing Race* next season."

"If you take one end and I take the other, can't we carry a canoe down the path?"

"I'd think so. Yes."

"And we could pile a few things inside. Just a few. Nothing too heavy."

Frank's straddling the end of his canoe. He's quiet. But he's not objecting.

"Frank, what do you think? Could we try?" Jen asks.

"It would make us feel as if we'd accomplished something." Okay, I may have taken it a little too far.

"Makes no nevermind to me if you women want to do it the hard way."

He rubs the muscles on either side of the laceration on his shin. Jen checks it as often as he'll let her.

"If you don't mind, I think I'll get myself a little snack before I join you on the trail."

"That's a good idea, Frank. Then you won't be pushing us faster than we can hoof it," Jen offers.

Bless her.

I've carried infant seats with twelve-pound babies. I've lugged a warehouse full of grocery bags over the years, including multiple two-liter bottles of ginger ale and five-quart pails of ice cream for hungry teens. I move my own furniture, inch-by-inch, so I don't have to answer Greg's questions about why I'm rearranging again.

But hauling a partially loaded canoe

through the woods and over roots and rocks is a new experience.

Jen's a trooper. I ask her if we can rest a minute every so often. My hand is cramped from gripping the flat part of the canoe that forms a triangle and a supposed handle. Jen's in back, so I'm not sure what she's found to grip. It occurs to me that we probably should have upped the insurance on Brent's brand new canoe before tackling this assignment.

"Slow down a little, will you, Libby?"

"Oh, thank you!"

"This was the right thing to do, wasn't it?"

"Absolutely," I say, swinging my free arm for balance on the irregular terrain.

"Save Frank's strength."

"Right."

"Oh, this is good news."

"What?"

"Look up."

"Jen, I can barely stand the way it is."

"Stop then and look up."

We grind to a clumsy halt, lower the canoe to the ground, stretch what isn't broken, and turn our faces toward the sky. Black fog in silhouette against the blue?

"What is that? A rain cloud?" I ask.

"That's no cloud, Libby. It's swarms of

insects. The warmth brought back the flying things. Black flies, maybe. Could be mosquitoes."

"Is it a state convention or something?"

"Provincial."

"What?"

"Canadian, dear. A *provincial* convention."

I reach for my end of the canoe again. "Let's get this over with and get back out onto the water."

Hustling proves counterproductive. I scrape my flailing arm on rough tree bark. My shirt sleeve catches on a stub of a branch. And, of course, the jolt makes me drop my end of the canoe.

"Oh, no! I'm so sorry."

"Are you hurt?" Jen asks.

"Is the canoe okay?" I drop to my knees and feel the skin of the canoe for punctures or dents, like a vet might run his hand over a lame horse's sore muscles. "Can you lift it up a little?"

She's already on the case, raising the front end — my responsibility — tentatively.

As smooth as ironed underwear, which I will never do — iron underwear. "I think we're okay."

"Made of good stuff," Jen suggests.

"Thank You, Lord. I don't think I could bear one more —" My breath is stolen.

"One more what? Disaster? Yes, I think we've had our fill for a while. I'd knock on wood, which there's plenty of, but I'd rather — Libby? What is it?"

The sight before me sends me into something bordering on arrhythmia. "I had to drop the canoe." My voice is hollow. It spooks even me.

"Well, sure. I understand. Your shirt caught on the —"

"I had to drop it here," I tell Jen. "In this spot." I'm not moving from my crouch, so Jen gently lowers the front of the canoe.

"Hon, what's wrong?" she asks. "Are you seriously hurt?"

I can imagine she's wondering how she'll cope with two patients on her hands for the rest of the trip. All I'm focused on at the moment is the slash of purple rising out of the primordial ooze. I reach to brush the debris from around it.

Not just purple, but "Grapes at Sunrise" purple. I teased Greg mercilessly about his decision to paint his Swiss Army knife housing the color of Tuscan grapes. I told him people would think he was a Vikings fan. We know how well that would go over in our part of Wisconsin.

"This is Greg's," I tell Jen, brushing away more debris.

She crouches next to me. "Are you sure?"

"He insisted it was a fitting color for a guy who'd just scored a major coup in the world of grape jam for Greene's Grocery."

"I've never heard of anyone painting his pocket knife." Her voice is taking on the air of a burned-out childcare worker.

"And here I am, in awe of a two-inch piece of purple metal that I know without question belongs to my husband."

Jen lays her hand on my shoulder. She squeezes. I think that means, "Glory to God."

"Fell out of his pocket?" she says.

"Looks like it. A downward trajectory for it to land nose-in like this."

"Downward trajectory? Well, aren't you just the consummate CSI!"

With crime scene investigator diligence, she and I comb the area for more evidence. We look at the position of the knife, trying to determine in our untrained way if it represents a drop made heading deeper into the wilderness or on the way out. Hard to tell without microscopes and laser beams, graphs, and computer programs.

When we've determined the area is hopelessly stingy with its evidence, I pocket the knife. Greg made it this far at least.

As we paddled past countless shorelines

and bays and inlets and islands each day, I wondered if we paddled right past him — beyond where he stood or lay. My eye sockets are bone dry from constantly scanning the shore for clues — a column of smoke from a campfire, a piece of familiar clothing left drying and forgotten on a rock or a low-hanging branch.

We've seen three other canoes since entering the Quetico. One was heading in the same direction. I would have told the canoeist to call his wife if I'd had the courage to speak when he came up behind us on a portage as if speed limits meant nothing to him. We gave him one of the cards Jen printed up with Greg's description and Brent's phone number. The canoeist only had time for the *Reader's Digest* condensed version of the story.

Our second encounter with people other than ourselves was an older couple — older than Frank — whose leathery faces told us this wasn't their first outdoor excursion. They passed us on the water heading out of the park a few hours ago. But no, they hadn't seen anyone matching Greg's description.

The third canoe belonged to a teenager and his dad, a guy with Greg's build but a potty mouth. So not my Greg. They'd fished up, down, and around the tangle of lakes and rivers for the last eight days. They'd seen a family of wolves, a cow moose with calf, and ancient pictographs — the early Native American version of hieroglyphics — but no sign of Greg.

He was here, though. This far at least. I have the proof in my pocket.

The regret of what we may have missed to this point washes away in an instant, as if we flipped the Etch-a-Sketch of worry and shook it to start a new picture. He made it this far.

"Do you suppose that's illegal? Taking the evidence with us?" Jen asks me after we've resumed our trek toward the light and water at the end of our woodland tunnel.

"Illegal?"

"Or unwise? I know it sounds dumb, but what if the authorities would need to finger-print it or measure distances from the trail or something? Have we just tampered with the evidence? Is that a prosecutable of-fense?"

Frank would get a laugh out of our con-cern over a purple pocket knife and jail time.

I have to work at not letting Jen's refer-ence to the possibility of foul play torment me. "Tell you what. I'll make Greg put it

back when we're on our way home."
Is there any real hope of that?

19

Retracing our steps down the portage trail to make another trip and another with canoe and packs and equipment seems equivalent to watching a baby's crowning head retreat between contractions. The agony! Let's get on with this! We need to move forward, not backward.

But there is no other way. We'll need every bit of this equipment, and we can't afford to overtax Frank right now. He's holding his own, but I don't need a degree in medicine to know he's exhausted. The heat isn't helping. Where's that cold front now when we need one?

I wonder if Estée Lauder makes a fragrance capable of masking what I smell like. Jen's running a close second. Frank, well, Frank has his own brand of "air freshener."

Everything we experience ignites my imagination. How is Greg coping with these same issues? If he's deathly ill, how is he fighting off the flies during the day and no-see-ums at night? My mind can't shake the picture of starving, emaciated patients lying in open-air African hospitals, while flies crawl over their matted eyes and oozing sores.

Jen would quote Philippians 4 and warn me to think about "whatever is pure, whatever is true, whatever is lovely, whatever is of good report."

Of good report? Let's see. We have a broken canoe paddle, empty sunflower shells, and a tiny knife with the world's smallest scissors and the best little tweezers for plucking eyebrows. I'm grateful for the clues, but can any of them qualify as encouraging news? Greg lost a paddle and dropped his knife. Both beg the question *why?* Both items held significance to him. Why did he abandon them? Or me? There may be some simple explanations. But good reports? I'll reserve judgment a while longer.

"That's odd," Jen says, as we slide from the rocky shore onto the satiny water.

I slip into my canoe seat without rocking the vessel or splashing our equipment. Sweet. "What is?"

"Getting back to paddling seems like a relief."

I agree. That is indeed odd.

After an hour of relief paddling, Frank suggests we temporarily lash our canoes together out on the water and eat a late lunch here, away from the worst of the insect convention. Good advice.

Strange as it sounds, we may have to take some time later today to fish. Noodles and rice and hash browns stretch a meal but we could use more protein. Frank, especially.

How long did Greg's supplies last? Is he nursing the last crumbs of moldy cheese or rationing raisins to survive? Is he harvesting wild blueberries? Is he conscious?

Worry is so much more natural than faith. I think I'd like to try living in the supernatural for a while. Would I have considered such a thing back home where everything around me bore the imprint of imperfect humanity?

Turning backward in the canoe seat to flash a breakthrough kind of smile in Jen's direction, I notice the sunburn on her bare arms. Mine sting when I scratch one of several dozen mosquito bites. Sunscreen would have been a good idea. It's buried somewhere in the side pocket of a pack that's tucked into the bottom of the canoe. Moot point now. Like so many things, once you feel it, it's too late to do anything about it.

"Do you think Greg packed sunscreen?" Jen asks from her position in the stern. The stern. I know this now.

"I'm sure he did."

"Good," she says. "Good."

We finish eating and pick up our paddles again. Stroke after stroke in silence for an eternity.

Another night in the wilderness. Another dawn. Another reason to let loose of our tenuous grip on hope.

We tear down camp with a marked absence of conversation. Frank hasn't said it, but we all know we should be heading out today, not deeper in. Even if Frank regains full strength, we can't keep searching and still manage to pull into the driveway at home when we said we would. We've missed our opportunity to keep our word.

But when the canoes slide into the water, they're drawn by the magnetism of what might lie deeper in.

Frank's going to have to call Pauline.

Our few conversations on the SAT phone each night haven't been long. It doesn't take much time to say, "Anything, Brent?" and hear, "Sorry. Nothing," in response. Over and out.

The Canadian authorities apprehended

the Jeep thief. That much we know. They're charging him with possession of a stolen vehicle, but have found no evidence he did more than lift it from the put-in point. Still no answers. They promised more passes with the search plane and will continue to chase down the stories of the thief's aiding-and-abetting buddies while we keep chasing hopelessness.

Last night, Brent related that Zack and Alex called from the central research facility in Santiago. They're fine. Survivors. When Brent told them the news, Alex broke down and begged to come home. Without thinking too long, I told Brent to charge their airfare home to Wisconsin. I'll find a way to pay him back. I need my boys near me.

Who knows? Maybe I have some small measure of strength to offer them.

If the cloud cover is thick, satellite phone reception is spotty. *Can you hear me now?* If the sky stays as cloudless as it is right now, we should have no problem getting through to Brent — and Pauline — tonight.

I'm not expecting Brent to say, "Oh, hey! Glad you called. Yeah. Greg's right here. We're watching the baseball game on ESPN. Let me put him on the line for you."

Not expecting that at all.

The wind is picking up. Appreciably. We

haven't had to fight waves to this point. Within a few minutes we feel as if we're in a scene from *The Perfect Storm.* I didn't know how blessed we were before the wind blew.

"Keep your nose into the waves!" Frank calls across the water.

Is that Jen's responsibility from the back or mine from the front of our canoe?

"Don't let them catch you broadside," he cautions. "Like that," he says after we're drenched by a rogue wave I didn't anticipate. Apparently, the responsibility of scouting is mine.

My body's blocking Jen's line of vision, so it's up to me to holler "right" or "left" or "big one coming" to give her guidance.

It takes twice as much effort to achieve half as much progress with the wind fighting us. We've lost so much time with Frank's injury and our need to slow down that it's troublesome to consider losing more. I dig my paddle deeper. Sit up straighter. Lean forward for better leverage.

My face stings and my eyes water from the pounding of the wind. We're tiring fast. Our only respite is the relatively quiet water behind well-placed islands that serve as temporary windbreaks.

If we were on a larger body of water with

more room for the wind to pick up before slugging us, we'd be traveling backward.

I can hear Greg's voice telling me, "Sometimes we voyageurs are forced to take a wind day, Libby."

Now I get it.

So much for fishing for a meal. What self-respecting fish would want to come out on a day like this and have to body surf for a nibble of a plastic minnow?

Behind me, Jen says, "I'm worried, Libby."

Please don't say that, Jen. I'm doing enough worrying for the both of us. "About what? You're doing great back there." I have to raise my voice and turn my head so the sound carries above the mini-gale.

"Frank looks exhausted. We're running neck and neck with him, and it looks like he's giving it his all."

"Can we pull over closer to him and suggest we sit this out?"

"I don't think we have a choice."

Before we can act on the idea, Frank heads his canoe around a point. We follow, overjoyed to find a sheltered cove with calm waters and a low, flat, postcard-scenic campsite. The cove's opening is so narrow we feel as if we've slipped into another world — a perfect, secret hiding place.

Not so perfect. Greg isn't here.

But we're protected. We all need the break. Frank doesn't fully unload his canoe. He uses the first pack he hauls out as a pillow and lies down on a flat rock.

I'm sad we can't travel any farther today, but I must admit I'm grateful for such a beautiful, easy-access spot on which to camp. Smooth, wide, flat areas for the tents. A great stone fire pit complete with a grill that none of the other camping spots have had. And a rough log creation that resembles a picnic table.

Jen and I know what to do now. We're content to let Frank rest while we set up camp. It's not as easy or efficient without him, but we do it.

The water's boiling for a rice concoction by the time Frank wakes from his siesta. He's into and out of the woods before he comments on our setup.

"Nice work, ladies."

It's enough.

"I wish we could have gone farther today," Jen says.

"Not much point in that," he answers.

Has he reached the end of his reservoir of "there's still a chance"? We've seen nothing to feed it since I stumbled onto a flash of purple. But how could we focus on much more than nosing into the waves for the last several hours?

"This is it," he says, not opening his eyes to speak to us.

"What's it?" Jen asks the question but we both want to know.

He lifts his chin and takes in the scene: the refreshingly still water protected from the wind that rages beyond the cove's tree barricade — water that reflects the picturesque cupped hand of Creation in which we're standing.

"This is as far as Greg planned to go. We're here. We . . . we missed him."

Hope won't get its security deposit back, considering the mess it left behind.

I scramble to cover its tracks. "Wait a minute. We've only been on the water a few days. Greg would have had more than a week of his trip left. Wouldn't he have gone at least another two or three days deeper into the wilderness before turning around?"

"Not what he said. He said he planned to get where he was headed and plant himself. Even adventurers get tired of tearing down and setting up camp, you know."

"But," Jen says, "it's possible he changed his mind, isn't it?"

"He has a right to change his mind." I'm defending an action my husband may have taken as much as three weeks ago.

Frank removes his cap and wipes his forehead with his sleeve. "How are we supposed to cover a million acres of woods and water, ladies, if he's not where he said he was going to be?"

A million? I hope he's exaggerating. But from what we've passed already in these days, I fear he's not.

"Needle in a haystack, I'm afraid," Frank says. He wobbles, then crumbles.

On his knees, he sobs like a professional mourner from a culture far from this corner of the earth. Jen and I join him in posture and tears. We're wetting with our tears the ground where at least one of us was sure we'd find him.

It's over. The search is over. It's final. He's gone.

20

Jen catches the cooking pot before it boils dry. Wouldn't want to set the woods on fire. She refills the pot, but I think we all know none of us will eat much tonight.

We gather wood because that's what one does. We start a campfire in the stone circle. It makes the scene even more beautiful than it was before. Somehow beauty seems wrong.

It also seems wrong that the darker the sky grows, the more spectacular are the flames.

As I stare them down, lost in their burning life, Jen asks, "Could we pray together?"

"What for?" Frank is beyond courtesy.

"Because," Jen says, "we're in a desperate place. We have no resources of our own. God's the only One who knows where Greg is."

"And He's not talking," Frank adds.

"He might." That's me. My voice. My

242

shaky but authentic conviction. "He might talk if we give Him a chance."

"It must be these bumps on my head. I halfway believe you."

Jen and I form bookends for Frank on his log. I take his hands in mine. "Frank, you know we love you, don't you?"

He purses his lips and exhales as if he's blowing out birthday candles. "You going to love me more if I admit I need God? Is that it?"

I fish for a satisfactory answer for him, a way to capture the concept of eternity. "Not more, Frank. Longer."

He's as still as the granite underfoot. Then he pushes himself to a standing position and says, "Well . . ." as if he has someplace to go or a chore pressing on his schedule.

Jen and I are left alone on the log while he wanders somewhere beyond the reach of the fire's glow. It's time to pray. Most definitely.

Far from a traditional "Lord, help us find Greg" prayer, we're moved to take a different tack. The search for Greg is over. When did we switch from rescue operation to recovery? It feels as ominous as it sounds when announced on a newscast.

Even recovery is unlikely.

From the shards of evidence we have and

the bulk of positive evidence we're missing, we can only conclude that he died somewhere in his beloved wilderness who knows how long ago. And who knows where. The fact that we've found no sign of his body or his canoe can only mean one thing. Both are lying at the bottom of one of these pristine lakes. Deeper than we can see or reach. Beyond rescue.

The thought stops my heart. One second. Two. Then it starts beating again. How is that possible?

Do. Not. Tell. Me. Life. Goes. On.

A kind hand uses a now-gentle breeze to brush stray hairs from my face and caress my shattered heart. On the breeze float the inaudible words, "Libby, I won't let you go."

My whole body aches to fall into their arms — Greg's and God's. Only one of those possibilities is still an option for me.

"I will never leave you nor forsake you," God says in His Word. When you give it a chance, faith remembers the important things.

Greg's gone. I prayed we'd find him. Now what? How am I supposed to pray? The answer is, apparently, flat on the ground near the water that claimed my husband.

I'm vaguely conscious of the presence of my traveling companions hovering nearby, like attending angels, bless them. Wisely, they leave me to my grief — my surrender.

It is indeed a prayer of surrender. What makes it all the more costly is the fact that a week ago I wasn't sure I wanted to spend the rest of my life with Greg. Not until I started to unearth who he really was and my own role in poisoning what we had together.

The rocks feel warm beneath my body, my arms, my hands spread out before me. The smell of terra firma fills my nostrils and reminds me how far I am from heaven — how far anything happening on this planet is from God's ideal.

"Never leave you."

I so desperately need to believe that. I choose to believe it.

Lord, I single-handedly turned the loss of our daughter into a double tragedy. My confession unleashes a new fount of tears. *Forgive me. Help me.*

Having to surrender Greg now, when there's no earthly chance of explaining to him what I've discovered about myself and about us could cripple me.

But I can't let it.

This flat piece of glacial granite is as good an altar as any on which to lay my broken dreams. Greg's not coming home.

Not to me anyway, Lord. He's come Home to You.

"Libby?" Jen whispers across the midnight darkness of our tent.

I poke my head out from under my sleeping bag like a turtle testing the safety outside his shell. "What is it?"

"You don't have to hide to read Greg's journals."

"Hide? I wasn't . . . I was afraid that . . . I didn't want the light to keep you awake."

"I know you need privacy, and I wish I could offer you some. But I assure you your flashlight is not one of the twenty things keeping me awake."

How long before either of us can sleep through the night?

"Lib?"

"Yeah, thanks. I wondered if I was starting to breathe too much of my own carbon dioxide under there."

"Find anything meaningful in your reading? You don't have to tell me details."

Meaningful? How can I explain what it means to read his words, to see his blocky, no-frills penmanship and discover that his heart had softer edges than I ever knew? How can I tell her how it feels to know he thought of me while he was here, but his thoughts were laced with pain?

"It makes me feel closer to him."

"Good."

"I can almost hear his voice as I read." I shift to lean on one elbow. "Jen, when we get home, memorize your husband's face and voice. You think you'll never forget, that he'll always be there to refer to when you need a reminder, but it's not always true."

Jen rises on an elbow too. An onlooker would think we're simply gabbing, slumber-party style.

"Maybe I should tell Brent and the girls to memorize mine," she says, her words floating like dandelion fluff but landing like anvils on my heart.

I didn't know she still thought of cancer as something that might recur. "What do you mean?"

Jen shakes her head. "Nothing. Just thinking about all the things we take for granted."

The things we take for granted? My personal theme song.

21

My throat is raw. I crawl out of my sleeping bag and slip on my shoes as quietly as possible to avoid waking Jen. It must be shortly before sunrise. There's barely enough light filtering through the sides of the tent to make out which of the shoes near the door are mine and which are Jen's.

I unzip the tent opening one tooth at a time. There's no sense waking the others because I'm restless and I've cried myself into clogged sinuses and a raw throat. When the opening's an inch larger than I am, I sneak through and zip it shut again.

It will take all the fortitude the Lord and I can muster to leave this place in a couple of hours. The finality of admitting defeat and heading home without Greg will make the trip back to civilization agonizing with every paddle stroke.

I find my canteen hanging from a low branch. Almost empty. I'll filter more water so we'll have enough to cook breakfast and fill all three canteens.

It's another "mist-ry" morning. Opalescent mists hang over the still water in this secluded cove. Through the narrow opening, I can see companion mists hovering out on the open water. If this were a movie setting, the accompanying sound track would have to be something with violins — no, deep-throated violas or cellos, and in a minor key.

Such rare, unspoiled elegance.

Oh, Greg! We could have watched this movie together. We should have. Ask me again. Ask me one more time to join you and I'll come to this window to watch the "mist-ry" unfold. I'll climb out of my sleeping bag at three in the morning to take in the star exhibit.

A loon glides through the mist into the protection of our cove.

"Don't say it," I whisper to the bird. "Don't tell me he's gone."

She doesn't listen to me. She lifts her pointed beak to the sky, stretches her neck to swan length, and ruffles the water with her wingtips while calling, "He's go-go-go-go-gone. Go-o-o-o-gone."

I've heard that if you tip your head up when tears threaten, you can keep them from spilling. Urban legend. It doesn't always work. And people you love don't always come home.

Nothing's left of the fire in the circle. Not even one ember worth fanning. I build a teepee of pine needles, dry leaves, and brittle twigs. I've never been good with lighters, so I use one of the box matches from the emergency supplies to ignite the kindling. It smolders and smokes, producing a smell I won't soon forget. I'll miss the campfires. I can't believe I'm saying that, but I will.

A seasoned fire builder after just a few days of experience, I carefully time the laying on of fingerling wood, then forearm-sized, then biceps. The fire crackles and spits. There's no point gathering more wood. We won't be here that long.

I untie the knotted rope holding our food pack and let it down to the ground. It's appreciably lighter than the day we entered the wilderness. Or am I stronger? Both.

A quick check of our remaining food supplies underscores the harsh reality that it's past time to head home. Our fishing rod case leans against a nearby tree. In minutes I have one of Greg's favorites assembled. I open the unused tackle box and choose a likely looking artificial lure, avoiding the ones that strike me as cute or fancy in favor of an ugly one that might tempt a fish used to looking at other fish all day long.

With two boys in the house and an avid fisherman husband, I couldn't help but learn a few things about fishing. It takes me several casts to get the lure away from the shoreline and land it with a kiss on the water rather than an uncouth swat — the "cannonball" of fishing techniques.

The sun manages to push itself through the birth canal of trees behind me and uses its laser beams to evaporate the mist. I twitch my rod tip like I've seen Greg do hundreds of times.

I'm not sure if I want to catch something as much as I want to experience the rhythm of the motion. Cast and retrieve. Wait and watch. Offer the bait. See if they're hungry. Fishing in a world so quiet I can hear the line slipping through the eyelets on the rod. I'm sure there's a name for those things. It really doesn't matter. I'm not here to understand fishing but the fisherman.

Something strong and determined says with a tug on my line, "Sure, lady. I'll play."

"Keep your rod tip up, Libby!" It's Frank, pulling his boots on as he stumbles toward me. "Don't give him any slack. But don't force him, either. Let him run for a bit."

I'm tempted to hand him the rod. He

knows what he's doing. But he may not need this as badly as I do.

The fish and I dance around each other for several minutes. Once, he explodes out of the water, shakes his angry, bug-eyed head, and dives unceremoniously back to the depths.

"I'd give that no more than an 8.5 with points off for lesser degree of difficulty," Jen says. So it's officially a party now.

My cheering section sounds a little like gamblers at the blackjack table. "Come on, little fish. Mama needs some breakfast," and "Bring it on home. Let's bring it on home."

I'm winning the battle. As I reel it in with a smoother motion than is natural considering the pounding of my heart, the fish edges closer to shore. Frank sneaks down to the water's edge and motions me to maneuver the fish toward him. He leans down, sticks his thumb in the fish's mouth, and raises it out of the water.

"That's a beaut, Libby. A fine fish."

Jen pats me on the back repeater-rifle style with several "I'm so proud of you" comments.

"Is it a bass?" I ask.

"Smallmouth bass. That's right." Frank has undone the hook from its mouth and is bringing it toward me. "Enough for all three of us to have a nibble and a half."

"Wish it was a walleye. Greg says there's nothing like the taste of fresh walleye in the morning."

My comrades stop in their tracks. A moment of silence for my fallen husband.

"I'm just saying," I continue, "that I wouldn't mind fishing some more if you two want to start the rest of our breakfast. The bacon's gone. But hash browns go well with fish."

Another wordless moment.

At length Frank asks, "Jen, you want to have the honors of cleaning this lunker, or do you want me to handle that?"

Frank, you're adorable. Jen relinquishes the privilege to my father-in-law and focuses on the cookstove.

With my next cast, I concentrate on the feel of the rod in my right hand, the reel handle then in my left. If I will my skin's nerve endings to cooperate, can I feel Greg's fingerprints, a faint remnant of the warmth of his broad hands? This would be a good time for my imagination to pull some overtime.

I close my eyes, waiting for a tug on the line. I want to feel *something.* Life.

It comes sooner than I expect. The drag on my reel squeals with pleasure. My rod tip is sufficiently elevated. No slack in the line. This one's a challenge. The rod bends toward open water like a divining rod.

"Oh, no you don't!" I pull back, calling on muscles taut from days of paddling. I reel steadily, evenly, quick to take up any hint of slack.

Then in an instant, it's all slack.

"Broke your line, did he?" Frank calls from the stump on which he's cleaning the bass.

I turn toward my companions, catatonic.

Jen says, "You should see the look on your face."

I stumble up the gentle slope toward the center of the camp, dropping the rod on the way. My hands press hard against my mouth, holding back the flood of a gut-deep scream. Tears blur my vision. The world's a fun-house mirror.

"Hey, girl. It's only a fish," Jen comforts.

I fall to my knees near the fire circle and bend forward, rocking as if keening, which I suppose I am. I clutch my stomach with both hands and cry, "Ohhhhhhh!"

"Sweetie, what's wrong?"

Both Jen and Frank are beside me.

"I know . . . I know why . . . why Greg didn't bring his fishing equipment."

22

Grief steals my words. Frank sits on a rock and pulls me into his lap as if I am twelve and needy. I can't tell if the spinning motion I feel is a remnant from the lumps on his head or from me.

Jen brings my canteen. "Here, honey. Take a drink. It'll help."

That's the world's answer for everything, isn't it? A drink of water. A cold washcloth. Sit down a minute, it'll pass.

Frank shifts his leg under me. My weight can't be helping his shin injury. I give him a "thanks for your kindness" hug and slide off his lap. Face to the sky. Still doesn't stop the tears.

"I need another minute," I squeak out.

"When you're ready, honey," Jen says.

"That's right, Libby. When you're ready."

I walk toward the water, pick up the rod from where I dropped it, and lean it against the tree where the rod case rests. Then I turn my attention to the scene before us. Towering pines. Glassy water. A brave sun plowing through all obstacles. A blue canopy of sky overhead. Rocks with bad toupees of lichen. An osprey nest in a limbless tree on the far shore.

Why didn't I realize? "I know why Greg left his fishing equipment at home."

"Why, Lib?"

"He didn't intend to fish this time."

Frank speaks up, "Well, we didn't think he forgot the stuff. That's not like him."

I turn to look Jen in the eye. "I know what's missing from his office shelf."

Jen's expression is a sea of pain for me and curiosity for herself, I imagine.

"His camera. He came here to take pictures, to be the photographer we wouldn't let him become."

"Libby?"

"What, Greg? I'm in the middle of something."

"I wonder what you'd think about my taking a couple of courses at the community college."

"More college? What for?"

"A hobby. An interest. I'd like to know more than I already do about photography. Nature photography, especially."

I leave the lasagna pan that isn't going to come clean without a good soak anyway and sit across from him at the table. "Photography's an expensive hobby, isn't it?"

"It can be."

I eye my pathetic countertops. He notices.

"I was actually thinking of getting into it on a deeper level than just a hobby. Eventually."

"What? A business? You have a job. It may not be glamorous, but it pays the bills."

He takes a breath, releases it slowly, then takes another. "I'm not looking for glamour."

"Then what?"

"Passion. Something to get excited about. Something to . . . to care about deeply. I want to wake up in the morning and bound out of bed because I can't wait to see what the day will hold. I want to capture some of the scenes that capture me. I want to care about something."

And then my zinger. "If you'd cared enough about our daughter, Greg . . ."

"What'd your dad say when you told him you wanted to quit the world and go find yourself in photography?"

Greg took off his jacket and spent a few extra seconds smoothing its sleeves before hanging it on the hook by the door.

"It wasn't so much my dad as Pauline."

"She agrees with me for once?"

"She's not known as a world-class encourager."

"What's that supposed to mean?"

"Nothing."

"Look, I'm sorry about what I said about Lacey. I know it's not that you didn't care."

"Thanks for the vote of confidence."

Another impasse.

"You can't seriously be thinking about starting a photography studio. Here?"

"Or maybe a little farther north. A nature photography studio probably has a better chance of making it in a tourist town."

"What about staying right here and doing weddings and senior pictures and things on the side nights and weekends?"

"Because that's not where my heart is."

"Obviously."

"That was harsh."

"So's life, Greg. Harsh realities. One right after another. Our daughter's gone. The boys will need college tuition soon. We have bills to pay. And although it may not put a sizzle in your step, you have a perfectly adequate job with Greene's and no hope of making it as a nature photographer."

"Lib, you know what I'd say if you told me you wanted to raise llamas or bike across the country or learn to hang glide?"

I know.

"I'd say go for it," Greg answered.

"That's where you and I are different, then. I have too strong a sense of responsibility toward this family to suggest any of those possibilities."

"What was wrong with me?"

Jen's voice breaks through my reflection. "You were hurting and didn't know how to cope with anything the least bit upsetting."

"What was wrong with *me?*" Frank echoes. "I knew better. I mean, we all grieved the loss of our Lacey, but when it comes to pursuing a dream, I ought to have known better than to let Pauline at him. Nothing kills a dream faster than a woman who thinks she's being reasonable."

"Frank!" Jen objects.

"Present company excepted."

The throbbing behind my eyes may have become a permanent part of me. I should be grateful. One more puzzle piece is in place. Greg came to the wilderness. That piece of information floated toward our camp in the form of a splintered paddle.

We know why he came. Not to catch fish but a dream.

I wish I'd known the difference between a dream and a whim when it mattered. If I'd encouraged him to pursue his passion openly, Greg might still be alive.

And there it is.

How were either of us to have known what a few simple words would net us?

"Lacey, you're going to school. Grab your backpack and an Advil if you need it and get out the door."

"Photography? Come on, Greg. You have a family to support. Give it a rest."

Lord, neither of us can hit rewind. What now?

I can't help viewing this wilderness through Greg's eyes or camera lens. Details that would have escaped me yesterday now whisper, "Wouldn't this make a great shot?"

Iridescent clouds, a pancake-sized island with a lone pine "flag" claiming its territory, a blue flame deep in the heart of a campfire, a single near-microscopic indigo wildflower that found a spark of life in a crevice of solid rock.

We didn't bring a camera. You know what that means. I have to come back here someday. Capture it all. For him.

"Ready to go, Libby?"

"Jen, I —"

"We have to go home."

"I know."

"Alex and Zack might be there already. They'll need their mama."

"Mamacita."

"What?"

"Never mind."

"We could put this off another hour, another day, but it wouldn't make any difference, would it?"

"No."

"Frank and I have the canoes loaded. We're just waiting for you."

"How's Frank doing?"

"Okay, I think. I didn't hear much snoring last night. Did you?"

"We could have taken off for home last night rather than chase sleep."

"We couldn't have gotten two feet safely in that inky blackness," Jen says.

"A few clouds this morning."

"I hope they don't decide to gang up and rain on us before the day's over."

"How far do you think we can get?"

"Paddling hard? Frank must not have had a genuine concussion. He's functioning better than I expected. I don't think we have to hold back for his sake today."

I know she's hoping I'll start moving toward the waiting canoes. My legs are steel posts driven deep into the unyielding rock.

"When Lacey was buried, it was all I

could do to pick up a handful of soil and toss it on top of her casket as it was lowered into the ground."

"Oh, Libby."

"Moving from this place feels like that, like tossing a final good-bye onto the grave that claimed my husband."

"God, help us all." Frank's voice joins the memorial service. "It probably wouldn't hurt at all if somebody prayed, would it?"

Greg, please forgive the irreverence, but I have to laugh at your father's attempt at spiritual leadership. I laugh not because it's silly, but because it's so precious I can't stand it.

"Good idea, Frank," Jen says while I attempt to compose myself. "Do you want to start?"

"You go ahead," he says. "Then I'll add to it if you forget something important."

She hits everything. Our loss, our pain, our need for strength, our desire to honor the Lord through our grief, our practical need for direction for the future, the ripples of Greg's loss throughout the community, and the ripples of his unwavering faith through his too-short life. All Frank adds is a hearty "amen."

When we open our eyes and lift our heads, we watch a bald eagle land on the tallest

pine in the cove. He must have been looking for a place with no people, no civilization, because he alights a few seconds later,
taking off with a whoo-whoo-whoo of air
forced down from his powerful wings. He
soars against the cloud-clotted sky.

We trace his path with our eyes. I trace it
also with my heart.

Turning in a wide arc with a grace that
speaks of unbridled freedom, the eagle
swings back the way he came, flying lower
now over the treetops along the little slice
of shoreline we can see through our narrow
view of the open water.

He calls in a voice strong enough for us to
hear from this distance, even with our human limitations.

Jen and Frank seem as taken by the sight
as I am. I reach out to grab them both by
the forearm when the majestic bird passes
between us and a thin column of smoke.

23

I can't avert my gaze from the wispy plume of smoke rising from the far treetops like a boneless finger of hope. "Frank? Jen? Do you see that?"

"Smoke, isn't it?" Jen says.

Frank adds, "Smoke. Campfire."

I risk glancing their way, but only for a second. "Seems as if it's coming from the middle of nowhere, doesn't it?"

Frank's hand on my shoulder is warm, fatherly, heavier than normal. "We're not alone out here. We've seen other campers. And I told you there are no restrictions in the Quetico about where a person can camp. The middle of nowhere pretty much describes the entire park."

"Do you think we should investigate?" Jen asks, and again I'm grateful she's speaking my thoughts.

Frank strokes his rough whiskers. They're well on their way to beard status. It's time to end this episode of *Survivor.* Frank must agree. He says, "Can't chase every puff of smoke on the planet."

We have to go home. I know that. We could spend the next three years checking behind trees and under rocks, around the next bend and under smoke columns. "Can we chase this one?"

He closes his eyes and drops his chin to his chest. He's been remarkably patient with us, all things considered. We may have reached the end in more ways than one. I consider apologizing but can't think what for.

Frank heads toward his canoe.

We follow.

With a quick zip he opens the outside pocket of his pack and removes his stash of laminated maps. "Do you know what the odds are?"

It doesn't take a statistics expert to know our odds are poor. A million to one? There's still a chance, then.

"Can you tell what's back there beyond that line of trees?"

"You're expecting a mall or something?" He flattens the map that holds his attention. "Trust me. It's land or water. Those are your choices."

We can't afford to snap at each other. We

need one another, particularly Frank and I, partners in pain.

You and Greg can't afford to snap at each other. You need each other. Was that Jen's counsel? Or Pastor's? Why can I not remember?

I'm still caught in the distress of memory loss when Jen says, "Can you see anything that would appeal to Greg, make him change his plans?"

"Something a photographer might want to investigate?" I add. Calling Greg a photographer tastes strange on my tongue, but not unpleasant, like my first bite of Pad Thai.

Frank studies a path he traces on the map with his finger and checks with quick glances in the direction of the smoke column. It's still there — the smoke. I feared it might disappear when I looked away, as Lacey did. And Greg. But it's still rising, meandering against the unsuspecting blue-and-white background as if unaware of its power to prolong our quest.

"This may be significant."

Jen and I lean over his shoulders before he utters the final syllable.

"What is it?" she asks.

I see it before he can get the words out. A waterfall. In print so fine it could pass for the bottom line on the eye chart. Lacy Falls. Spelled differently, but would Greg have considered it a sign from heaven? Would he have seen the possibility on his own maps and felt compelled to capture the scene forever on film?

"How long would it take us to get there? How far is it?" We haven't mentioned the spot on the map. Jen noticed it on her own.

Frank refolds the map with Lacy Falls showing. He looks in the direction of the smoke. "Be there in an hour or two, I figure. If you ladies can keep up."

"So, are we agreed to pursue this?" I ask. A wave of determination sweeps over me. I'm going, with or without them.

Frank shrugs, his way of saying, "Absolutely. How could we just walk away from what is obviously our X-marks-the-spot? Sooner we get there, sooner we slap Greg with a few hugs, a couple of versions of 'My boy, you near scared us to death,' and load his gear to head home." He shrugs again, punctuating his enthusiasm for the idea.

Jen hesitates. Hesitates? Why should I have to talk her into this? I finally have a feeling — a sensing from God. The smoke. The eagle whose flight path alerted us to the smoke. In the nick of time. What's her problem?

"I need to call Brent," she says.

"Sure. Tonight. Like all the others. If there's no cloud cover."

"I'd probably better try to connect with him now, before we chase smoke signals." She stuffs her hands into the front pockets of her cargo pants. Her shoulders head north, toward her ears. What is that expression on her face?

"Jen, if you think we're foolish to try to find out where the smoke's coming from —"

"It's not that."

Frank shoots us a look that says, "Time's a 'wastin.' "

"Jen, believe me, I know I've asked a lot of you, more than any person has a right to. And despite his friendship with Greg, Brent must be more than a little weary of my hauling you all over the wilderness. I can't imagine how much the girls must miss you."

Actually, that's not all that hard.

"I can't hope to find a way to repay you, any of you. And I can't pretend to have a logical reason to keep searching. It's a hunch. Just a hunch. A puff of smoke that could be from a couple of tree huggers on their honeymoon. Or a Boy Scout troop. Or Girl Scouts."

She slips her hands out of her pockets and

places each one on its opposite shoulder, as if streamlining her body for a bungee jump. "It's not that my family misses me too much. That's not it."

"Then what? I trust your judgment, you know. You're well-endowed."

"Excuse me?"

"With wisdom."

She's still poised for bungee jumping. But her face registers an emotion I haven't seen on her for a long time.

"I have an appointment."

"We know. I'm sorry about that. Can Brent call and reschedule it for you if we take another couple of days to get home? Another inconvenience, but —"

"It's the first session in a new round of radiation treatments. I . . . I have a spot on one of my ribs."

Cancer has its own dictionary. It changes the meaning of the word "spot."

What happened to all the oxygen in the air?

24

Jen says the spot on her rib is small, minuscule. In my mind, it's a sulfurous, undulating, dagger-toothed monster against which I have no weapons.

Reining in my distress is also impossible. "How could you not tell me?"

"I'm really sorry. I probably should have."

"Probably?" Would it be tacky to wring the neck of someone who is about to be sent back to Iraq for another tour of duty? "When did you find out?"

Jen toes the bed of rusty pine needles at her feet. The smell of pine resin rides the last few oxygen molecules not sucked out by her announcement.

Frank's voice floats into our circle of pain. "I imagine the girl was trying to spare you more grief." His words are laced with an empathy richer and sweeter than it was even a few days ago. What's happening to us?

"Spare me?" Tempering my frustration

takes more energy than I have in reserve. "In what rush of rationale did it seem prudent not to tell me?" If I had a mirror, the varicose veins in my temples and along the sides of my throat might scare me. We're a trio, aren't we? Jen needs radiation and who knows what else? Frank needs a prostate exam. I'm ripe for a stroke.

Jen draws a deep breath. "I made a judgment call. Brent and I talked about it. We prayed about it. Both of us felt it would be best to wait until . . . until we knew something about Greg."

Oh, my beautiful friend. I can't lose you too. My heart's not that strong. If Jen could read my mind, she'd call that "stinkin' thinkin' " and threaten to disown me.

"When? When did you first know?" I've lost a few decibels. Good.

Frank retreats. Suddenly every zipper, clasp, and closure of our equipment needs checking. I don't blame him for choosing that over this.

"The Friday Greg was supposed to come home."

"How could you keep that kind of news to yourself all this time?"

"I felt I had to."

Jen's explanation sits like curdled milk in my stomach. Not because of her, but because of me. She's right. I couldn't be trusted with that kind of information during those early days of the siege against my sanity.

"Are you in pain?" That's the question I should have asked many minutes ago. God, forgive me.

"No."

"Oh, Jen!"

She touches a place a few inches under where her left breast used to be. "No pain. We wouldn't know about the spot even now if it weren't for Brent's new health insurance. The company demanded a chest x-ray for both of us, even though I had a clear one not six months ago. Guess I should be grateful, huh?"

"Jen, I'm so sorry."

"Me too. I don't want to add to your burden right now."

"*My* burden?" How long has it been since I exhibited even a fraction of the selflessness that comes so naturally to her?

Jen heads toward the canoes. "Let me try to catch Brent at work."

"Stop it!" I call after her. "There's no way he'd let you skip radiation, even if we would. We're going home. It's time to —" I choke back my final two words and a grocery cart full of sorrow.

I can't see. The flood distorting my vision started building years ago. How is it that I'm still upright? Ignoring the solid rock foundation beneath me, I drop to my knees, shuddering as if febrile. My mind embarks on a frantic search for a Scripture pill, a biblical capsule to ease the crippling distress. All that rises to the surface is the idea of scraping my boils with pottery shards.

Her rib. A bone shadow. Not good. When we get home, I'll get Zack or Alex to help me search the Internet for information about survival rates — right after the funeral or memorial service or whatever it is we'll call the service we hold in Greg's honor. My boys will stay home a couple more days beyond that, won't they? Or a couple of weeks? Could they miss the first few weeks of the new semester? I may never be ready to send them back out into the world again.

Independent and self-sufficient as they are, the loss of their dad will cut deep. My attempts to close the wound for them will feel like straddling a section of the Grand Canyon.

Nerve endings are curious things. The nerves in my skin ache for my husband's touch. Now more than ever, I need to feel the weight of his arm around me, to press myself against his wide chest, to bury my face in his shirt and breathe his confidence into my lungs.

I need to tell him about Jenika.

He doesn't comfort with words. I could live with that if I just had his touch. His warm hand against the small of my back as he steers me forward. His hand covering mine when I crave a reminder of his presence. The silent blessing of his body curved around mine when sleep eludes me. His hint-of-mint breath lifting the hairs on the back of my neck. The brush of his whisper-kiss when he knows "I need you, baby" won't score as many points as "I'm here for you."

The scent of his aftershave embedded in the threads of his pillowcase. As powerful as any aromatherapy.

The sound of his voice on the phone. My constant.

My earth-constant. Heaven has its own version — the Lord from whom Greg learned how to give.

The Lord from whom Jenika Morgan learned how to do friendship. And joy. And stamina. And hope.

My nerve endings must have eavesdropped on my mind's meanderings. I feel the weight of an arm around my shoulders.

"Honey." It's Frank.

"I'll be okay."

"We know you will. But we have decisions to make. Jen's on the phone with Brent. You want to get in on this conversation?"

I've imposed upon their lives, thrust the dagger of my neediness into the stab wound of their own pain long enough. This is between the two of them. Regret floods through me. Of all weeks for me to keep Jen and Brent away from each other. What must have been going through her mind when I whined about a mosquito bite or hangnail or sunburn?

"Sorry, Libby. It's a little hard to sympathize when cancer's eating holes in my bones."

But that's not what she said. She smiled and supported me and swallowed the scream clawing at her throat. If there was no scream, that says all the more about her character, her faith, and the God of inexhaustible hope.

My God.

It's time for me to step up to the plate and live like I believe it. Jen needs me to represent Him to her.

25

Jen replaces the SAT phone in its waterproof case and turns toward me. "What did you say?"

"Mumbling to myself. How are the girls?"

"Good. They're good." Rather than return the case to the backpack tucked into the canoe, she hugs it to her chest. I know the feeling. I considered sleeping with my canteen — Greg's canteen — last night just for the connection with him.

I choke back a hundred thoughts. What's the appropriate thing to say right now?

"Jen, I love you."

"I know. I love you too."

"We'll get through this."

"By the grace of God. Just like last time." She pulls her fingers through the honey-toned hair at the back of her neck — the hair that had to start from scratch after chemo.

A Canadian jay, as gray as my thoughts,

invades our space. He lands on the spot we called the "kitchen" little more than an hour ago. Searching for crumbs? He can join the club. I'm searching for something with which to rebuild a life and help my dearest friend negotiate the bone-rattling rapids in hers.

"This is really weird," she says.

"What is?" A better question would be "What isn't?"

"I read about that eagle we saw this morning."

"What? Where?" I pat my breast pocket. Greg's journal remains tucked there, close to my heart. She couldn't have read about an eagle sitting on those pages.

"My Bible. Revelation eight."

"You're reading in the book of Revelation on this trip?"

"It fell open to that spot." Jen looks away from me.

"Are you going to tell me what it said?"

"Not sure I should."

"Yeah, look how well it turned out the last time you decided not to tell me what you knew." Spilled words are like spilled mercury. Retrieval is a nightmare of futility.

She stands with her palms open in front of her and her gaze fixed on the sky. "Then I looked," she recites, "and I saw a solitary eagle flying in midheaven, and as it flew I heard it crying with a loud voice . . ."

"What? What was it crying?"

"You have to take a thing like that in context, Libby."

I lower my gaze and my voice. "What was it crying?"

"Woe, woe, woe to those who dwell on the earth, because of the rest of the trumpet blasts which the three angels are about to sound."

Glad I asked.

Wishing Jen wasn't quite so good at memorizing depressing passages of Scripture, I snatch my life vest from where it waits, leaning against the base of a tree. As I zip into it, I speak the words I've avoided. "We'd better get going."

"Right," Jen says. "We can't afford to keep Greg waiting."

I ram the teeth of the zipper into a chunk of my shirt. Stuck.

"We're not pursuing the misguided Greg Rescue anymore. We're getting you home."

She lifts her chin. Defiance does not become her. "Look, it's decided. We can't go home yet. God gave us a sign. How could we ignore it?"

"And how am I supposed to bear the guilt of delaying your radiation? How can I look

Brent or your daughters in the eye?"

"He's in agreement." Jen tugs on my life-vest zipper while I hold the shirt fabric out of the way. Free at last. "Brent knew something like this could happen. He was ready for it."

"No!"

"It's a done deal. Brent's already on the phone with the clinic, rescheduling my appointment."

"Your oncologist will kill me if the guilt doesn't!"

She sighs. So do I. "It's an extra day or two at the most. That's all we're talking about."

In the murky recesses of my mind, I see cancer cells multiplying exponentially while we discuss the issue. I don't want to hear Jen's doctor say, "If only we could have caught it sooner."

A couple of days. A couple of zillion cancer cells versus the chance that my husband is still alive and that we are only a few hundred paddle strokes away from finding him. Some choice.

"Greg, you'd better be there."

"What?" Jen is climbing into the canoe as she speaks.

"Sorry. Thinking out loud." I move closer

to our launch point. Where's Frank? There. Returning from another trip to the open-air lavatory. "I'm not comfortable with this, but I appear to be on the losing end of every battle these days. Let's go chase a puff of smoke."

Jen smiles. It's not her usual full-faced smile. It's more like a slice of mandarin orange, a look that acknowledges she won this battle and hopes she can win the larger one at home.

God, help us.

"Mute point now," Frank says. We turn toward where he stands with his feet spread and his hat cocked back on his head. He rubs the back of his neck. What is so interesting on the ground at his feet? Nothing I can see from here.

"That's a *moot* point, Frank." He made it this far in life without knowing or caring about the difference. Why did it seem important for me to correct him?

Frank doesn't lift his gaze but points with one arm toward a spot away from our camp. *The* spot. Where we first saw the smoke. Smoke that is no longer visible.

26

A stone in my shoe pokes at my heel as I leave the water's edge and join Frank to gain his vantage point. It's gone. The faint column of smoke is gone. What does that say about our one-in-a-million chance?

Three sets of eyes are trained toward a phantom smoke plume. Nothing.

"Well, I suppose there's no point standing here looking cute," Frank says at length. He recenters his cap and brushes past me on his way to the water.

"What do we do now?" I'm aware that my words sound whiny. I follow Frank with my feet but not my heart.

Jen moves toward me, lays her hand on my forearm, and mouths the words, "I'm sorry."

The once-sharp edges of my heart are worn smooth from the jostling. A shred of hope invades my world with despair close at its heels — despair deeper than ever. We discover what might be a clue. It disappears before we can trace its origin. The column of smoke appears in our line of vision just in time to prevent our leaving this wilderness to head home without noticing it. Now it's gone.

Should it comfort me that odds were the smoke had no connection to Greg in the first place?

We're heading home empty-handed, empty-hearted. I know my Redeemer lives. I don't know if my *husband* lives.

Sunflower seeds and a failed woodworking project told us Greg came to this wilderness. Oh, and an odd-colored pocket knife. But I'd discovered I wanted him back before finding those clues. I wish now I'd realized how much safer it would have been if I'd not let the Lord rekindle the embers I'd allowed to grow cold.

That's not true. I just lied to myself. I'm grateful to care again. So grateful.

Wish I could tell Greg.

■ ■ ■ ■

GREG'S STORY:
THE DAY HE LEFT

■ ■ ■ ■

27

Greg Holden checked the clock again. In his position and after all these years, he had every right to treat the time clock as a general guideline. Who would object if he left work a few minutes early?

His conscience. It wouldn't let him get away with anything. Five o'clock meant five o'clock.

Funny, how he was more flexible with others than with himself.

"Mr. Holden?" His administrative assistant poked her goose-down head around the doorway into his office.

"Yes, Manda?" Had she caught him daydreaming? He shuffled a pile of file folders into a neat stack.

"Do you think it'd be okay if I clocked out early? Lloyd's taking me to the Legion Hall fish fry for supper, and you know how ornery he gets if a line's already formed."

Greg didn't know, didn't want to know

the level of Lloyd's orneriness. "Not a problem. Go ahead. Fish, huh?" Soft on others. Hard on himself. Was that a virtue?

"Batter dipped. Best in Franklin County if you ask me." Manda stepped fully into the doorway, revealing the purse slung over her Pillsbury Doughboy shoulder. " 'Course it won't compare to the fresh Canadian walleye you'll be eating in a couple of days."

"Right," he said, prompting a muscle twitch in his left eyelid. He'd have to schedule a sit-down with the Lord to discuss the line between white and black lies. God ought to know. He drew the line, probably a good distance from where Greg tiptoed these days.

"You heading back to this spot?" Manda asked. She pointed toward a framed photo on the office wall near the door. Her fingers sported more rings than a raccoon tail. He forced his vision to focus on the scene to which she referred. One of his favorite photos. The view from his favorite island campsite on Pickerel Lake. He'd considered moving that picture. It lay right in his line of sight every time he looked up from his desk. The idyllic scene didn't help make him more content with his present landlocked life.

"Mr. Holden?"

"Different kind of trip this time. Exploring new territory. New to me, anyway."

"Well, enjoy yourself. Anyone deserves it, it's you."

Deserves? I might deserve a vacation. Okay. Why do I have such a hard time accepting that I might deserve the kind of trip I've planned this time?

"Thanks, Manda. Oh, before you go, did you have a chance to contact Mr. Stenner about the —"

"Done. Faxed him a copy and asked him to email his assessment. It's not in your in-box yet?"

"Haven't checked. Saved that for my last order of business before leaving."

Manda hoisted her purse strap higher on her shoulder. "Sure that's wise?"

"What do you mean?"

"Sure you want your contact with Stenner to be the last taste in your mouth before vacation? That's like chasing down a nice piece of double fudge cake with a final nibble of lima beans, isn't it?"

She winked at him, the Bambi eyelash a little loose in the outer corner. Greg considered offering her a drop of SuperGlue before she headed to the Legion Hall but thought better of it. Manda was the kind of character who could make a brooch the size of a Tupperware lid and one floppy false eyelash endearing. She'd steal the show at the fish fry.

"Part of the job," he answered. And not by any stretch the least appealing part, he wanted to add. "You take care while I'm gone. No crises, okay?"

"Do my best," she called back as she exited.

Others might worry that their secretaries would mark time while the boss was away. Not Greg. Truthfully, Manda could do his job as well as he could. The knowledge added to his guilt and the ever-churning restlessness that Alka-Seltzer could no longer quell. Somewhere along the line he'd guessed wrong when listening for the Lord's voice to tell him what he was supposed to do with his life.

Was it fair to offer Libby and the boys a reasonably decent paycheck delivered by an unhappy man? Did they even realize how unhappy?

He knew other Christian businessmen who started their workdays with a quick prayer for the Lord to guide them and bless their efforts. His morning prayer sounded more like a death row prisoner's appeal to the governor. "Get me outta here!"

For Christmas last year, Manda gave Greg

a motivational poster — *The longest journey begins with the first stroke.* One would think a woman Manda's age might have considered that the word *stroke* holds a medical meaning most hope to avoid. The artwork helped straighten the words: a solo canoeist paddling a glassy waterway toward a rosy sunset. Or was it a sunrise? It matters, meteorologically speaking. *Pink sky in morning, sailor take warning.*

The first stroke? Was that the mantra Greg needed?

More like, "Nevertheless, not my will but Thine be done."

Greg identified with the Gethsemane words of Jesus, and with the sweat drops of blood and the anguish of heart. He empathized with Jesus' disappointment that those closest to Him couldn't bear the weight if He told them the whole truth behind His internal wrestling match.

Lacey had something to do with it, to be sure. Before her death, he could tolerate boredom and meaningless work assignments. But since that beautiful child's head hit the satin pillow in the coffin, he couldn't stomach walking away from beauty, passing by as if there would always be another chance for that particular scene, that curve of water on shore or twisted leaf or wrinkled rock. Another chance? Not always.

Greg dismissed his thoughts as a king might dismiss an annoying servant. The office was for work, not thinking. He'd have plenty of time for pondering once he got on the road and the water, especially on a solo trip.

Now was the time for all good men to check their email messages. Then he'd shut things down, turn out the lights, head home, and try to find a satisfying way to say goodbye.

28

Libby didn't watch while he loaded the Jeep. That helped. She stayed in the kitchen. He appreciated the supper she'd prepared. Had he told her that? Meatloaf and twice-baked potatoes. Two of his favorites. Two things he wouldn't see or taste for a while.

He'd offered to help with dishes when the meal ended. Libby scrubbed the butcher block countertop with an exuberance bordering on abrasion and insisted she didn't mind handling it alone. He needed to get on the road.

That, he did.

He almost broke down and grabbed his fishing equipment. But that would defeat the purpose, wouldn't it? He couldn't be distracted by the lure of a lunker. Not this time. He'd postponed it too long for all the wrong reasons — expectation, routine. And that insipid cliché called the comfort zone.

A solo trip. He should have made this

move years ago. It could change everything.

What price would he pay when Libby found out the truth? He still had time to tell her. But when a marriage is missing a few planks in its hull, it's not a good idea to volunteer to take on more emotional cargo.

Zack and Alex would enjoy a trip like this. Game for anything, they'd listen to his plan, pause a nanosecond, then start packing.

Still alone in the garage, Greg tugged on the tie-down straps for his Mad River canoe and let thoughts of his sons play in his mind. Man, he missed those guys. Nobody had told him the empty-nest syndrome affected dads too. He presumed it was more Libby's territory. How could he hope to prevent his boys from failing the women they'd marry? Some great role model he turned out to be.

The wilderness heals. A God-appointed tonic. *Oh, please let it be true this time.*

"All set?"

Libby stood in the kitchen doorway, holding the screen open with one hand and a dish towel in the other. Screen doors. Dish towels. Attached garages. Civilization. Civil, emotionless question. He'd answer her. That was the polite thing to do.

"Yeah, guess so."

"And you'll be home two weeks from

tomorrow at the latest?"

"That's the plan." He looked at his wife's concrete face. What did he expect to see? Tenderness? Longing? Her eyes said something in another language. He'd never been good at languages.

"Well . . ." she said, and then let that one word ricochet off the garage walls. The screen door moaned. Did she intend to close it or open it wider?

He knew the answer.

Now what? Allow her to retreat into the house? Mumble, "If that's the way you want to be," and climb behind the wheel, shaking the garage dust from his feet?

"Libby?"

"Yes?"

He crossed the space between them, expecting an echo from his childhood to chant, "Warmer. Getting warmer," as he neared her. No voice. No sound but his rubber-soled hiking boots on cement.

He'd once patched a boat leak with chewing gum — a temporary fix, but effective. He went through rolls of duct tape like some men down six packs. He'd repaired the upstairs toilet mechanism with a plastic chopstick and one of Lacey's elastic hair things. But he had no skills that could mend what was wrong between him and Libby.

You can't fix what you don't acknowledge.
Where'd he heard that before? Manda quoting Dr. Phil? Got news for you, Phil. Sometimes you can't fix what you *do* acknowledge.

"You take care while I'm gone."

"Sure. Will do."

To kiss or not to kiss? That is the question.

Greg stood on the stoop one step lower than the threshold on which Libby was rooted. He reached for her. She leaned into him with what felt more like exhaustion than desire. He held her, breathed in her green-apple shampoo and the heady aroma of homemade meatloaf.

"Greg?" Her voice, soft as unlit dynamite, begged something. If only he understood what.

"I know, Lib. I know." But he didn't, did he?

A longer embrace would only prolong the awkwardness. Greg loosened his grip, pulled back enough to look into her eyes, and made the critical choice. He pressed his lips into the sweet hollow under her cheekbone. "I'll be back before you know it."

He was a mile down the road before he realized he'd forgotten to say, "I love you."

29

He knew this route as he might a well-worn path to Grandma's house. Pick any one of a handful of roads as long as the choice landed him on State Highway 53 North, then set the Jeep on automatic pilot toward Duluth. Cross from Superior to Duluth — from Wisconsin to Minnesota — over the scenic bridge, Great Lakes freighters anchored in the harbor on the right. Weave through Duluth's white-knuckle hills. No way around it. One more gas-up — cheaper Minnesota gas — and restroom break before heading into the true North.

Ten-thirty, an hour and a half until midnight, after a long day at work and last-minute packing. And the stuttering good-bye.

Greg took his position behind the steering wheel, deciding to use his freshly purchased twenty-ounce bottle of diet cola as a cold pack for his neck. He'd just negotiated a couple of hundred miles of deer crossings and was about to traverse a couple hundred more. One of the planet's most successful tension producers — deer in the headlights. Or worse, deer just outside the circle of light.

Two Harbors. How many more miles? He could stop at that cheesy-but-pleasingly-cheap motel on the outskirts and catch a few winks. Did he pack earplugs in his overnight bag? The foghorn may protect Great Lakes vessels from crashing on the shore but it also keeps weary adventurers from crashing for a good night's sleep, whether in a tent, camper, or shore-view motel.

Greg flipped on the radio. "Okay, someone. Anyone. Elvis, Backstreet Boys, Third Day, Rebecca St. James. Someone keep me awake a few more miles."

He should enjoy the radio while he could. Once he crossed the border, station choices would become scarcer than sale prices on Kobe beef.

Ugh. A stray grocery store thought. Distance couldn't free him of the place? Now, that was a depressing thought.

Although he couldn't see any farther into the scenery than the headlights would allow, Greg knew what lay beyond their reach.

Sun-crisped grasses and wildflowers in the ditches. Postcard-worthy branches of tamaracks fluttering like green feathers against the solid porcupine quills of the white pines. Marshes and bogs. Bald hillsides stripped for the sake of the iron ore and the country's thirst for steel. Thumbprint-sized lakes. Million-dollar vacation homes and scruffy cottages existing side by side.

Somewhere off to the right, deep in the shroud of blackness of night, lay Lake Superior. Soon the road would swing near its shoreline again. Two Harbors. Three-hundred-dollar-a-night vacation condos and his choice, Wilsonaire Motor Lodge and Bakery. Bakery air, he didn't mind. Far from it. But what marketing genius told these owners they'd make money advertising the smell of Wilsons?

It always gave him a laugh thinking about it. Tonight his laugh didn't reach any farther than his throat.

Libby.

Distance had no impact on freeing him from thoughts of the woman he left at home.

Distance is overrated.

Greg cranked open the driver's side window. Maybe the night air would steer his thoughts in a more productive direction.

Smack! His temple stung from whatever

had flown in the window. There, crawling on the dashboard, a June bug the size of the Medjool dates the produce department carried during the holidays. An insect Lacey would have dubbed "super gross." He couldn't disagree. Nasty things, June bugs. Had this one not heard it was August already?

His instant reaction had been to brush it off when he felt it assault his temple. Apparently, that's a declaration of war in June-bug speak. Flying, dive-bombing, no-respect-for-a-person's-personal-space warfare. He slowed the car more abruptly than was safe, pulled off onto the gravel shoulder, and opened his car door.

"Okay," he told it. "You or me. One of us is leaving this vehicle."

Alex and Zack were probably fighting insects four times this large and threatening. Or collecting them. Or studying them. Or analyzing their mating habits. Greg just wanted this one gone.

The dome light of the Jeep stayed on while the door was open. Nice feature. Normally. Tonight it became a marquee for a mosquito convention and a neon sign for moths and various other winged things.

"I love it when a plan comes together," he told the damp, musky night air. "By contrast, this is exactly how my plans have gone the last few years." He stood alone at the edge of the highway, watching most of the entomologic population of the Upper Midwest congregate in his party vehicle. "I try to solve a problem and create forty more. Forty?" He eyed what was beginning to look like a sick mosquito orgy. "They're multiplying as I speak."

A car whizzed past him so close the draft ruffled the hairs on the back of his neck.

"Thank you for not stopping," he called after it. "No, sincerely, I'm grateful you didn't see me paralyzed by a bug and his inbred cousins twice removed."

Is it only bad to talk to yourself if you talk out loud?

He could cut back on that, couldn't he?

Greg tried to recall what technique he and Libby used when they convinced Zack to give up his imaginary friend, Tank. Or were they truly successful? At their advice, did Zack plant his feet solidly in reality or did he just stop talking to Tank *out loud?*

"*I* will never leave you nor forsake you," he said, quoting his invisible but very much real Friend. The reminder became a prayer. "God, you promised."

Another set of car lights came upon him from the south. The car slowed as it neared

Greg. He turned, faced the center line, and motioned the driver on with a wave that said, "No big deal. I can handle it."

When the Good Samaritan's taillights faded into the night, Greg opened the remaining doors of the Jeep, rolled down all the windows, and found the little button on the doorframe near the steering wheel. Depressing it, he snuffed the dome light.

"Take that."

Cocooned in darkness now, he could only hope the insects would pack up their instruments and go home. If not a yard light or porch light, they might seek out the few vacancies in front of his still-lit headlights.

He'd drive the rest of the way with all the windows open to promote insect escape.

Mile after monotonous mile ticked by. He lost a fast-food wrapper to the vortex created by driving with open windows. As time elapsed, his cola lost its fizz and its ability to cool.

With Two Harbors still too many miles away, Greg rationalized that he could leave one eye open and shut the other for a few seconds. Then switch.

The crunch of gravel woke him.

"Good night, Charlie!" He wrenched the steering wheel and swung the Jeep back into his own lane from where it had drifted.

Heart pounding, eyes bulging, he scanned the traffic in his rearview mirror. Nothing. Grace of God. He could have killed someone.

Lacey's face flashed on the big screen of his memory.

"In Libby's eyes, I already did."

30

The key to his motel room was weighted with what looked like an artificial musky lure, minus barbs. Clever in a touristy overkill sort of way. Since his last stay at this particular establishment, management must have changed hands or had a visit from the health department. The bedspreads looked almost new and almost clean.

He dropped his overnight bag on the nearer bed, opting to drop his body face down onto the one closer to the bathroom and the air-conditioner unit mounted high on the back wall.

"A vacancy. On a Friday night. Thanks, Lord."

Greg used his right foot to nudge the heel of his left shoe until it plopped noisily onto the cheesy carpet. Repeated with a stockinged left foot to the right shoe. Untying laces was a job for the energetic.

He buried his face in the crevice between

two pillows, arms flat against his sides. The coroner could find him just like that in the morning, should the scare on the highway cause a delayed-reaction heart attack.

The aged air-conditioner compressor wasn't exactly white noise. But it did help mask the rhinoceros snore leaking through the thin wall between Greg's room and the one next door. He fought a twinge of jealousy that some unnamed motel guest was deep in slumber.

"I'm right behind you, buddy."

But he wasn't.

Not a half hour later. Nor an hour. Not after peeling off his jeans and shirt. Not after two trips to the bathroom and a swig of iron-laced water to wash down a Tylenol PM capsule. Not after checking the setting on the alarm clock four times and his backup wristwatch alarm.

"A guy can tell the difference between heartburn and a heart attack, can't he?"

He sat up in bed and propped the pillows behind him so he could lean against the pressed wood headboard. A deep rumbling clawed its way up his throat and out his open mouth in the form of a belch.

"Excuse me," he apologized before realizing he'd offended no one. "Well, that's it then. Simple heartburn." But the heaviness in his chest lingered.

Finding sleep impossible the night before heading into the Quetico was nothing new. Excitement often claimed the victory. Tonight, excitement ran second or third behind other emotions. Shame for not telling Libby the truth. And what's the word that means self-loathing but not quite so violent?

Mild self-loathing? That's like being a little bit pregnant.

He couldn't lose another night's sleep to what-ifing the day he sent Lacey to school. He'd sought and received forgiveness from the One who — unlike Greg — knew the end from the beginning. He'd sought but not received forgiveness from the one he'd vowed to love and cherish.

Is that all he'd vowed? Maybe she thought he pledged to make her happy every day of her life or to shield her from disappointment or prevent grief from touching their family. If so, she was wrong. He was incapable of any of that.

All he could do was love her. Not enough. Never enough.

The mercury-vapor lamp in the parking lot outside his window cast eerie shadows around the room when filtered through less-than-classy fiberglass drapes. If he closed just one eye, then the other . . .

■ ■ ■ ■

"This is the day, this is the day that the Lord hath made, that the Lord hath made" sounded less than comforting at the loudest volume setting on the clock radio's alarm function.

"Can it!" Greg growled as he slapped the offender into pre-dawn silence. "So I escaped a heart attack last night only to have a Christian radio station give me one this morning? Nice."

His neck ached. Reaching for the alarm had sent a spasm of pain across his shoulder and down his arm. He'd slept folded. Not good for the spine. Could have been worse. He could have slept long enough. Imagine how stiff his neck would have been then.

Greg sat on the edge of the bed. He needed to get on the road. But a hot shower might loosen his cramped muscles.

His hair still damp from his shower, Greg checked out at the front desk, then wandered into the Wilsonaire Bakery to make his breakfast selection.

One would think a motel/bakery combo would offer continental breakfast at the very least. A Danish and coffee? Donut? One lousy free donut?

"What's your best seller?" he asked the flour-dusted woman behind the counter. Mrs. Wilson, he guessed.

"All of 'em," she said, her filmy eyes giving away her age despite the jet-black hair that shouted, "However old you think I am, shave at least a dozen years off that number, mister!"

He eyed the filled and frosted long johns. Couldn't help chuckling. He almost had "filled and frosted" his long johns on the winter camping trip with his boys — then probably ten and eleven — when the wolf pack wandered into their territory, or vice versa. Northern Wisconsin gray wolves lost their endangered species status, huh? Plenty of them. Is that right? How lucky for the Holden family.

The wolves lost interest. Eventually. The boys stuck to Greg like leeches the rest of the weekend. Had he ever admitted that his fear level matched — if not exceeded — theirs? Wild animals. Fascinating, but unpredictable.

"Never underestimate the beauty of predictability."

"What's that you say?" the bakery woman asked.

"Two chocolate frosted long johns, please. Unfilled."

"That it? You want coffee?"

"You have coffee?"

"By the cup or the gallon. We'll fill your Thermos or canteen, if you want."

"Great. That's new."

She dropped two portions of bakery heaven into a white waxed paper bag. "New?"

"Free coffee. I've stayed here before. Under the old management."

"Did I say anything about free?" Her mouth puckered and her eyebrows drew up into the folds of her forehead.

He pushed aside the foot in his mouth and said, "Sorry. I —"

"Oh, don't take life so serious, my friend." She handed Greg the bag. "Of course it's free. Help yourself." She pointed toward a giant pump Thermos near the exit.

He reached into his back right pocket for his wallet. "How much for the long johns?"

"If you were a Wilsonaire Motel guest last night, you're entitled to one free bakery item."

"Okay. Great. And for the second one?"

She leaned over the glass display case, her ampleness resting just above a harvest of glazed donuts. "It's complimentary."

"Excuse me?"

"Look, mister, you gonna analyze my

307

marketing methods or you gonna take the loot and run?"

Greg marveled that a crazy, older-than-she-wants-to-admit woman could lift his mood a little. The pound of flesh he'd gain from the baked goods would be worth the sacrifice.

By now, he wasn't the only customer. Courtesy and an eagerness to head even farther north prevented his sticking around to see how Mrs. Wilsonaire treated them. He rested his overnighter on the floor at his feet and set the white bag on the counter while he grabbed a cup of coffee — just one — and capped it with a plastic lid. He retrieved his two bags and headed out the door.

Mental note: Plan a stop at Wilsonaire Motor Lodge and Bakery next time through. If there is a next time.

31

Dawn sneaks up on a person who is locked into a track on the highway of monotony. Far off to the right of his vehicle, the horizon emerged slowly, as if the sun were suspicious of what the day might hold. The Controller of the universe cranked up the dimmer switch in tiny increments until Greg's headlights became redundant. Another cloudless day. Swell. No clouds, no rain. No rain, no campfires. Too bad. As much as Greg respected the fire bans and their necessity, he did some of his best thinking near a campfire.

Maybe before the trip was over, the Quetico would get enough rain for the ban to be lifted. Did he dare pray for a convincing deluge? Would it be worth it? He could make a fire in the fireplace at home if he wanted to think.

Home. The word just didn't feel right these days.

Greg wondered what Libby would be doing at this moment — the first few minutes of dawn. Still in bed. No question. Was this — ? It was. The first time the house was empty for more than a day's stretch. Libby was alone. Completely. His boys wouldn't drop in until the new semester started, and probably only then to show pictures of their summer's adventure and beg their mother to do a hundred loads of laundry.

God, I don't know what she'll need while I'm gone, other than You.

How arrogant of him! To think that Libby might struggle in the absence of her husband. As if he'd meant anything significant to her recently. She'd probably wake a couple of hours from now feeling nothing but relief.

What I am to her right now and what I want to be are polar opposites, Lord. Any hope of a cosmic miracle while I'm gone? A little shock-and-awe in the polarization department?

In response to the lack of a direct answer, Greg reached to turn on the radio. An oldies station responded first to the seek feature. Two words into the song — "Fifty Ways to Leave Your Lover" — Greg knew *that* was a mistake.

Seek. Elevator music. Seek. Screaming guitars and angry drums in simultaneous seizures. Seek. "He's always been faithful to me." Sara Groves.

Better.

What am I doing? Running? Deception is hardly a desirable character trait. I should go home and tell Libby the truth.

Greg rubbed his hand over day-old whiskers. "Yeah, I can picture how that would go."

"Libby, can we talk?"

"Sure, my beloved. You mean the world to me. If something's on your mind, I'm ready to listen."

Rewind.

"Libby, can we talk?"

"What about?"

"I . . . I need a change."

"Change? You mean, with us?"

"With me. And us. I'm not happy."

"You're *not happy?*"

"I know. What right do I have to feel more miserable than you do?"

"What's that supposed to mean?"

"Nothing, Libby. I know you're unhappy. So am I."

She'd pause, cross her arms, then ask, *"You want out?"*

"Yes." The word soft but unmistakably clear.

"You want to leave me?" she'd ask.

"Leave? I would never leave you."

"Then what?"

"I want to leave my job."

No. Telling her the truth would only add to her pain. And his.

Greg shifted in the driver's seat and focused on the highway ahead of him. First things first. The trip, then the truth. First he had to know if he could live with photography. Then he'd know if he could live with himself.

32

Eager for a chance to stretch his legs, grab a snack, and use indoor plumbing one last time, Greg pulled into the gravel parking lot of The Last Chance Convenience Store.

The men's room boasted nothing special except hot and cold running water and a flush toilet.

"It's all about perspective," he said to his reflection in the mirror. "Good-bye, porcelain. Good-bye flush handle. See you in a week and a half or so."

Nothing would move Libby to give up indoor plumbing in the name of adventure. Nothing about this trip would appeal to her. How many times have the words "Why don't you come with me?" died on my lips?

Greg used an extra squirt of liquid soap when washing his hands and snatched two paper towels from the dispenser. Then a third for good measure.

One last glance in the mirror. The awkward stage. Patrick Dempsey could pull off a day's growth of beard and make it look sophisticated. On Greg, it lay like steel wool shavings stuck to the business side of masking tape. He needed a few more days of beard production.

And a reason to go home at the end of the trip.

But he'd settle for an icy diet cola. On his way past the car air fresheners, windshield washer fluids, outrageously priced canned soup, and limited assortment of first-aid products, Greg paused and reached for a bag on the snack display.

His canoe slid into the water the way a foot finds familiar toe-shaped curves and depressions in a well-worn shoe. Greg sat for a moment, not paddling, letting the momentum of his push-off from shore carry his vessel out into the lake, away from his land link to reality.

His spirit floated just above the surface of the water and ran parallel with the canoe's hull. It drifted above small waves and left a wake of little note.

"And so it begins," he said to the lethargic breeze. "I'm here. Work your magic."

One deep breath. Another. Dead in the water now. He'd have to start paddling if he hoped to get anywhere.

His initial stroke felt like the first dip of the knife in a fresh jar of peanut butter, satisfying for reasons unexplainable.

Within minutes, the rhythm returned from where it had hibernated since his last trip. With an efficient J-stroke he could paddle a straight path through the water without switching sides. A half hour or more. Greg Holden — Master Voyageur. Water pioneer. Inadequate in every other way.

Each switch of his paddle from one side to the other — in-frequent as they were — left a dribble of cool lake water that crossed in front of him. He'd make a few changes in the way he packed the canoe after the first portage. The nose was a little high in the air, creating a drag he didn't need when solo paddling. He'd shift more of the cargo toward the front to balance things out, and he'd position under his dribble pattern an item that could bear getting wet.

His maps — both standard and topo-graphical — hung from the canoe thwart in front of him, their ink marks holding a different attraction than they had on other trips he'd taken. He needed to know where he was going, yes, but this time weed beds and underwater drop-offs and fish habitats mattered far less than marked pictographs on cliff faces, rapids, waterfalls, and the ever-present portages.

Protected by a waterproof sleeve and a clear viewing window, the maps led the way like a guide dog would lead the sight impaired through a busy intersection. He'd be lost without them.

Maybe it hadn't been the smartest move to choose unfamiliar territory for his first solo trip. He pushed the thought aside with his next paddle stroke and conquered another few feet of water.

Is it okay, Lord, if I don't think about Libby for a few days? Don't think about her pain and my inability to fix it? Or am I a world-class moron for asking?

Greg straightened his posture and scanned the scenery for something worth photographing.

His digital camera hung from a lanyard around his neck. Not the world's most expensive camera, but it would do for now. Tucked into the waterproof carrying case were two extra memory cards. He wouldn't have to worry about preserving enough film to last until the final days of his trip. He planned to use his evenings in the tent to scan the shots he'd taken each day and delete the imperfect.

That'd be a nice feature for life, if You're

looking for something new, Lord. Delete the imperfect shots, imperfect words, imperfect decisions. "Oh, that didn't turn out like I'd hoped. Delete."

Thoughtful and *pathologically pensive* share some common DNA.

Two portages and a dozen pensive thoughts later, Greg realized he hadn't taken a single photograph yet. Not that volume was his goal. But he still acted like a grocer on vacation rather than an adventurer seeking a cover shot for *Boundary Waters* magazine. He'd hoped to get a shot of a campfire at twilight, the hot flames silhouetted against the blue-black sky. The fire ban doused that idea. Even a camp stove could threaten dry tinder. He'd have to exercise extreme caution. All he needed was to create trouble and give Libby more reason to berate him for not taking a satellite phone for emergencies.

Greg decided to hug the shoreline for the next leg of his journey, hoping it would prove the scenic route for photo ops. He also wondered if a person could find a cheap satellite phone on eBay.

His paddle felt good in his hands. It would get a workout this trip. "B minus, my foot," he said, slapping it hard on the water. The sound echoed off the wall of pines on the far horizon. "Beaver tail," he lied to the stillness, instantly conscious that you can't fool the Creator of beaver tails.

At the end of the next portage, Greg laid the last of his equipment in his canoe, straightened to his full height, and gave his puffed chest one fist pound. "I am man, hear me roar!" he said to his pine tree companions and the waterway that stretched before him. He turned back to survey the route over which he'd hauled his canoe and equipment. Alone. All the effort, his. All the decisions, his to make. He considered punctuating his accomplishment with an über-manly grunt, but feared unintentionally mimicking the mating call of something furry and large. With claws.

He drank in a long draft of virgin air. No diesel bus fumes. No car emissions. No mingled grease smells from the kitchen exhaust fans of competing fast-food restaurants. No evidence of other humans and their habits.

No reason to hurry.

Getting settled into camp for the night — a worthy goal — held no deadline but the one imposed by darkness. This far north, light lingered as late as eight-thirty or nine in August. Nothing pressed him to hustle but his eagerness to sample all that the wilderness promised.

His test run on Lake DuBay at home taught him how to use a canoe-built-for-two as a solo unit. He climbed into what normally served as the front seat — the bow seat — and turned to paddle the canoe with its stern now forward. The weight of his supplies rested far ahead of him in the canoe to counterbalance his own bulk in the "back."

The lone exception was his camera case. It stayed close at hand, like a faithful golden retriever waiting for instructions.

Greg pushed off into navigable water, but laid his paddle across his lap before venturing farther.

Lord, he began, dropping his chin to his chest as if the weight of his thoughts was too heavy for his neck muscles, *I need to meet You here. Audible voice would be nice. Handwriting on the cliff faces. Bolt from heaven. Anything.*

With an exhale and an "amen" echo, Greg gripped his paddle and slid it into the waiting water. Yesterday's page of the flip calendar on his desk claimed, "Faith is expecting an answer from God when you can't even define the problem." He didn't recall memorizing that entry, but there it was, imprinted on his mind.

Like a photograph.

He dug deep into the water, propelling his canoe forward. His muscles stretched and yawned, then expressed their gratitude for the opportunity to get back in the game. His shop-class paddle's sleek handle belied the rough ridge on the blade beneath the water's surface. How many strokes, how many water miles would this imperfect paddle measure if paddles came equipped with odometers? How many adventures? How many fish had he cleaned on the blade over the years?

A tandem canoe converted to solo use lacks grace. Greg's path through the water wouldn't win him any style awards, but as the northwoods breeze evaporated the perspiration on his face, he moved farther into unfamiliar territory, leaving a small, untidy wake.

Unfamiliar territory. The thought returned. Was that wise? Would it have been smarter to choose a familiar trip route? Probably. Smarter. Safer. And routine.

"Fie on routine!" he said, leaning into his next stroke.

As he pulled the paddle through the water, he envisioned pushing all remnants of normal life behind him. Time clocks. Lunch boxes. Mindless meetings. Memos. Negotiations. Paperwork.

In his wilderness world, he'd push no papers. Except for the maps. And his trip journal. No alarm clocks. No business suits. No pasted-on smiles for the church family that still thought he and Libby had bounced back better than ever after their loss.

Maybe that's where they slipped off the rails. Was keeping their pain private a mistake? What could the church have done for them? Pray more?

Directly ahead lay a turtleback island no larger than a Volkswagen Beetle, a single pine tree — long dead — its only inhabitant. The tree leaned awkwardly toward the water, as if it lacked the strength to stand upright.

Greg stopped paddling and removed his camera from its case. The interruption in nature's symmetry caught his photographer attention. The other trees in the background stretched vertically, held tall by invisible strings connecting them to heaven. This one sagged.

He lined up the shot, grateful for a good interplay of light and shadows and the relative calm of the water.

He slid the camera back into its case, zipped it shut, and fought off the sensation that he didn't deserve to make a living doing something from which he derived joy.

Fantasies were for teenage boys and the unmarried.

Responsibility kept many a prospective dragon-slayer's sword sheathed. It might well keep Greg's camera locked within the dark coffin of its case.

Like an addict drawn to the feel of the cigarette in his hands as well as the nicotine hit, Greg turned again and again to his camera. Scenes begged him to capture them. The otter with obsessive-compulsive disorder, cleaning his catch-of-the-day at the water's edge. Black trees against the sunset sky. The shimmering dawn. A twisted branch. A jay feather lodged between two rocks.

For ten sweet days he focused the lens of his life on whatever beauty he could capture. He ate and slept at will. Paddled when necessary. Floated when he could. Explored. Lingered. Napped without working around anyone else's schedule.

Low water levels turned creeks into mud holes and stretched access points farther out into the lakes he traversed. He faced the portages with a viewfinder, stopping often to take pictures of scenes he would have walked past if fishing were his goal, if conquering distance mattered.

As his smooth strokes pulled his canoe around a point of land, a marshy shallow bay came into view. A brown mass near the shore caught his attention. In slow motion, Greg laid his paddle across his lap and unzipped the camera case. Was it — ? Yes. A cow moose. She raised her regal yet decidedly bulbous head from drinking at the water's edge. Her ears twitched. Greg floated closer, hesitant to make sudden moves or noises that might frighten her away.

The cow bent to take one more quick drink, an overflow of water pouring off her chin when she jerked her head back up and turned in Greg's direction.

Greg pulled off his best imitation of driftwood as his canoe drew closer. As slow as a turtle on Valium, he raised his camera to line up the shot. Thumbing the telephoto toggle brought Greg's perception of her so close he could tell she wasn't wearing false eyelashes. They were real.

As he framed the picture and poised his finger over the button to capture the shot, the moose pounded through the water toward Greg's canoe.

"What in the name of — ?"

The low water level kept her from having to swim to pursue him. The lumbering animal charged through the weeds and water.

Half a ton of angry hurtled toward him. What could he do but paddle backwards? He knew she held every advantage over him — size, speed, power. But a person does not sit and let a moose bully him into paralysis.

Greg's heart mimicked a machine gun in his chest. With every panicked stroke, he willed his trusty canoe to sprout wings, or a motor.

But just as suddenly as she'd waged war against him, the moose pulled back. Greg continued to retreat, but she gave up the pursuit.

"Can a moose contract rabies?" Greg wondered as he slowed his departure. "That thing's crazy. Fascinating, but crazy."

With the cow a safe distance away from him now, Greg plied his paddle on the other side of his canoe to turn it so he could move forward out into the main body of water. He'd get a photo of a moose another day. As he turned, he heard another splash-dance coming from the other side of the bay. A moose calf.

He watched as the calf loped through the shallow water toward his mother. No wonder she was upset with Greg. His canoe had drifted between her and her calf, unintentionally, but the results were the same. *First rule of nature: never come between a mother and her baby.*

He'd failed that test at home too.

Midday Tuesday he ducked his canoe into a sheltered cove. He'd come as far as he dared if he planned to make it home by Friday night, or Saturday at the latest. The threat of a deadline crept back into his vocabulary. If he started back on Thursday at dawn and pushed hard, he could make it home in time for a few hours' sleep before church Sunday morning.

He hadn't gained what he'd hoped. Insight still eluded him. He'd lost a few things, though. Somewhere along the way he'd dropped his pocket knife. Maybe when he'd reached for his handkerchief to mop up the blood from the gluttonous mosquito he'd swatted a pint too late.

And his paddle. Poor, sad thing. As faithful as it had been all these years, it couldn't bear the weight of a misplaced foot. The boulder underneath it served as a splitting wedge when Greg lost his footing and landed on it when he was heading back down the portage trail for another load. He shouldn't have laid the paddle against the rock. Should have tucked it into the canoe.

Splintered, it was useless. He probably should have flung it into the woods. Or burned it.

His life was full of "should haves."

As he set up his tent in the idyllic cove, Greg worked to push aside the debris of regret. He'd found no answers. The joy of catching nature in candid poses underscored the uselessness of a photo with no audience. If a tree falls in the woods — ? If a snapshot's never seen — ?

Only fifteen more years until he could retire. At the earliest. Fifteen years of purchase orders and haggling on the phone and crunching numbers and sitting through business meetings. Maybe then he could think of his camera as a companion rather than a tourist's accessory.

Who was he kidding? Responsibility trumps dreams every time.

If it weren't for the fire ban, the night would be a good one for poking at embers.

33

Clouds. The morning sky sported clots of white and gray clouds.

A false alarm, no doubt — teasers. The earth cried out for rain, but every cloud Greg had seen the entire trip flirted but refused to give in.

He fried up the heel of the summer sausage and a package of hash browns. Not the Tremendous Twelve special breakfast from Perkins, but it would do. He'd have to be careful on the way home. Meals might be a little skimpy. Usually at this point in his wilderness adventures, he started craving home-cooked meals and fresh vegetables. But the thought of vegetables reminded him of the produce department at Greene's and nothing with the word "home" attached to it brought comfort.

One good thing about the return trip: the food pack weighed decidedly less than at the start.

If anything, his heart weighed more.

No one had to tell him he was dragging his feet around camp. Starting home seemed so final. Terminal.

He toyed with the idea of taking another day to explore. He'd face the wrath of Stenner if he didn't show up on Monday morning for work, but if he drove straight through and got home late Sunday night, he could manage it, sleep or no sleep.

A strong wind could destroy the perfection of that plan, unless it was a tail wind.

If he had the time, he'd go check out that spot in the crease of his map — Lacy Falls. Probably not a spectacle, as falls go, or it would warrant larger print and a marked portage into it. But still . . .

34
LIBBY

"Shouldn't we see a portage put-in point somewhere in here, Frank?"

I'm getting pretty good at finding them tucked into the endless miles of wooded and rock-strewn shoreline. Unlike the cement boat landings that give public access to lakes in Wisconsin, here every attempt is made to hide the evidence that humans sometimes share this wildness. No sign markers. No postings announce, "Great campsite." No arrows point the way. No "Caution: Bear Crossing" benefits.

Still, as green as I am in the ways of the wild, my overactive powers of observation prove useful here. When we're still many paddle strokes away, I often catch a glimpse of a slightly paler place on shore, a slight widening, a less formidable border to the water.

But after crossing the lake that threatened us when the waves were high, skirting around islands and peninsulas of rock and trees, and following a barely-there creek that hardly qualifies as a body of water, we see no hint of a portage or a column of smoke. No portage is marked on the map, but we hope that was a cartographer's mistake. A simple omission. Who would need a portage here? Who would venture this deep into nondescript lakes and channels? For whom would the promise of an ultra-fine-print Lacy Falls serve as a destination worth pursuing?

I still cling to hope that the answer is my husband.

As we troll slowly along the shore, looking for a phantom portage through which we can reach what we wordlessly acknowledge is our "last place to look," I try to stay focused on just this crisis. The other one, raging through the body of the woman sitting a few feet behind me, is further out of my control than this one.

We haven't spoken about it since Jen and Frank pointed our canoes toward Lacy Falls. A curtain of discomfort dropped between us. She hadn't told me. She should have told me. I should have known. It might have changed everything.

Not the cancer, but the fact that she's searching for my husband when she could be lying on a table, letting an army of radiation soldiers beat back the enemy.

Maybe this *is* her way of beating back the enemy.

"Jen?"

"Yes?"

"I want you to know —"

"What?"

My eyes don't leave the shore we're scanning, but my heart jumps over the packs in our canoe and lands near my best friend's. "I don't understand your decision not to let me know what's going on in your body."

I hear her sigh, so I hurry my next comment. "But I respect you. I love you. And I'll support you no matter what."

Her "thank you" is almost engulfed by the sound of waves licking glacial granite.

"Let's tie up here," Frank calls back from ten yards in front of us. Ten yards — enough for a first down. Greg would be so amazed that the comparison that came to my mind related to football. My tolerance for the game rates about as high as the percentages for Hail Mary pass completions.

Lord, football season starts in a few weeks. What am I going to do if Greg doesn't spend it in his recliner with that ridiculously huge — ginormous — Packers mug at his side?

"Here?" Jen asks.

The shoreline is as unforgiving as the shoreline of my heart — nothing soft, flat, or remotely beach-like on which to land. But a hint of a beaten-down path through the shore-hugging underbrush catches my attention too.

"Let me go on ahead, just to see if this spot's worth pursuing," Frank says.

I look at Jen, wondering which of us will be the first to object.

"Besides," he adds, "nature calls."

Again?

He vaults out of his canoe onto the lowest and closest pile of rocks and ties his canoe to the branch of a low-hanging cedar. Before we can voice our objections, Frank disappears into the underbrush.

We sit with the paddle handles resting across our laps. The blades dangle over the side of the vessel where they can drip without affecting our personal comfort.

"Libby?"

"Yes?"

"Do you know the name of a good urologist for Frank? That man has a genuine problem."

"Agreed. I'll talk to Pauline when we get home. Maybe she can convince him to see somebody."

In cahoots with Pauline for Frank's health.

Bonding over urination issues. It's a start, I guess.

I'm making plans for what happens when we get home. The three of us. Once we get past the bodyless funeral. I'll have more time to devote to Jen's needs. I know the way to her oncologist's office. I can pull out my recipes for mild foods she can tolerate during chemo, if necessary, and casseroles Brent and the girls like.

When Jen's energy wanes, I'll take her girls shopping and invite them over to make cookies and teach them Cat's Cradle and any jump rope moves I remember and can pull off without wrenching something important to me.

The sun is too bright. Blinding. It reveals everything. The sunburn on the backs of my hands. The smudges from last night's campfire on my pants. And the distance my heart is from home.

The gentle waves rock us like a kind hand on a cradle while we wait for Frank's return from the men's room. The breeze whispers a snatch of heaven's lullaby — "It'll be okay. It's going to be okay."

Lord, I can only believe that because You said so.

Jen must have heard the lullaby too and drifted with me. She and I startle in unison when we hear a branch do a drum riff in the woods.

It's Frank, crashing out of the brush with a wild-eyed look on his unshaven face. He's breathing unnaturally. Great gulps of air. "I . . . I found . . . my boy."

35

"You found him?" Jen's voice and mine hit the same decibel level.

He draws another stomachful of air. "I found . . . his . . . canoe. I didn't . . . I couldn't . . . see him. Saw . . . footprints."

"Oh, Lord Jesus!" I'm ashore before Jen by a nanosecond.

Frank waves his arms like an agitated gorilla. "Tie it down! Tie it down!"

"Jen!"

"Got it." She snags the nylon rope attached to the nose of the canoe just before it floats away to a happy life in oblivion.

As soon as I reach him, I grab Frank's sleeves. "You found his canoe? Where?"

"In the woods."

"What?"

"No more than about thirty yards in. Upright. And —"

"What? What is it?"

Jen's arm around my shoulders helps

335

lower my heart rate by a beat or two per minute.

"The canoe . . ." Frank says. He swallows whatever chunky thing had camped in his throat. "It's been there a while."

Jen squints at him, as if that will help draw clarity from his words. "How can you tell?"

"Upright, Frank?" The words tumble out of me as realization dawns. Why would Greg abandon his canoe in the woods? And why upright? "Was anything in it? His equipment? Packs?"

Jen adds, "There's no trail here. How did he get the canoe into the woods in the first place?"

"You said it had been there a while. What did you mean by that?"

Frank takes a step back from us, turns toward the woods, then back again. "His . . . his stuff's in there, some of it, anyway. And it's been . . . messed with."

"By whom? Or what?" I can't let my imagination drum up an answer. I can't.

"It was his food pack. Bear, I suspect."

Jen tightens her grip on me and then says, "Shouldn't we be moving faster?"

My legs try to perform their duty without the benefit of bones. Not the way God designed things. My lungs are frozen on inhale mode. How long before I pass out?

"I don't think there's any need to hurry," he says with funereal solemnity. "And . . ."

Frank's hesitations may drive me the last few feet to insanity.

"And what?"

Jen pats my forearm with her free hand. Is she about to apologize to Frank for the edge in my voice? I pull away from her and ask him again, "And what?"

What happened to the tan Frank developed on the trip? It's gone.

"I looked around the immediate area. Not much for footprints. No more clues."

He would tell us if there was blood, right?

"We have to look farther," I tell him, annoyed he hadn't thought of it himself.

"Yes, of course," he says. "But in light of what the contents of his canoe look like, it might be best if I . . . if I went on alone."

"No!"

"Libby, it's not pretty."

"No! You're not going alone, for a hundred thousand reasons."

Jen straightens her shoulders and adds, "You're looking at two of them."

Every hard edge on Frank's face softens like glass at its melting point. "Now look, I love you women."

He does?

"But you have no idea what we might find."

We can imagine. I'm trying not to, but —

Jen presses her hands to her stomach. A pain? "Frank, we can't stay here and wait. Please understand. We have to go with you. We'll go crazy either way."

Frank eyes us as if calculating the logistics of hog-tying us to a tree to put us out of *his* misery. Are those tears in his eyes?

"I wish I could spare you this."

"Frank," I say, "sometimes there is no other way but through." Now. *Now* I learn this.

"Okay, how are we going to handle the search?" Jen asks. "What do you want us to do? Spread out so we can cover more territory?"

Please say we have to stay together.

Frank lifts his hat from his head and wipes his forehead with the back of his wrist. "I think we should hang close to one another. Then none of us will be alone when —"

I can finish his sentence for him. "— when we find Greg's remains."

Jen's head snaps in my direction. But she doesn't correct me.

As we head into the woods together, Frank warns us to look before we step. Every bent twig or indentation in the moss could mean something.

"Frank? The footprints you saw?" Jen asks.

"Yeah?"

"Human or — ?"

"Human. One way."

"What?"

"I saw a few footprints going in one direction only. In deeper. Nothing coming out."

What did I eat for breakfast? I'll know in a minute. It's on its way back up.

"See?" he says, pointing.

Why do we see so few footprints? One here. Two several yards farther on.

He anticipates my question. "The sporadic appearance tells us they were made a while ago. Only the ones that were in deep moss or mud are still visible. The rest, the ones that connect the dots, might have been washed away with the rain we had."

"Just a couple of days ago?"

"Or earlier," he says. "A week ago."

Silence seems a reasonable response to that possibility.

The underbrush is so thick, I can't imagine Greg trying to carry his canoe through this. He didn't get far with it. I wish I could ask him if he just intended to store it until he found out if Lacy Falls was a glance-and-a-wow spot or if it warranted an overnight stay for which he'd need to haul the

rest of his equipment on a subsequent plow-
your-own portage.

"Greg, what kept you from coming back
for the canoe?"

A few steps later, I know.

The claw marks that made strips out of
Greg's heavy canvas food pack and scattered licked-clean debris scream "bear." We
have to check for human remains.

Don't we?

"Frank?" I manage to say through a pool
of lumpy bile. "Is there any chance he could
have survived this?" I make a megaphone
with my hands. "Greg? Greg!"

All three of us scan the scene. A flicker of
hope. That's all I'm looking for.

Frank bends to pull away a piece of wreck-
age. Is he moving in slow motion?

Jen and I watch as he moves things I can't
imagine touching. I shiver as he digs deeper
into the refuse that once belonged to my
husband. Then he stands, wipes his hands
on his pants, and takes a shuddering breath.
"This is a good sign."

A good sign? "Frank, how can you say
that?"

"No blood."

Which the rain would have washed away.

"Or bones."

Oatmeal. That's what I had for breakfast.

It's boxing with my epiglottis.

Frank paws through the debris again. "Things are missing."

Jen steps closer and wraps an arm around me.

Frank gestures with his hand toward the destruction. "I think Greg took a few things with him and, for whatever reason, didn't come back for the rest. I don't see any trace of his tent or any pack but his food pack, or what's left of it. That's all the bear was interested in anyway."

Crazed bears sometimes masquerade as merely hungry bears. Even I know that. And crazed bears do nontraditional things, like attack innocent humans. It makes the news. And documentaries.

"Are you ready?" Frank interjects into my distress.

"For what?"

"Following the trail," he says, already engaged in the process. Jen's right behind him.

"Wait a minute. Wait!"

The two turn in unison to face me, the uncooperative one.

"If Greg wasn't anywhere near here when this happened," I say, gesturing toward the crime scene, "wouldn't he have come back? Wouldn't he have returned, discovered that his food pack was shredded, but take the canoe and hightail it for home?"

Birdsong — light, delicate, comical — mocks the silence that falls between us.

One Mississippi. Two Mississippi. How many seconds will pass before someone breaks free with a viable thought? What must a lost eternity feel like? These brief moments of silence stretch interminably around us, like a cloak too heavy for our shoulders, a dark river of reality too deep and threatening to risk crossing. Hopelessness burns like a fire that grows fiercer with everything I try to use to extinguish it.

Frank turns, wordlessly, and walks away from our pool of despair.

"Where are you going?" If I breathe next time I speak, the words might have some power behind them.

"You women can do what you want. Me? I'm following footprints until there are no more."

Jen looks at me. Then we step into Frank's wake. I don't know about Jen, but I'm overcome with concern that I won't survive our finding that final footprint.

36
GREG

Greg smelled ozone, saw only pale gray light filtering through the tent walls, felt a washboard of tree roots under his back and clammy dampness on exposed skin, heard an uneven percussion pattern on the tent roof, and tasted swamp sludge. The sludge had nothing to do with the rain. It testified to the inadvisability of hot-and-spicy beef sticks as a snack.

Rain. Good for the thirsty land. Bad for taking pictures. Good for dispelling fire bans. Bad for finding dry wood. Good for reading. Good for thinking. Bad for making it home in time. Ah, there's the rub.

That guy in *Cast Away* had a volleyball to talk to, to help him wade through his thoughts. His friend, psychiatrist, and sanity barometer — Wilson. Greg looked around the interior of his rain-pelted tent. His ripe hiking boots. No. His quickly ripening sleeping bag? No. His flashlight? Possibility.

"What do you think, Sparky?" he asked it. "Could you use a friend?"

After unsuccessfully trying to dodge raindrops on his visit to the "men's room," Greg grabbed some snacks he'd tucked into his daypack and slipped back into the tent. If the rain kept up, that's where he'd spend the rest of his day. The pages of the book Greg brought with him were limp from the humidity, as if made of flannel rather than wood fibers. He propped his backpack behind him to form a makeshift recliner for a storm-long reading marathon but soon found himself drifting off to the rumble of approaching thunder.

In a blinding flash, hot streaks of pain shot through Greg's body and exited through his eyes. A guttural scream scraped his throat raw. Into what abyss had he fallen? And why?

A tympani crash of thunder shook his world. He swallowed convulsively but his saliva was gone.

Like an animal in a cramped cage, Greg thrashed and clawed at his inky confinement. What was that smell? Burnt nylon? Burnt feathers? Burnt flesh?

As awareness replaced panic, Greg stopped thrashing and fought to gain his bearings. Unimaginably deep blackness told him night descended long ago. Moonless. Comfortless. Thunder shuddered, too loud and too close. Where was the lightning? Lightning should have given him sporadic strobes of illumination to help him figure out what happened to him. Where was it?

He reached for his flashlight. His hand patted the tent floor. Nothing. Nothing as in no tent floor. His palm touched bare dirt and tree roots. Where was he? He scooted sideways in his sitting position until he could feel the tent walls — walls, but a hole in the floor?

The bulk pressed up against his leg was his sleeping bag. It stunk like a singed chicken — a reminder of summers at his grandmother's. As he searched the bag for his flashlight, his hands landed on a patch that felt crisp to the touch. Crisp?

He ached on a cellular level. Every movement sent new currents of pain to his nerve endings. He wasn't seriously hurt, was he?

A Genesis cry split the darkness. "Please, God. Let there be light!"

Greg's voice scared him. Raspy, thick, a smoker's voice. What had happened?

The bare ground. A hole burned into his sleeping bag. The smells. The pain.

As his hand closed around his flashlight,

reality hit him in the gut. Most likely a bolt of lightning followed a tree root into his tent. That explained everything — the highly charged air, the smoke residue, and the fact that even when he pressed the switch on the light, Greg's world remained dark.

37

Greg spread his sleeping bag flat, burnt side down, and lay on it, backside down, face toward what he knew from his dry condition was an intact tent roof. The sounds of a pelting rain soothed one concern. If the lightning strike started a fire in the woods outside his tent, it stood no chance against the downpour.

Limb by limb, muscle by muscle, he assessed the damage. As the minutes passed, the intensity of the pain he'd first experienced dropped from boiled-in-hot-oil to a deep, all-encompassing ache. But he could move his fingers and toes, arms and legs. Trembling, he let his hands examine the rest of his body for burns, but there were none. How could that be?

If he could lie still, listening to the thunder retreating as it moved the storm to points east, would the assault on his body retreat too? Wary of sudden movements that might hamper his body's ability to rebound from the near miss, Greg reached again for the flashlight. He tapped it against his palm in case the batteries hadn't made a good connection the last time he tried. Then he prayed, opened his eyes, and flicked on the switch.

Nothing.

Greg felt everything and saw nothing. He waved his hand in front of his face. Where do shadows go when life itself is blacker than a shadow?

I just need to give it time. My body's in shock.

A wave started in his toes. Up through his loins, stomach, chest. When it reached his throat, Greg raised up on one arm, leaned to the side, and wretched.

Suffocating and potent, a new smell filled the tent. The odor of his fear.

Like Libby breathing through her labor pains, Greg pressed back the thoughts that engulfed him.

Temporary. This is temporary. When daylight comes, I'll probably see a hint of something at least. I'll have to be careful getting around camp with limited vision, but if I can just make out shapes or light-and-dark, I can do it.

He wouldn't let himself consider how long

it might be before he could find his way out of the wilderness.

Or what it might mean about his condition if daylight had already dawned.

Sleep seemed pointless but unavoidable, an organic painkiller. His body begged for it. His brain fought for time to worry. Exhaustion won.

He woke again, opened his eyes — not that it mattered — and "observed" the distressingly familiar blackness. The rain was long gone. Greg could tell from the way the air temperature had risen that the sun had probably punched in hours ago. When had the rain started? Yesterday?

He remembered the sound of rain. He'd settled in to read his book. Fell asleep. For how long? A few minutes? Hours?

And when the lightning struck, did he lose consciousness? For how long? How could he tell what day it was?

Libby. He had to tell Libby. No matter how limp and lifeless the connection between them, it was still a connection, in God's eyes at least.

But at the moment, God was the only one taking calls.

He was thirsty, but first things first. As his bladder spasmed, Greg felt his way toward the tent door, missed by a dozen inches, but eventually he found it. He couldn't afford to miss camp by a few inches when he returned from his outing. Time to make a plan.

He felt along the bottom of the tent flap for the zipper pull. As each tooth of the zipper responded to the pull, Greg tried and discarded possible ideas for how not to get lost in a shapeless environment. He recalled reading all the Laura Ingalls Wilder *Little House on the Prairie* books to Lacey when reading chapter books by herself was still a year or so beyond her abilities. Laura and her family used a rope guide during blizzards. Holding tight to a rope attached to the house and the barn enabled them to safely maneuver from one to the other even in whiteout conditions.

It could work for blackouts, too, couldn't it?

He had a good length of rope. It was attached to his food pack. Through the darkness, hiding under his canoe.

Under the circumstances, most people would understand if Greg chose a spot just a few feet from the tent door for his bathroom. He ventured outside the tent and discarded Sparky with a right-fielder's effort. The most useless piece of equipment he'd packed in.

The moss and rocks were slick underfoot. That's all he needed. Greg stuck his arms and hands out in front of him. He'd rather catch a tree with his hands than his forehead. If he'd camped longer in this spot, he might have grown more accustomed to the terrain. Thinking back to when he set up camp, he tried to remember major landmarks. Fallen trees. Rocks. He shuffled in the direction he assumed would take him a short distance into the woods. With memory alone as a guide, he pressed on.

Why hadn't he paid more attention to the layout of the camp?

It was probably senseless to regret leaving the rope behind. Wouldn't his sight rebound soon? Any minute now. He'd had the equivalent of a paparazzi-load of cameras flashed in his face. Eyes are resilient, aren't they? He'd recovered quickly from his dad's camera-happy holiday gatherings with those insipid blue flashbulbs. The optical shock or whatever it was would settle down, and he'd be able to see something soon. He needed to give it time. No reason to panic.

Except for the absence of light.

Greg shuffled farther into the darkness. When he judged he was a safe distance away from his tent, he stopped. The edge of his world. He relieved himself, then retraced his invisible steps back. He didn't find the center of the tent wall as he'd hoped, but caught his foot on one of the tie-downs. Close enough.

"I should have been an engineer," he said as he considered viable options for maneuvering through his temporary darkness.

The chalkboard of his mind registered a mockup of a log-hemmed path, with the logs like gutter guards on a bowling lane for kindergarteners. If he laid downed logs end to end along the left and right sides of the path, he could feel his way toward his bathroom area. If he kept one foot in the path, he could step out with the other to search for firewood. Ban or no ban, he needed to make a signal fire.

What was he thinking? A lot of good a signal fire would do if he burned the woods to the ground. No matter where he built a fire, without sight he had no clue about overhanging tree branches. He wouldn't see a stray spark catching on dry pine needles, if any remained dry after the soaking of the storm. He couldn't even detect a runaway flame chasing the length of a piece of firewood for a quick escape from the fire ring.

A fire was too risky under the circumstances.

Libby won again. She accused him of not stopping to mourn a loss or grieve a crisis but instantly flipping into fix-it mode. He'd done it again. Already he found himself engaged in the business of surviving, making his camp more accessible and safer, inventing a plan to navigate the crisis when he hadn't given himself much time to consider what had happened to him.

Starting down that trail of thought promised to prove as risky as starting a fire.

All of his resources — books, doctors, online medical information — were out of reach. Out of sight. No phone. How many times would he kick himself for not forking over the money for a reliable means of communication? Especially on a solo trip.

"Smart move, huh, Greg?"

Talking to himself. The least of his concerns.

Greg took a few tentative steps in the direction of the water. He'd set his tent with its only opening toward the cliff and water to catch the best views. How ironic. From the tent door he counted ten paces slightly left, then bent down to feel for the place where the rocks sloped toward water. He listened to the sound of the waves and moved toward the slurp, slurp, slurp against rock. The ground's unevenness unnerved

him. He'd skipped over this terrain yesterday, but that was when he could see. Today
the smallest obstacle could send him tumbling into a heap if he didn't watch his step.
Watch. Awkward faux pas. He needed to
heed his steps. Take care. But he wouldn't
watch anything for a while, apparently.

Five more paces. Plant one foot, draw the
other up to it. Plant the foot. Draw up next
to it.

He hoped no one passing by his peninsula
campsite observed his halting steps. Wait!
He did want to be seen! His rescue depended on it. How would he know if a
canoe came near enough to flag down?

"Another wise move, Gregory. What are
the odds anyone else is likely to venture
back this deep? No portage. No footpath.
Not much of a reputation for fishing or it
would have been marked on the map. Way
to go. You managed to get into trouble in a
place so remote no one will ever find you.
And you're not due home for two days, so
no one even knows to look! Brilliant move,
Greg."

Two more steps and he knew he was close.
He lowered himself to the ground and
crawled the rest of the way on his hands
and knees. When he felt the lake lick his
fingers, he laid flat on his stomach, reached

out for a hand-scoop of water, and pressed it against his eyes. Cold. Refreshing. But not healing. When he opened his eyes, the world was still black.

38

Greg crawled back to the tent. He should be hungry. Maybe he'd eat later. A headache poked at the back of his eyes. Where was his canteen? Staying hydrated was especially important at a time like this.

How long before he stopped trying to see? He'd turned his head to "look" in the direction he thought he'd left his canteen hanging from a hooklike broken tree branch. Holding his arm out at shoulder level, he moved into the darkness. Like a man with a metal detector attached to his shoulder, he swung his arm in a wide, slow arc. His wrist hit what felt like a sapling. Not the right tree. Sweep and step to the right again. Nothing. To the left. A rough-barked trunk.

He tapped the trunk with his palms as if patting down a suspect after a high-speed chase. Nothing. Arm extended again, he pressed on to find the right tree among the dozens scattered throughout the campsite.

"Since when did this happen?" he asked the darkness after stubbing his toe on another tree root. "Yesterday, I would have told you I'd picked a nice flat spot to camp. I didn't notice the obstacles. Was that yesterday?"

It helped to talk. He'd probably need assistance to break that habit once he was rescued.

His hand brushed against a tree, bumping into something that banged against the trunk. The cool aluminum sides of his canteen. With his fingers, he traced the strap until it reached the hook. Once the strap was free, he lowered the canteen, unscrewed the lid, and took a sip.

Lukewarm, with an iron aftertaste. He let the liquid slip down his throat and envisioned it climbing through among the honeycomb of his cells to rehydrate anything the lightning had evaporated. His mouth was dry again after the first swallow.

"That can't be a good sign."

He took another swig. Then he replaced the cap and hung the canteen strap over his shoulder. He'd have to keep the important items close to him from now on.

Close to him. From now on.

Libby.

Before he could stop its onslaught, a

legion of marauding thoughts warned him he might not have a chance to try.

Blindness didn't kill him, but the aftereffects might.

What if he impaled himself on the sharp point of a fallen branch he didn't know was in his path? What if he misjudged his position and walked off the cliff? What if no one knew or cared to come looking for him? What if his paltry food supplies ran out before his sanity? What if wild animals sensed he was injured and vulnerable? What if he had to wait for the lake to freeze over in a few months so he could slide across the ice to a position where he'd be more visible to low-flying planes?

A few months.

He couldn't imagine God asking him to bear this for more than a day or two before sending help.

What Bible character could he recall who contracted a dreadful infirmity but found healing the first day or two? None. The only situations that came to mind were peppered with words like "She suffered for twelve long years" or "It rained forty days and forty nights" or "born blind."

Where were the stories about *temporary* blindness, other than Saul? One-day crises? Here today, gone tomorrow trials?

When Lacey died, Greg resented the Bible characters who got their dead children back. The poor, heartbroken parents plunged neck-deep into mourning. Then here comes Jesus onto the scene, and the child is restored — alive — to his or her parents' arms. Nice. A well-timed miracle. As it should be.

Greg had waited for his miracle in the hall outside the trauma center three years ago. As he paced and prayed, doctors fought to bring his daughter back from the precipice.

What did he expect to hear?

"Mr. Holden, we're happy to report that the paramedics jumped the gun a little. Oh, sorry about the bad choice of words. They were a little premature in their assessment of your daughter's condition. Lacey isn't dead. Far from it. In fact, she's behind those doors right now teaching the nurses how to jump rope with IV lines. Man, that was a close call."

"She's not . . . not dead?"

"Nope. Our bad. Hope we didn't scare you."

"She's alive?"

"That's pretty much what 'not dead' means, Mr. Holden."

"And she's not injured?"

"Funniest thing. Well, not funny funny, but you know."

"No. Tell me."

That would have made a great Bible story, wouldn't it? Twelve-year-old girl fatally wounded in school shooting lives to tell the story. Doctors baffled by remarkable return from the brink of death.

But while Greg ripped out his insides praying, "Please, God! Spare her life!" she died.

Not a temporary death. The real thing. Forever.

By the time Libby arrived at the hospital, the doctor had already pronounced a time of death and pulled a hospital sheet over Lacey's face. Libby ripped the sheet back with a look that shouted, "How dare you risk suffocating my child!"

Lacey's lips were cold and blue. Both parents bent down to kiss their only daughter as they stood on opposite sides of the hospital gurney. Their child's body already bore the trademarks of a mannequin. Stiff, unyielding, unresponsive, lifeless.

"Why didn't she qualify?" Greg remembered debating with God.

"Excuse me?"

"Why wouldn't Lacey have qualified for a miracle? Why couldn't she have been raised from the dead like Jairus's daughter or the Shunamite's son?"

"Qualify? That's not how it works."

"Was it me, then? Is it my fault? Did I not qualify to have my prayers answered?"

"Greg, My son —"

"No platitudes, please. I need to know why those other people received what they asked for and I didn't."

Greg had broken down at that point, one of the few episodes of weakness in a lifetime of testosterone toughness. He cried over Lacey's death and over the fracture in his relationship with a God who had never given him any reason not to trust Him.

He figured it was about time that he formally apologized for seeing it as a fracture, not a bridge.

And what was this — this new challenge, however temporary? Another bridge? A thorn? A cross?

Or a twisted way to tell him to give up the last of his passions? His marriage was all but buried. His daughter danced beyond his reach. His job required life support. And now he'd lost what he most needed in order to pursue photography. His sight.

How far could he travel on *in*sight?

With his forearms resting on his knees, Greg sat on a rough-barked log and stared at the relentless blackness. The effort to try to see fueled a persistent headache. But giving up trying seemed tantamount to admitting defeat. Unthinkable.

He was startled when something brushed across his cheek. He turned toward where he assumed it landed. The leaf or pine needle or feather or bug or whatever it was would remain an unknown unless he felt compelled to search for it with his hands to confirm its innocuous nature. What was the point?

"Day and night are the same to You, aren't they, Lord? They're the same to me now too. For You, it's all light. For me, darkness. Ever-present darkness."

Greg supposed it didn't matter if it were day or night at the moment. He would sleep when he was tired and eat only when hunger forced him to deplete his meager supplies.

He thought he'd been so smart to leave his food pack with the canoe and take a minimum of food in his daypack when he blazed a trail through the woods in search of a waterfall named Lacy. It wasn't a surprise to find the remnants of a waterfall but no active flow. The stains of water left their imprint on the rock face, but nothing remained that he could touch or photograph or hug to his heart. Like his own Lacey.

So smart. Just a few food items. How long would he have to make them stretch?

What made him grab his tent when he abandoned the canoe and food? The last things he needed for a short jaunt to snap a couple of photos were his tent and sleeping bag. Given the choice, should he have chosen the food pack instead? Staying out of the elements and having a place to sleep sounded good. But the idea of starving to death in the comfort of his tent offered no comfort.

When the rain started, he'd been grateful for a roof overhead. Now it promised only deeper darkness — and little more.

He pushed himself up from the log and shook off his lassitude. Could he use that word in a sentence? *His weariness and diminished energy grew into full-fledged lassitude.* Rehearsing vocabulary words could only fill so much of his day. He'd have to find a worthwhile way to occupy himself while he waited for deliverance.

Recite Scripture? Days ago, he hungrily devoured what he read in God's Word. The black ink on the white pages spoke with an almost audible sound, a Voice reassuring him of The Presence despite how things appeared.

Only what lived on the fleshy walls of his heart and mind could speak to him now. Too few words. Too late to commit more to memory. Too late for a lot of things.

Where was his solo trip notebook? In his clothing pack. He felt his way to the tent. He let the flap hang loose as he patted his way around the interior in search of the pack. His hands found the pack and searched its surface. Belts, buckles, straps, zippered compartments. His mind oriented him to the scene invisible to his eyes. This one? No. One compartment lower on the right side of the pack. Yes. There it was.

He sat back on the tent floor, removed the pen from its nest among the spirals and flipped the notebook open. His fingers moved over the pages, searching for one without the subtle indentations that let him know he'd pressed his pen into its wood fibers. When he regained his sight, he might laugh at where he'd started writing and at his distorted penmanship. At the moment, all that mattered was writing, getting the words — God's words — recorded. As if that mattered to a sightless man.

After a minute with his head bent over his work, Greg chuckled at his folly. Without eyes, he could write lying down with his paper on his stomach if he wanted. He didn't need to see, but he could feel the words scrolling onto the page.

He resisted the easy ones — "For God so

loved the world . . ." "The Lord is my Shepherd, I shall not want . . ." "Behold I stand at the door and knock . . ." — certain he could bring those familiar verses to mind without thinking later on when he'd exhausted himself trying to dredge up other passages of Scripture he knew he ought to know.

The sound of the pen tip on the paper soothed him as he wrote.

"The godly man does not fear bad news nor live in dread of what may happen. He is settled in his mind that God will take care of him." Psalm something or other. Living Bible paraphrase.

"Be strong and take courage." Joshua or Deuteronomy or one of those books.

"I will never leave you nor forsake you." New Testament, he was fairly certain. Or was it?

"Thou wilt keep in perfect peace whose mind is stayed on Thee." King James. Sunday school memorization contest when he was in fifth grade and the family next door hauled him to church with them — to his dad's chagrin.

"Faith is the evidence of things unseen." The book of Hebrews. Chapter twelve, if he wasn't mistaken. Or was it eleven? "The evidence of things unseen."

When had those words meant more than now?

A wolf howled somewhere in the distance. The echo drifted on the air currents. Greg's prayers hitched a ride.

39

Greg stretched the kinks out of his arms and shoulders and back. His wrist rebelled against his efforts to loosen the cramp from the writing marathon the "night" before. He'd slept with the notebook in his other hand. Before he closed the cover and slipped it into his breast pocket, he bent up a bottom corner of the last page on which he'd written. When he thought of more verses, he'd know where to start.

Crawling out of the tent, he was greeted with radiant warmth on his face. Sunny day. Good to know.

He lifted his face toward the direction the warmth was strongest and opened his eyes, straining for a hint of light to reach his retinas. Nothing.

A low growl quickened his heartbeat. His pulse settled almost instantly when Greg realized it came from his empty stomach. He'd have to eat something. Part of a fruit leather? He'd divide it in fourths. A little for breakfast. More for lunch. Some for supper. And he'd save the rest for tomorrow's breakfast.

First things first, though. Bathroom break.

Without thinking, he lifted his left arm to check the time. Just like a sighted man would. He slipped the pointer finger of his right hand under the watchband and prepared to fling it toward the flashlight graveyard when it occurred to him he had a ropeless method of finding his way back to camp. The alarm on his watch.

It took some finagling to set it up by feel only, but Greg managed to configure the watch to beep, a sound he'd found annoying before he lost his sight.

He set the watch on a flat rock near his feet and shuffled into the woods, arms extended, memorizing the position of the trees and roots. When the sound of the beeping grew too faint to hear, he backed up a couple of paces. That was far enough. When he was done with his morning routine, he followed the sound of the beeping until it was right underfoot again.

He lifted the watch and kissed it before slipping it back onto his wrist. "Good boy," he told it.

Sparky hadn't been near the friend his

watch promised to be. It needed a name. Taking a cue from the biblical method of naming characters like Isaac, whose name means "laughter," and Ishmael, whose name means "God hears," Greg christened his watch, "In His Time."

Certain elements of his memory were razor sharp in this land of photogenic light and shadows. He recalled that Hagar, a woman rejected and condemned, adrift in her own wilderness experience, reached out to the Almighty and called Him "The God Who Sees."

"My Lord. The God Who Sees."

He spread his arms wide and invited the sighted God to walk him through his wilderness.

Suicide.

He chewed the last mini-bite of fruit leather, using his tongue to dislodge a piece that got stuck between two molars. He needed every morsel.

Suicide, he thought again. The idea of finding his way back through the twist of woods to his canoe, then back across the remote lakes to one that was more well-traveled spelled certain suicide. The exertion of the trip didn't frighten him, nor did the fact that he couldn't keep his normal pace. The journey deal-breaker lay in the impossibility of finding his way without the benefit of sight.

Willingness, he had in abundance. But his internal GPS system was missing a key component. Sight. Hard to triangulate without sight.

The danger of wandering deeper into hopelessness kept him imprisoned at his camp.

"Secure the perimeter," he told himself and any woodland creatures listening in. "If I'll be here a while, I need to make it as safe as possible, as convenient as possible, and easier for someone to find me."

He drew a slow breath. It didn't imply a lack of faith if he felt he needed a more permanent camp setup, did it? He'd gladly abandon it all at the first sound of a search plane. Or another human voice. "Hey, buddy? You okay? Need help?"

Sweet words.

The only ones he could imagine holding greater sway for him? "Greg, I love you. From the depths of my heart. We can make this marriage work."

Rolling and tugging, crawling when necessary, Greg moved a series of downed logs and soccer-ball-sized rocks to form a two-foot-wide runway leading from camp to the water's edge. When finished, he stood tall and felt his way down the slope, tapping first one side then the other with his feet.

When he reached the water, he lowered himself to a rock-bench. He stripped down to his underwear, grateful for the penetrating warmth of the sun. His workout hauling logs invigorated him. He lifted one arm, turned his head, and sniffed. He couldn't see. But he could smell. And he did.

He left his socks on. What a sight he must have made. The socks provided some small protection against the uncertain lake bottom.

Small rocks no more threatening than a pebbled pool lined the approach. Good. Sand would have meant greater difficulty in scooping drinking water. He had no choice. He'd have to risk water-borne diseases like Beaver Fever and drink straight lake water. His filtering kit rested comfortably and unused in his food pack underneath his stashed canoe.

Greg slapped his forehead with his palm. He should have filled his canteen with water before his open air bath. Now he'd have to wait for any silt to settle after he climbed out or look for another route to the water's edge, farther away from his Jacuzzi.

He felt his way with his feet as he ventured deeper into the water. Knee-deep. Thigh-deep. Deep enough. He squatted, lowering most of the upper half of his body into the icy water. He splashed it over his shoulders, shuddering as he did. Bending forward, he submerged his head and used his fingers to comb the water through his wiry hair. No soap or shampoo. Those, too, were in his food pack.

If he'd guessed right about the sequence of amorphous days and nights he'd lived through since the lightning, Libby would have expected him home days ago. How long before she started to worry? Would she worry? Or would his absence serve only as yet another annoyance? He scrubbed hard at his scalp, then shot up for air, spewing like a whale.

He couldn't risk floating on the water. Without the gift of sight, he could easily become disoriented. No. Straight out from shore, carefully counted steps, and straight back. That's all he dared attempt.

He squeegeed his hair with his hands, sloshed more cold water on his armpits, and headed back the way he came. It comforted him to feel the water lapping lower on his legs as he walked. The right direction. Closer to shore. A simple knowledge. More valuable than a Harvard degree in this place under these conditions.

Would Libby call the police first or his dad? She would call someone, wouldn't she? Only Providence could tell them where to look for him. He'd made his own twisted detour, blazed his own trail. No one would expect him to venture this far off the traditional routes through this region. Only Providence.

"Jehovah Jireh, my Provider. Jehovah Shalom, my Peace. Jehovah Rapha, my Healer."

Greg pulled his pants over his wet body, grabbed the rest of his belongings, and walked sock-footed through the gauntlet of fallen logs toward the living room of his camp.

His balance was improving. He cringed at the thought that he was getting used to being blind. Maybe someday he'd look back on this time with no more clarity than he remembered two semesters of high school Spanish. *¿Donde está el baño?* could elicit a response to let him know the location of the nearest restroom if he were stranded in a Mexican village, but that was about the extent of his recollection of those semesters.

That one important question remained in his mind, plus the amazing taco parties

Señora Carolina threw for her students twice a year.

Was there any hope he'd live long enough to forget how this trip ended?

The sun dried the beads of lake water from his skin and hair as he sat in its warmth. When the breeze picked up, he slipped back into his shirt. He'd been heading out of the park when he took this detour. Nothing in his clothes pack was any cleaner than the shirt he'd worn earlier. When his rescuers came, they'd find him dressed in crusty clothes.

Message in a bottle. Could he put a message in a bottle and launch it on the lake, hoping someone somewhere along the line of the waterways would find it? How many years from now?

One of the empty water bottles lying on the floor of the Cherokee would work perfectly — a few too many miles away to be of any help.

Like the last straw in an already groaning wagonload, it dawned on Greg that he'd left his keys in the ignition of the Jeep. Another in a string of smart moves. He'd heard Libby call him *clueless* under her breath once. Maybe she was right.

Clueless. Sightless. Hopeless. And hungry. His stomach rumbled again.

"And for your dining pleasure this evening," he told it, "we have an excellent vintage lake water. For an entrée the chef recommends the sun-baked fruit leather, small but succulent."

He felt in his shirt pocket and added, "And for dessert, a single, salt-encrusted sunflower seed."

After his meal, he crawled straight forward toward the cliff edge, found it with his fingertips, then scooted back a couple of yards and planted a couple of medium sized rocks as a warning barricade. Two or three more trips and he had built something that must look like a caveman's guardrail.

Hunger made him weaker than he thought it could. He'd lost a day to the storm, then who knows how many to the lightning strike and its aftereffects? Three days — or was it four? — since he ate anything that resembled a legitimate meal. His body would adjust to that, too, wouldn't it? Every time Libby embraced a new diet, she'd complain hardest the first few days. Then she fell into a couple of weeks of tolerance before deciding it was her duty as a Wisconsinite to support the dairy industry and pork farmers, most particularly through consuming frozen custard, sharp cheddar, and bacon in all its forms.

"Greg, get your mind off food."

So, the list of unmentionables now included food, anything having to do with vision, death, and happily ever after. Not necessarily in that order.

A low roar interrupted his thoughts. Closer. Closer. An airplane! Probably one of the forest service float planes.

"Hey! Hey! Over here! I'm here! HELP!"

Greg jumped up and down, swinging his arms in wide, frantic arcs. "Down here! HELP!"

He needed a way to signal the plane. Was it night? It felt like night. The temperature had dropped considerably in the last few hours. He'd start a fire, no matter what the risk of setting the woods ablaze. No. No time. The plane sounded as if it were almost directly overhead.

His flashlight. He could flash an SOS-like signal into the air. That would draw the pilot's attention. But he'd tossed Sparky aside as worthless to a blind man. How wrong he'd been. Somewhere tangled in the underbrush lay the one piece of equipment that could help him. The drone of the plane's engine faded into nothingness while he searched for it.

40

The sun on his face. Warm. Penetrating. Black as the stone lining of a burned-out tomb.

Another day. Another colorless, lightless, sightless day. He'd lost count of how many dawns he hadn't seen. Eight? Nine? Stretches of warm and cold, dry and drizzle, a patch or two of rain again, twisted together with no defined edges.

Was it too much to hope he'd wake one morning and have to shield his eyes from the blinding sun?

Blinding?

Sight impaired. He was sight impaired. Temporarily. The word *blind* was for people who stayed blind. Not him.

Introspection held the potential to sour his existence or sweeten it. Somehow he had to find a way to keep the sour at bay. The hours stretched into days with little to do but think and calculate. How many days without any more protein than the bugs and bacteria floating in his drinking water?

Purchase orders scrolled through Greg's mind. Cases of canned peaches. Spaghetti sauce. Flats of hamburger buns. A gross of Bibb lettuce heads. Freezers full of turkeys.

What he wouldn't give right now for the overripe bananas the produce guy at Greene's tossed in the dumpster. Or the slightly expired lunchmeat. Or less-than-fresh fish.

Fish. He could have fished, if he'd brought his fishing gear rather than his useless photography equipment. His camera. Brilliant move. What was he thinking? How long did that dream last? Not quite the two weeks of his dream solo trip. All the fabulous shots stored in his camera might as well remain there. What was the point of capturing such incredible beauty if he could never view it?

His mind traced the contents of the digital memory of his camera. The island with the lone pine sentry. The fireball sunset threading its flames through the line of trees. The mist hovering over the surface of the lake like a downy blanket too light to settle. The leaf caught in the back eddy between two rocks. The columbine's regal crown-blossom, claiming sovereignty over its domain. The rich mosses. The otters at play. The loons in dance mode. The eagles outstretched against a cobalt sky.

The memory card in his mind still held the shots. For how long? If this blindness lasted, and if he survived long enough to be rescued, how soon before the darkness snuffed out memories of sights and colors and vastness and grandeur?

Maybe it was the hunger talking, but Greg decided to make a plan, to orchestrate his own rescue operation. How much more trouble could he collect if he set out on foot — albeit slowly and blindly — until he came close enough to another camp or a canoeist who could help him?

"A wilderness full of trouble." He said the answer out loud. Someone had to say it.

Could he fish? What in his meager possessions could morph into a hook and line? A shoelace? Quite a lot of overkill and quite a lot of underlength, but possible. Did he have a pin? A paper clip?

His spiral notebook. His handwritten Bible. The blindly penned journal of his demise.

He could fashion a hook from the metal spiral. A few rings of it.

And what would he use for bait to catch this mentally challenged fish who wouldn't mind chomping down on part of a notebook tethered to eighteen inches of shoelace tethered to a desperate man?

Does a fish that bright need bait?

Time for another math lesson. How much food was left? A few crumbs from the last breakfast bar. A piece of fruit leather the size of a Boy Scout badge. Two sunflower seeds, coated with lint from his shirt pocket.

He couldn't be more than a quarter mile from the canoe and his food pack. He could eat if he could get to it. Not a lot in the pack. A few meals at best. He'd assumed he was heading out of the Quetico after his sightseeing detour. *Not much left* sounded a lot better than his current pantry, though.

The pack was on the ground under the canoe. Enough protection for what Greg figured would be a couple of hours at the most. After multiple nights within easy reach of woodland nightlife, what could possibly be left?

Greg brooked no sympathy for hungry wolves — wolves whose mournful cries seemed to draw a tighter circle around his camp the longer he remained their accidental guest. Was his hearing more acute? Or were they truly moving closer? Did they watch for him to give up as they might watch a fawn struggling against quicksand?

"Morbid, Greg Holden. You are morosely, pathologically morbid."

He shook the dust from the throw rug he was using for his mind. "Happy thoughts. Happy thoughts." The phrase nearly gagged him.

"Bacon cheeseburger meatloaf with onion frills on top."

His plan for happy thoughts lacked a healthy focus.

He rose and paced the perimeter of his compound, his steps slower and shakier than a few days ago. Ten paces across the front, waterview side. Five paces along a right angle toward the woods. Nine across the back to the largest of the trees in his limited domain. Definitely a pine, not an aspen or birch or poplar or cedar. When he touched its trunk, his hand came away sticky and smelling like industrial-strength cleaner. Turn. Six or seven more steps, depending on his level of frustration, and he'd completed the odd geometric shape that probably had a legitimate name recognizable only to math geeks.

His foot kicked against something, sending it scooting behind him a short distance. He heard it roll and bang along the edge of the guard rails. Probably a fallen branch, although it had greater heft to it than a small branch.

He hadn't fallen when he stumbled over the object. Not even close. Then where did the dizziness come from?

His pulse pounded in his ears. Since when was blood loud? His heart rate shot up and stayed up. Greg lowered himself to the ground, not waiting to find a log or rock. On his hands and knees he crouched, waiting for the sensation to pass. It didn't.

He rolled onto his side. The contents of his skull followed a split-second later, as if it hadn't gotten the memo in time to move in sync. "Lord, what is this? Is this what starvation does?"

Was it foolish to think his vision was the lone casualty of the lightning strike? Maybe dehydration made him weak. No matter how uncomfortable the sloshing of water and gastric juices in an otherwise empty stomach, he'd have to make it a point to drink more frequently.

Pine cones. Are they edible?

"Any time You want a test subject for modern-day manna, Lord, I'm your man."

Greg stayed on his side until the spinning stopped. Then he pushed himself up, worked the kinks out of his neck, and decided he had no choice but to limit his physical activity even more than normal.

Normal. What an odd word for his current existence.

He took a step forward, then stopped. The water was to his back, right? Or had he gotten turned around? The confidence he'd gained in memorizing the footprint of that plot of land fled into the darkness.

"God, help me!" he cried.

All he heard in response was a whispering, mocking pine.

Sheets snapped and flapped, straining against the wooden pins that secured them to the clothesline. He'd bury his face in them later that night, drinking in the preserved sunshine. Like a kid making snow angels, he'd slide his arms and legs over the crisp fabric. One of life's simple pleasures. Sun-baked sheets.

He'd have to be careful mowing. Grass clippings discharged in that direction would not be good. Maybe Libby would take down the laundry before he reached that part of the yard.

She stood in the doorway, propping open the screen door with her hip. In her hands she balanced a wooden tray with a pitcher of homemade lemonade and five glasses. One for each of them.

She smiled his way. Smiled. He shut down the mower and leaned on the handle for a moment, drunk with the wonder of it.

Snap. Snap.

Greg opened his eyes. His rank sleeping bag smelled of sweat and smoke and dampness, not the sun. He pushed himself to a sitting position. Snap. Snap. Snap.

He crawled over to the tent door and felt around its opening. The tent flap caught the wind again and skirted away from his grasp as soon as he snagged it. Like a tightrope walker inching his way along the high wire, Greg moved his hands along the nylon until he caught the loose edge again.

No lawn mowing today. No lemonade. No sheets on the line. No smiles on Libby's face.

He growled at the frustration of not knowing if he'd slept an hour or a day. Not that it mattered.

The tent walls buckled and puffed, as if trying to breathe.

"I know how you feel."

He left the flap open and lay back down on his anything-but-crisp-and-sweet-smelling nest.

"Wind that stiff —" he said, "I pity anyone out on open water."

He tried to make a snow angel on top of his sleeping bag, but the effort wore him out.

What was wrong with him? The profound weakness. He shouldn't actually starve to death for weeks yet. Wasn't it true that a person could live without food for a month or more, as long as he had water?

Without food. Strange thought for a guy in the grocery business.

He reached into his shirt pocket and pulled out the spiral notebook and pen. On the last page with a bent corner, he wrote:

"Man does not live by bread alone." — words of Jesus.

Then he slid his hand down the page the equivalent of several lines and wrote:

"Man does not live by bread at all." — words of Greg Holden.

Words. Of Greg Holden. Someone should find his words after . . . an explanation of why he died here. Why he came.

He reached across the darkness and flipped to a fresh page. His pen hovered over the paper. He wished he could remember if it was blue ink or black. Blue seemed more "him," more legitimately his own thoughts.

As he pressed the pen into service, it occurred to him that what he was about to write would last far longer than he would, barring divine intervention.

To the ones I love — Libby, Zack, Alex, Dad and to the One who showed me how little I knew about love . . .

He stopped writing when the only unused paper was the inside of the back cover. Then he composed an addendum and filled the cover too.

I couldn't have loved you more, although I could have loved you better. I hope you'll forgive me for that. I pray God has.

Greg closed the notebook, tucked it into his breast pocket, laid his hand over it and his heart, and prayed himself to sleep.

41
LIBBY

As we walk toward an unknown future that will make me an official widow when we cross the finish line, I tweak the funeral plans I started the day Greg failed to come home.

We're moving forward as if there's hope. And I do see glimpses of it. Not hope we'll find Greg alive. That boat — canoe — sailed long ago. But hope that I'll survive.

My robotic steps break through the underbrush not tramped down or pushed aside by Jen or Frank. There are four of us on this faux trail. The One who walks beside me says, *A shekel for your thoughts.* God's using Frank's sense of humor?

Lord, I thought I needed my daughter spared in order to fully trust You, I tell Him. *It didn't happen.*

I hold back a sapling and duck to miss another as I press through. *I thought I could believe You were good and righteous if you spared Jen further pain.*

Stumbling over an exposed root, I flail then regain my balance. *I thought finding Greg alive and well and wanting me would be the key to fixing my faltering faith.*

Jen turns back as if reading my prayers. That's not possible, is it? Her eyebrows lift like those of a sympathetic cocker spaniel. I return the look, then nod an "I'm okay. Let's keep going."

Lord, I don't need my daughter, or my friend, or even my husband as much as I need Your mercy.

The words pull the lining out of my stomach. All the broken pieces of my life congeal at the base of my throat. I double over. And over.

When I straighten, I'm surprised to see that Frank and Jen haven't pulled away from me. They stand — stooped — no more than a dozen yards ahead.

Jen calls back, "Libby? We need you, hon."

I jog to where Frank crouches and Jen hovers with her arm around his shoulders. "What's wrong? Frank?"

"I can't go any farther."

Jen and I lock eyes. Heart attack? Stroke? Have we pushed him too hard after his head injuries?

I bend to Frank's eye level and grasp his

large hands in mine. "Tell us where the pain is."

He wrenches one hand free and presses it against his chest. "Here."

Oh, Lord God! Now what do we do?

"It's . . . in here," he says, tapping his breastbone. "I can't do it anymore. I can't handle stumbling over my boy's body."

Jen rubs her hand across his back. "We don't know for sure that Greg's dead."

He raises his head, not to her, but to the skies. "Yes, we do. We all know it. He's a bright boy. He had to have been badly hurt not to try to get word to us, not to *try* . . ."

He doesn't have to mention that we aren't even following a trail. We're crashing through untouched forest. He doesn't have to point out that we're flailing wildly in our search with even less hope than when we thought it was utterly hopeless.

Greg said it was always Pauline who buried the family pets when they expired. Frank couldn't do it. He refused to stand in the family receiving line at Lacey's funeral. Said he had to "walk off a charley horse." Can a heart muscle get a charley horse?

Greg and I didn't risk having pets. But I know what death looks like. If I don't find it, it will find me. So I have to go on.

"Will you stay here with him, Jen, while I

go on a little longer?"

"That's crazy. It's going to be dark soon."
Jen looks from Frank to me as if struggling
to keep both tightrope walkers from falling
off the edge of the earth.

"Can I see the map?" I stretch my hand
toward Frank, palm up. The other hand I
raise — palm up — over my head, asking
God to drop fresh wisdom into it.

Frank sighs. "I'll come."

"No." My voice holds power and gentle-
ness in what I hope is Jesuslike balance.
"No, I think I'm supposed to go on alone
from here."

Jen grabs the hand waiting for a map.
"You can't do this."

"Why? Because it's hard? Because we
don't know the outcome? Because how this
turns out might be the opposite of what we
think we need?"

"Those are some good reasons right
there," Jen says, withdrawing her hand.

I reach to grab it back. "I don't want you
to go through what's waiting for you back
home, Jen. Because it's hard. Because we
don't know the outcome. Because when
God answers our prayers, we may not like
His choices. But you're going to walk
through it anyway, aren't you?"

Jen's eyes glisten. The earth's rotation

seems to hiccup, then catch again and turn as it has since God's Hand started the first spin. "How long will you be gone?"

"How long will it take us to find our way back out of here?" Frank asks with an instructor's tone. "Too long. We should have started back an hour ago."

I press my hand an inch closer toward him. "The map, Frank?"

He's a resistant dad, handing the keys to the good car to his freshly licensed teenager. I take the map reverently, understanding what it cost him to let me see it. The faint pencil markings swim before my eyes. "Where are we now, as near as you can guess?"

Frank stands and leans toward me. "Wish I knew."

Jen levels her gaze at him. "What exactly does that mean? We're not lost."

"No. Not lost," Frank says, dropping his chin. "I just don't know where we are. Exactly. But if we leave now, we can retrace our steps. They're the only footprints out here, you might have noticed."

We've all noticed.

I press trembling fingers to my lips and look beyond Frank and Jen, deeper into the friendless woods. I'd hoped it wouldn't come to this — a decision to stop searching. The sands of time drained long ago. Frank needs rest. Jen needs radiation. Brent needs more time with his wife. Zack and Alex need reassurance that life will go on.

And I need mercy.

Through the shadows, a flash of light.

"Did you see that?" I breathe.

"See what?" Jen asks a fraction of a second before Frank does.

"I saw a light. There."

The others turn their line of sight to the trajectory I indicate.

"I don't see anything," Frank says.

"Sorry, Libby. Me either. What kind of light?"

"Just a little flash of something."

Frank turns his eyes and emotions back onto our makeshift trail to leave this place of pain. "Probably the sunset sending out a caution warning through the trees. It's time to go, Libby."

"I have to agree this time," Jen says. "I'm so sorry. We need to go home."

I stare into the approaching darkness. "God, please. Either take away this urgency to keep pursuing this or show me the light again."

Nothing.

I breathe out all hope and drink in two lungsful of fresh air that I pray will bring meaning to a life devoid of Greg's bedrock love.

Still nothing.

I begin to take the first step to reverse course and follow Frank and Jen. But there. A mere pinpoint of light. Logic says it is a stray ray of a dying sun, as I've been told. My heart tells me different.

"Fifteen minutes. Or a half hour. Give me half an hour, okay?"

Without waiting for an argument, I quickly increase the distance between myself and the others.

Frank growls something foul, but doesn't try to stop me. Not that he could.

As I tear through the untamed woods, I keep my eyes on the direction from which I last saw the flash. Like headlights on a sunny day, the light seems faint at best. Weak. But real.

And annoyingly intermittent.

As I pursue the phantom, I steel my heart for the revelation that what I saw originated from a piece of tinfoil long ago abandoned by a camper. Or a shard of mirror dropped by a novice canoeist who didn't realize a mirror is the last thing she would want after a few days in the wilderness.

I press ahead another few steps, ready for

the disappointment but compelled nonetheless.

The light — when it appeared — was low to the ground. Not knowing its source, it startles me to break through a tangle of waist-high brush and see it there before me on the forest floor.

A pocket-sized flashlight, stuck in the "on" position. Surviving on what are probably its last few seconds of battery power. I bend to pick it up. The light dies in my hand.

As weak as its light was, how could I have seen it from the point where I left Jen and Frank?

A dying flashlight.

In the "on" position.

Someone was here. I don't know the life expectancy of the newer kinds of batteries, but I find it remarkable that I saw the light at all.

"Greg? Greg Holden! Is anyone there?"

I scan the section of woods where I now stand. Left to right and back again, like a metal detector might sweep a portion of park lawn. Where? Who? Why is an abandoned flashlight lying in a remote, uninhabited spot? And working?

A sudden breeze lifts the branches of the trees as if pulling back a curtain, revealing an opening in the thick undergrowth. Curiosity draws me forward to get a better view of a jarring pattern. Downed logs lined up end to end. This smacks of human intervention. I lift my eyes and catch sight of a tent twenty yards in front of me.

No movement. No sign of life. The fabric has a smoky cast, as if someone once lit a fire inside.

It has to be Greg's tent, doesn't it? I step closer, overdosing on adrenaline. *God help me with this. Help me handle it if he's not here. Or . . .*

As I approach, I survey the campsite area. The logs form an ankle-high fence around the perimeter. This isn't the work of a sane man. Not Greg. Who would build a fence only four inches high? Or tackle a landscaping project here?

I'm in over my head. A possibility we hadn't considered is a madman serial killer camped in the woods, stalking people like Greg — cereal purchasers. That is *so* not funny.

I should wait for Jen and Frank. But I won't.

"Greg?" I call out softly, then more insistently. "Greg?"

Nothing.

A couple of strides from the tent door, I call out again, "Greg?"

"Libby?"

I stop and fall to my knees where I stand. How far has imagination taken me this time? I thought I heard his voice.

"Libby?"

An unseen hand unzips the tent flap from the inside.

"Greg? Oh, dear God! Greg, what happened to you?"

I watch him ease his body through the tent opening, his movements tortured. Jumping to my feet, I rush forward to meet him as he emerges. What is that expression on his face? He's turned slightly away from me. Why can't he look me in the eye? What's going on?

It doesn't matter right now. By the grace of God alone, I found him, and he's alive. I press my embrace upon him, hugging gingerly. He seems so thin and frail. My strong rock of a husband nearly collapses in my arms.

"Libby, I can't believe it. How . . . how did you find me?"

His words hold the quality of a message forced through a drinking straw. Pinched. Laconic.

"I would tell you that Frank and Jen and I did it together, but truth be told the Lord deserves all the credit for this one. I saw your flashlight."

"Sparky?"

"What?"

"Would you tell it I'm sorry?"

I pull back from Greg without letting go and search his eyes for some confirmation that he isn't as unstable as he sounds. He looks intently at a stretch of my forehead. I brush at the spot, wondering what is so fascinating up there.

He's alive. Talking. Not making sense, but he's making words.

"Do you still have Sparky?" he asks.

I reach into my pants pocket and pull out the now lifeless beacon.

"Do you?"

"Greg, it's right here. Can't you s—"

The dazed look on his face. His slightly off-target gaze. The logs — not a ridiculously low fence but guide markers. "Greg?"

"Libby, is it daytime?" He steps to his right three short paces and with effort lowers himself to an ottoman-shaped rock. "Or is it night again?"

My intestines tighten. What horrific ordeal has he been through? "It will be night soon." I choke back the question I'm aching to ask, one for which I already know the answer. Instead I scrape together a few splinters of courage and say, "I don't want to leave you, but I have to tell your dad and Jen that we've found you. Will you be okay if I'm gone for just a couple of minutes?"

He clutches his stomach and rocks forward. "I . . . I don't think so."

I kneel beside him. Hold him. Cry with him.

He cradles my head in his hand and burrows his face in my neck.

"Oh, Greg, I smell like a —"

"Like a little breath of heaven," he whispers into my skin. "Actually," he says, pulling back slightly, "you kind of smell like fish."

"Long story. Doesn't matter now." Ignoring its abrasive quality, I cup his face and stroke his McScruffy cheeks with my thumbs. "I need to know your story. What happened?"

He encircles one of my hands in his, then lifts it away from his face and kisses my palm. His answer floats into my lifeline wrinkle. "Heart transplant."

"What?"

He presses his lips together in a thin line that quivers, as does his voice when he finally speaks. "It never occurred to me you'd come looking for me."

"It didn't occur to me either. For most of three years." My throat tightens. I stroke his damp eyelids with my fingertips. "No matter what happened to you, or what this means for our future, we'll get through it together."

His lips lean toward mine. I move my head to the side and lift my chin so as not to miss the connection.

42

"Libby?"

"I'm here, Greg."

He knows that. He can feel my back curled into his chest, my arms drawing his tighter around me.

"Did you need something?" I whisper into the dark.

His fingers play my ribs like piano keys. Pianissimo. "Found it."

I don't know how Frank and Jen had the energy to backtrack to our canoes and haul our tent and packs here so we could camp — together — along the place where Lacy Falls once flowed. Joy has a way of recharging a person's batteries.

Before night had a good hold on our world, we'd fed Greg and ourselves a hot meal and settled in. I intend to kiss the inventor of satellite phones when we get back to civilization. We're too far in for a float plane to land. And darkness doesn't help. On our own for another night, we'll head toward an open spot for rescue in the morning. All of us.

"Libby?"

"I'm here, Greg. Try to get some sleep."

"I thought I was dreaming."

I lift his hand and press it to the beat of my heart. "Did you feel that?"

"Yes."

My elbow to his stomach. Gently. "And that?"

"I'm not paralyzed. I'm blind."

I hate that word already and I've only dealt with it for a few hours. What vile thoughts must he harbor against it?

"Greg, we have a long couple of days ahead of us." To say nothing of the ones through which we've just clawed our way. "We need sleep."

"I'm afraid of the dark."

"Good one."

"I am, Lib. Not of the night. Of the dark. This edgeless black."

One of us is trembling. I can't tell where he ends and I begin in our conjoined fetal position. If he's afraid of the dark, so am I. "Can we talk about this in the morning?" And the morning after that and the next and the next as we adapt to this strange new life?

He shifts away from me. Not far, but someone could definitely slide a dollar bill between us now. "I'm not sure I can do this. The blind thing."

I close the gap. "I'm sure enough for both of us that you can."

Father, forgive me, for I have sinned. I'm barely sure enough for me, much less him too. I trust my husband. I don't trust the world in which he'll have to feel his way. You helped us find him, Lord. Now help us find our way home. All the way home.

He's playing with my hair. Like a toddler would rub the satin binding on his favorite blanket. I didn't realize how much the blanket benefited from the arrangement.

Is it just me? Do all women race ahead in their thinking? Planning funerals for husbands whose bodies haven't been recovered? Making lists — the pros and cons of selling the house? Wondering what life's supposed to look like with a husband who can't see?

I hope he sleeps sooner or later. Me? I'm mentally rearranging the family room so he won't stumble and wondering if it's worth it to learn Braille at his age and contemplating the red tape of filing for disability and praying that our insurance covers laser surgery or whatever he needs.

"Libby?"

"I'm here."

"Just checking."

How many unsung heroes hover just offstage in the Bible? I remember reading about blind men whose sight was restored by Jesus. I don't remember reading about their mates. Heroes? Victims? It's a fine line sometimes. I'm both, I suppose. I found my husband, but lost part of him. I'm not the one with the disability, but I am disabled. He's the one who can't see. I'm one of the things he can't see.

Am I the worst belly-creeping slug for thinking of myself at all? We're one. Divine design and all that. Part of me can't see. And it's killing me. He doesn't deserve this. I probably do.

We'll get through this. Together. I've said the words a dozen times since he stumbled out of the tent and into my arms. It's my theme song for Jen too. I should tattoo it on my forehead. Do they do Braille tattoos? And ewww if they do!

"Libby?"

"Greg, I'm right —"

"Move, will you? My arm fell asleep."

Ah. So sleep is reserved for appendages only. Minds are off-limits.

I scoot away a couple of inches. My back chills instantly.

I'm not so much afraid of the dark as I am afraid of reacting badly to the darkness he knows. What if I'm a lousy caregiver? What if I caregive when he's capable of more than I think? What if I guess wrong about who needs me more on any given day — Jen or Greg?

An acrid smell tickles the hairs in my nose. Smoke. It's his sleeping bag, the one opened underneath us. Not cool. All I need to induce sleep is a reminder that Greg could have died when the lightning used him as an outlet.

I slide back toward him, and by the Braille method discover he's lying on his back. His chest rises and falls in a deliriously comforting rhythm. I think I'll spend what's left of the night trying to match my breathing pattern to his.

It's so much like the rhythm of my paddle in the water. Stroke. Stroke. Stroke. Smooth. No splashing. More efficient that way. Stroke. Stroke. All the way home.

EPILOGUE

I feel it before I see it. Warmth in the palm of my hand. Pressed there by a loving husband who still thinks a cup of coffee holds healing powers.

"Thanks, Greg. What am I going to do if — ?"

"Shh," he says, laying one broad finger on my trembling lips. "Let's just see."

See. Yes, let's. Let's all just *see*.

Waiting room coffee. Miserable stuff. Not decaffeinated but de-taste-inated. The vending machine somehow extracts the flavor and ramps up the bitterness factor. Or is that my imagination? Maybe the coffee's fine and my stomach acid is the culprit.

He's here. Beside me. The husband I wished away. The sight of him medicates me.

Frank would be here, too, but his surgeon understands prostate cancer far better than he understands a man's need to be supportive so soon after the scalpel removed what it could.

God bless Pauline Holden. She's watching Brent's girls so he can drink waiting-room coffee and pray.

Greg must have forgotten that my peripheral vision is stellar. Does he not know I can see him slip off his dark glasses and rub his eyes?

We're supposed to be at the awards banquet tonight, but we won't make it. Even when the doctor walks through those doors to pronounce a verdict, it'll be too late to drive all the way to Minneapolis. Too late to find silver-shimmer pantyhose to match my all-sparkle-all-the-time gown. Too late to pick up the tux we rented for Greg. Priorities dictate that we're in jogging suits now. My hair's in a ponytail. Not my most flattering look, but how can that matter?

Alex promised to send pictures of the ceremony on his cell phone. Am-Can Nature Photographer of the Year. Greg's spread in *North America Wild* magazine clinched it for him. For us.

I wish I knew my Bible better. I can't recall an incident of a half miracle, but maybe there is such a thing. When Greg's vision returned, it didn't make it all the way. He sees shapes without details. I see details without shapes. We're better together than apart. Both of us.

A half miracle. No.

"What do you see?" Jesus asked the blind man at Bethsaida.

"I see people, but they look like tree trunks," the man said after a touch from the Healer.

"Good enough," Jesus answered and walked away.

No. That's not how it ended. Jesus touched the man again and restored his sight completely.

Why not Greg?

Is the other half of our miracle yet to come?

Will the complete return of his vision depend on another lightning bolt during a late summer storm? Will it steal into our bedroom in the middle of the night? Will it serve as a glorious aftereffect of a sneeze? Will it pour down on him while his face and hands are raised to heaven in worship of the God we call Rescuer?

I shift in the vinyl chair I've occupied too long. Greg reaches over to grab my hand.

"No matter what, Lib, we're going to make it."

I don't want to argue with him. I want him to be right.

Brent left the room long ago, with our blessing. Maybe the doctor will let him bring us the news. Brent deserves something happy to report.

As long as we've waited, I'm caught off-guard when I see him standing in the doorway. He's shaking and crying. A grown man like that. Greg sees clearly enough to know we can't stay seated. We move to either side of him, acting as his human crutches as he stumbles farther into the room.

"It's . . . a boy," he whispers. "He's small, but healthy, as far as we can tell."

I can't form a word, much less a sentence.

"And Jen?" Greg manages.

Brent's face contorts, then returns to the grace-shape it usually wears. "Holding her own. Her obstetrician turned her over to the oncologist. They'll up her pain medicine now. Then, we'll see."

Does the birth of this child mean God knows Jen will live to raise him? She says they took every precaution to ensure her cancer treatments weren't in danger of compromise from a pregnancy. A pregnancy that happened anyway and that resulted in a "small but healthy" baby boy who is going to need his mother. Almost as much as I do.

Greg extends a hand toward Brent, then reaches with his other arm to embrace the new father. "Congratulations, man. A son. What an amazing gift."

The sound of my husband's voice — my husband, being normal — anchors my runaway thoughts.

Life. What a gift. The breath of life.

"Then, we'll see," Brent repeats.

Yes. We will.

DISCUSSION QUESTIONS

1. What lies did Libby believe about her marriage, her husband, her daughter's death, her faith? How did those lies cripple her, blind her?

2. At what moment in the story did Libby realize her vision of the truth was skewed? Was it a moment or an unfolding?

3. All creation seems designed to endure hardship. We humans are included in that plan. We're designed to persevere and push through solid rock to give glory to God. What situation in your life right now seems like a "through solid rock" experience? What comfort can you draw from realizing you were built for endurance and tenacity?

4. In some ways, Libby was a "motherless child." How did that influence her at-

titudes toward her children? Her mother-in-law? Her best friend?

5. Symbolically, lightning played both a subtle and an in-your-face role in the book. How did it affect Libby's relationship with her daughter?

6. The many references to "bathroom breaks" in the wilderness may have seemed crude, but represented both Frank's distress and the harsh reality — no matter what the crisis, the necessities of life persist. If you've lost a loved one, even temporarily, you know the added pain. Laundry and meals and mortgages and dirty dishes and bathroom breaks don't stop for your grief. How has that raw reality played out in your own life?

7. Imagine finding yourself marooned in unfamiliar territory, your resources and resourcefulness drained. Not only are you in trouble, but no matter how brave or inventive, you cannot save yourself. The author intended that as a symbol of humanity's desperate need for a Rescuer. In the story, God's Word became an umbilical cord, pumping pulses of hope until rescue arrived. And even then, it was a

long trek home. When have you been most conscious of your inability to provide your own rescue?

8. Strength is made perfect in weakness, according to the Bible. Libby discovered she was stronger than she knew, weaker than she realized. In some respects, each of the characters made the same discovery. What drew them to those conclusions? What draws you?

9. What compelled Jenika to risk so much to stay by Libby's side?

10. Do you think Frank's heart would have softened toward faith issues if Libby hadn't struggled with her own? How was her battle key to his awakening?

11. In the pre-wilderness relationship between Greg and Libby, how did the grief/blame cycle hamstring their healing? How might it threaten their post-wilderness lives? What proactive measures would you advise them to take?

12. What was the one thing Libby discovered she needed?

So let us seize and hold fast and retain
without wavering the hope we cherish
and confess and our acknowledgement of
it, for He Who promised is reliable (sure)
and faithful to His word.
— Hebrews 10:23, Amplified Bible